BONNIE DUNDEE

Claverhouse urged his horse forward to the very brink of the water, and shouted to them. He was a quiet-spoken man, but his war-shout was a clarion, that could carry from one end of a battlefield to the other. 'This is an unlawful gathering! Lay down your arms in the King's name; yield up your leaders; and the rest of you may depart quietly to your homes.'

A kind of low angry snarl that was the voice of the crowd made him answer; and in the midst of the gathering, a tall man in black with the white flash of Geneva bands at his throat – like enough it was Renwick himself, certainly he seemed to be the leader among them – stood with arms upraised, his grey hair blowing about his face, and shouted back, 'In the name of God be gone from us, ye sons of Belial! For we own no king save God himself and no law save His Covenant. Unbelievers! Boot-lickers and tame butchers to a papist so-called king and his hell-spawned bishops! Get you gone and leave the righteous to their peaceful prayers!'

ROSEMARY SUTCLIFF BOOKS
PUBLISHED BY RED FOX

Beowulf: Dragonslayer
The Hound of Ulster
The High Deeds of Finn MacCool
Tristan and Iseult
Sun Horse, Moon Horse
The Light Beyond the Forest
The Sword and the Circle
The Road to Camlann
The Witch's Brat
The Armourer's House
The Shining Company
Knight's Fee
The Capricorn Bracelet

BONNIE DUNDEE

Rosemary Sutcliff

To the Lords of Convention, 'twas
Claver'se who spoke,
'Ere the King's crown shall fall there are
crowns to be broke,
So let each Cavalier who loves honour and me
Come follow the bonnet of Bonnie Dundee!

Walter Scott

RED FOX

A Red Fox Book
Published by Random House Children's Books
20 Vauxhall Bridge Road, London SW1V 2SA

A division of Random House UK Ltd
London Melbourne Sydney Auckland
Johannesburg and agencies throughout the world

1 3 5 7 9 10 8 6 4 2

First published in Great Britain by The Bodley Head 1983

Red Fox edition 1994

Set in Times New Roman by SX Composing Ltd
Printed and bound in Great Britain by
Cox & Wyman Ltd, Reading, Berkshire

RANDOM HOUSE UK Limited Reg. No. 954009

ISBN 0 09 935411 X

CONTENTS

1

The Covenanters

Maybe I could go back now. Some among us gained leave to return home years ago; but I've no stomach for Scotland under Hanoverian George. Oh, there's times I grow homesick for my own hills, and I should be glad to think that you laddies might come to know them one day; but that will be for you to decide when you are grown men. Your grandmother and I do well enough here in Rotterdam. With all the Scottish merchants and the captains of the cross-channel trading vessels and tall East Indiamen that come and go, we are never out of touch with our own roots, and nor do we go hungry for the clack of the good Scots tongue among the broad flat speech of the Low Countries.

Sometimes there's too much of either tongue, when the women get together. Aye.

Not three days since, as I was cleaning up my brushes and palette after the day's work, your grandmother came in upon me with her eyes stormy and the colour flying like flags in her cheeks; and when I asked her what had put her in such a bonnie taking, 'I was talking with Mistress Seton over a cup of chocolate,' said she, 'but I'll not be entering her house again! She was asking me was it true, as she'd heard, that Claverhouse was used to hang men with his own hand for the pleasure of it, aye, and that he caused two God-fearing women to be tied to stakes on a sandbank in the Clyde, to drown when the tide came in.'

'That's nothing,' said I, rubbing the last of the poppy-seed oil into my palette – a good mature palette, properly oiled after every use has a surface like satin, and to my mind should never be left to the journeyman's tending. 'Folks have talked about their betters since Adam and Eve were driven out of the Garden. I've heard it said before now that Claverhouse was in league with the Devil, and could not be killed save with a silver bullet. Aye, and that that great raking sorrel he used to ride was his Familiar.'

'It is no laughing matter!' said your grandmother.

'Is it not? Whisht, woman, let the Whigs and the Covenanters tell what tales they please. *We* know what manner of man he was, and the truth of the stories.'

Your grandmother sat herself down in the big carved oak chair with the mermaid on the back, that I put my sitters in when they come to the house. 'Aye, we know,' she said. 'But Johnnie and Jamie never saw him, and as for their bairns' (that's you) 'how will they know what to believe, when folks tell such wicked lies, naming him Bloody Claver'se and all?'

'I've told the true tales to John and James, often enough to weary them, Heaven knows,' said I, 'and I'll be telling them to the bairns no doubt; they're good tales for telling round the fire on winter nights.'

'Telling is not enough,' said she. 'Folks forget, and stories get twisted, and memory tangles itself. What tales do you suppose the bairns will be telling *their* grandsons, by and by?'

I said nothing. I had not thought as far ahead as that, and she went on, 'No, I was thinking all the way home from Mistress Seton's – you must write it all down!'

I stared at her. 'Write it down? Woman, if it's a book you're wanting, Philip of Amryclose did that long ago.'

She sniffed. '*The Graemiad*? All high words and

2

heroics and written in Latin, forbye? No, Hugh Herriot, I was thinking just the tale, just the truth, for the bairns and their bairns after them. And *now*, before one day you begin to forget, too.'

'Och away!' I said.

But I began to think. And I thought what a sore pity it would be if all that I could tell was lost; for it is not many that followed Claverhouse and are yet alive and have the painter's eye to tell of those days so that others may see them too. It is not many that made the great Highland March with him in the spring of 1689.

So here I sit, beginning the task; setting down on a ream of fair new paper the story of the Claverhouse I knew; Colonel John Graham of Claverhouse that became Viscount Dundee; him that the Covenanters called Bloody Claver'se, and the Highlanders called *Iain Dhub Nan Cath*, Black John of the Battles – which, come to think of it, is the story of my own youth as well.

It began in the great farm kitchen at Wauprigg, with the table pushed back, and the household and farm folk and neighbours gathered to hear Ezekiel Grey, the minister who had come to hold service for us. It was not the Sabbath. At that time the minister came when he could, and the word went round and the people gathered; sometimes just a handful in a farm kitchen, since our own kirks were forbidden to us; sometimes folk from miles around crowding in to one of the great conventicles out on the open moors under the sky, with lookouts posted against surprise by the King's troopers.

I was standing among the farmhands well back against the walls. I was used to that, though indeed I was one of the family; for my mother had disgraced the name of Armstrong, so *they* thought, by running away

3

to wed with a travelling painter, and roaming the country with him like a Tinkler lass. She had died when I was five, and even my memories of her were hazy, though it was a sunny haze. After that I had gone on stravaiging up and down Scotland like a dog at my father's heels, as he plied his trade. Mostly it was just shop and inn signs, a pair of gilded spurs for a lorimer or a unicorn for a tavern of that name. But now and then some country squire would ask him to paint a favourite dog or horse or a new house. Those would be the times when we would bide more than three days in one place and have full bellies the while. The times when nobody wanted even a shop sign painting, we held horses for travellers and went hungry. My father was not as good a painter as he longed to be; but he always believed that one day I would be a better painter than he was; and beside teaching me all the things that belong to a painter's boy – cleaning his brushes and grinding the paint and boiling up the black walnut oil – he taught me how to look at things, and even began to teach me how to draw their shapes in the soft brown-black paint called ingres. But when I was eleven he took sick with the lung fever – the winter was bad that year, and we had been sleeping hard – and went the way of my mother.

But before he died, he contrived to get word to my mother's folk; and my grandfather came all across Scotland to Edinburgh to fetch me from the old besom in the cheap lodging-house – aye, and paid her again for my keep, though my father had left a fine just-finished sign for a silk mercer's shop in our stinking room, that must have fetched more than enough for a few days' keep for one laddie.

So here I was at Wauprigg, with my mother's kin,

4

and had been for upward of two years. And I had food enough, and a dry place to sleep, and even did lessons with the village dominie when I could be spared from work on the farm. That was a thing I had my grandfather to thank for; I'd have had no schooling but for him. For the rest, my Aunt Margaret never forgave me that my mother had shamed the family. And I daresay my looks, for I was narrow-built and dark like my father, among those big tawny-gold Armstrongs, made it easier to forget that I was kin of theirs.

Aye well, standing back with the farmhands against the wall, I could see the whole crowded kitchen as though it were a picture; and it was a picture that held the eye my father had trained in me.

There were the best wax candles glimmering on the chimney-piece, and the shutters tight closed over the windows though outside it would be scarcely dusk of the windy March day. My aunt's finest linen cloth on the back-pushed table, and in front of it, Master Grey in his rusty black gown and Geneva bands, the candle-light haloing his thin hair with silver while it left his long narrow face in shadow. But it seemed to me that even in the shadow, as he launched into his sermon – I misremember what it was about, but it must have been about Hell-fire and the sins of the English and their bishops, for his sermons always were, which is why I had mostly given up listening to them and taken to following my own interests inside my own head – I could catch the fanatic blaze in his pale blue eyes. It's a look I misliked even then.

And all around the kitchen, their faces lit by the candles that were at his back, kneeling with their hands folded before them, were the folk who had gathered to hear the Word of God. Folk from the few farms roundabout, Forsyths and Patersons and Carmichaels, and

5

the Wauprigg folk, my own folk, though I never felt them to be just that; my Aunt Margaret, beautiful but bleak – a bleak and bitter woman, and grown more so, I guessed, in the years since the soldiers had killed her man when Alan was but ten years old. Alan was fifteen now, and standing beside his mother; and 'twas he that held my gaze most strongly of all the souls in that room; aye, and something of my heart as well. A tall callant with a white freckled face under a burning bush of hair, and grey-green eyes that oft times had the Devil looking out of them; but he had tossed me a kind word from time to time, and whistled me to heel as a man whistles his dog. And I was aye a good follower, in my young days, and needed someone to follow.

There should by rights have been one more of us there, in the space kept clear for him by Aunt Margaret; but my grandfather, Armstrong of Wauprigg himself, was busy in the byre with a sick cow.

I had noticed before, how often my grandfather had some good reason for being elsewhere when the conventicles gathered. He had told me once how, when he was a laddie and the Covenant first came into being, the great Montrose himself, him that raised the Highlands for the first King Charles, had ridden the length and breadth of Scotland, with a knot of blue ribbons in his bonnet and the bonnets of his followers, heartening the folk to sign it, no matter what the cost, for the love of God and the freedom to worship Him in their own way, and not in ways forced upon them against their conscience by an English king who had forgotten that he was also a Scot and the bishop of his church. And how folks had flocked in from far and wide to sign, some in their own blood – my grandfather had shown me the tiny white nick-mark on his own wrist. But that had been in the shining days at the beginning, and the shine had gone, and things and folk had changed until the people who had been ready to die for the freedom of their faith sought to deny that same freedom to the English. And the thing had gone black and bitter, and when the Covenanters came to power they had driven the Episcopalian kirk into the wilderness in their turn. And Montrose had torn the blue ribbons from his bonnet and ridden south to carry his sword to the King. That had been more than forty years gone by, but the blackness and the bitterness remained. And now, with the second Charles upon the throne in London, we must again worship God in secret, and now we were willing not only to die for our faith but to kill for it in ugly ways. Only five years ago Archbishop Sharp had been pulled from his coach on the Edinburgh road, and his brains beaten out of his old grey head before his daughter's eyes; and every good Covenanting house in Galloway and all the South West had smuggled Dutch muskets in the thatch or under the hearthstone. And Claverhouse was in the West again, and his troopers were for ever trampling up and down to keep the King's peace and root out the forbidden gatherings.

My grandfather had small love for the Government troops who had killed his only son at Drumclog. But he was not a good hater, the like of my Aunt Margaret, and I'm thinking he had small love either for what the Covenanters – 'The Saints' as some of the leaders called themselves – had become. He was a peaceful man who wanted to be free to tend his own land and beasts in peace. He wanted an end to killing. And so he found a sick cow that needed him as often as might be when the Covenanting congregation gathered.

I did not know at that time whose side I was on. I

7

would have liked to join my grandfather with the sick cow, and yet there was a cold excitement that drew me to the gatherings and the danger and the shuttered windows and hidden weapons. And Alan was for the Covenant. 'We are fighting for Scotland's freedom from the English yoke, as well as for our own way of worship,' Alan said.

I suppose none of it was quite real to me as yet.

But it was to become real to me, that night.

I found that the minister was done with his preaching, and all the folk were getting to their feet; and the big smoke-darkened kitchen was filling with the deep murmur of the next psalm. Generally it was the more fierce and grievous of the metrical psalms we sang, but this one I joined in with sudden surprised delight, for it was one I loved well.

'The Lord of Heaven confess,
On high his glory raise.
Him let all angels bless,
Him let all armies praise.
Him glorify
Sun, Moon, and Stars;
Ye higher spheres
And cloudy sky.'

What had possessed the minister, what had possessed the Godly congregation, to choose anything so joyful, I wondered.

'Praise God from earth below,
Ye dragons and ye deeps:
Fire, hail, clouds, wind and snow . . .'

8

I looked across at Alan, wanting to catch his eye and share the splendour of the moment with him. But even as I looked his head whipped round towards the windows, and I saw that he was listening. A second or so later I caught it too, above the voices of the good folk; the sound of someone running, desperately, stumbling as they ran. A few seconds more and everybody heard it. The rhythmic murmur of the psalm dwindled and died away.

'Douse the candles,' said my Aunt Margaret.

Master Grey shook his head, 'Yon's no trooper. 'Tis one of our own – you can hear the brogues on his feet.'

For an instant the whole scene seemed frozen in the candlelight as I have seen a bee caught and held for all eternity in a drop of Baltic amber; while the running footsteps drew near and nearer yet, swung in through the steading gate and crossed the yard. The door burst open, and there in the dusk on the edge of the candles' reach stood Willie, the cowherd from High Fold way. He dived in and slammed the door behind him – no one stood in an open doorway with a conventicle gathered within – and stood panting against it.

'Willie,' said Master Grey sternly as the scene melted back to life, 'you come late to the worship of your God!'

We all knew what Willie would have been up to; he was the best poacher in those parts, and a fat hare would hold him from divine worship at any time. He did not even attempt to deny it, but stood there puffing and wagging his head until he had enough breath to speak.

'I came by old Phemie's alehouse,' he got out at last. 'Phemie Saunders has four of Claverhouse's men inside. Three troopers an' a wee drummer!'

There was a blink of silence; and then Master Forsyth from Arkle said one word, 'Carbines!'

'Three carbines, there'd be,' said Willie, 'no' the laddie, of course, but three carbines is better than naught.'

'Three would go halfway to replacing the muskets we lost when they searched the kirk last month,' said Master Carmichael. 'Right, then, Reverend, let's be away!' And together he and the minister heaved up the table – not the Lord's Table any more, but the table of Wauprigg kitchen, and hauled it aside.

Underneath, with the loose flagstones that covered it laid by, was the shallow space before the hearth where the congregation put their weapons when they came to worship – quickly covered in case of need, and quickly got at also. Man after man stooped and came up with his own weapon. Two muskets, a carbine and a couple of old muzzle-loading hand guns, and several knives and hangers of one kind and another. But I was watching Alan as he stood in the inner doorway holding one of Grandfather's pair of horse pistols – a fine breech-loader, old but in well-loved condition. Grandfather had shown them to me once; he had carried them when he followed Montrose and they were a part of his youth and the old shining days of the Covenanting cause.

I saw Alan's face as he looked down at it in the candlelight. It was already loaded, but he cocked it to make last-minute sure, then pushed it into his belt. For a moment his eyes did meet mine, across the ordered bustle of the big crowded kitchen, and I saw the brightness in them that was somehow cold and unchancy like marsh fire.

Then they were all heading for the door.

'Go forth in God's name and do His work!' cried my Aunt Margaret, as Willie pulled it open and they shouldered out with the minister in the lead, into the deepening dusk.

One of the bairns began to cry. The women left behind stood and looked after them, listening to their footfalls until they were swallowed up in the gusting wind. One of the farm dogs barked, and was silent.

And there I stood, left among the women and the bairns. And part of me wanted to accept the shame and bide there; and part of me wanted nothing to do with what was going to happen. But another part of me was filled with a rising tide of excitement, and that part would be out and away after Alan, heading with the other men through the gusty March gloaming with Grandfather's pistol in his belt. And in my inner ear was that light quick voice of his, "'Tis not just for our way of worship, 'tis for the freedom of Scotland that's crying out under the English heel!'

And I knew that where Alan was going, I had to go too. That whatever was going to happen, I had to be a part of it. I had at least to be there . . . I had to see . . . I mumbled something about going to see did Grandfather need any help with the cow, and bolted out into the farm garth.

No one said me nay, or seemed to notice my going. Indeed I am thinking that nobody cared much whether I went or stayed.

Outside, darkness had taken the valley, though there was still light in the sky, and a lopsided moon caught in the swaying still-bare branches of the rowan tree by the gate was pale and insubstantial as a bubble. From the doorway of the byre dim lantern-light spilled out over the straw-wisped cobbles, where Grandfather kept company with his sick cow, and I wondered if he had heard the comings and goings. There was still time to turn aside.

One of the dogs came padding across and thrust her muzzle into my hand. I fondled her for a moment, then pushed her away. 'Back wi' ye, Jess. Good lassie, get back.'

Then I was out on the driftway and heading down towards the burn. The wind was hushing through the whitethorn trees along the edge of the out-field. I kept well among them, and took care not to get too close to the knot of dark figures I could just make out ahead of me on the track.

They were down to the cattle-ford now, stringing out across the timber foot-bridge beside it. On the far side they clotted again, and by the cobweb light of the moon I could see a handful more figures coming down the braeside to meet them where the track forked on the far bank. Seemingly Wauprigg was not the only place to have received the word. I hung back until they had crossed the low ridge and dropped out of sight beyond it, then made for the bridge myself, and went after them, top speed.

On the far side the track dropped to join the drove road. Left hand below me a few half-hearted flecks of light showed from the huddled cottages of the clachan; right-handwise the way climbed up towards the moors, and far up that way a single glim, lonely in the dark billows of the land, shone, I knew, from old Phemie's alehouse.

I turned up towards it, and again saw that flicker of dark movement way ahead of me. A sort of shadow-loping that made me think of a pack of something, wolves maybe, on the hunting trail. Then it was lost among the thorn trees that arched over the lane. But a few moments later I glimpsed it again, among the furze of the rough pasture. They were leaving the drove-way, spreading out like a hunting pack to surround the quarry.

It came to me for the first time in that moment that there were living men where that light was, and the hunt closing in on them out of the dark. Then part of me was for shouting and making a warning uproar; part of me was for heading back to Grandfather and the cow, and hoping that it was all a dream. In an odd way it was like a dream, but suddenly I was caught up in it and I could no more have broken free than spread wings and flown to the moon.

There was a cold clemmed sickness twisting in the pit of my belly, but still I headed on towards that nearing blink of light, and the thing that was going to happen there.

The alehouse crouched beside the lane, its roof of heather thatch like the back of some big crouching beast against the sky. I did not dare get too close for fear of being discovered by the dark shapes – I had long since lost all thought of them as human folk I knew, and the feeling was in me that if they found me in their midst they would tear me to pieces. But I saw the smoky light leaking out through the gaps in the ill-fitting shutters. And somewhere inside I heard laughter and a snatch of drunken song.

And then it was as though the night with its creeping shadows blew up in my face. From away to the right and left of me – I must have been closer among them than I knew – owls began to cry, and away beyond the alehouse others answered them. There was a small red glow as somebody brought out a tinder-box from under their plaid; other, sharper flecks of light from slow-match for the old-fashioned muskets. Someone dipped the corner of a bundle of rags – pitch soaked, they must have been – into the tinder-box, and as it flared up I saw faces springing clear for a moment out of the dark. And the one with the bundle of rags was Davy Meickle the blacksmith, and the one with the tinder-box was the minister.

Then all in the same moment as it seemed Davy was kicking in the ramshackle door, flinging in the burning bundle, while someone else crouching behind him lobbed after it something in a flask. There was a whoof of flame – dry rushes there would be, on the floor. Somebody shouted, 'What of old Phemie?'

And somebody shouted back, 'She can run for it with the rest! If not, let her burn for the accursed witch she is!'

There was ragged shouting from inside the alehouse, and old Phemie screaming, shrill and high like a hare in a trap; and shadows lurched to and fro, maybe they were trying to quell the flames, but with the rush-strewn floor there was no hope of that.

And then old Phemie came running out, skirling and beating at the flames that fringed her shawl as she ran. They let her pass. But in the same instant there came a ragged rattle of shots from the back of the alehouse. There was no door that side, but there were windows, and on that side too there would be shooting-light, for the inside was well ablaze and the shutters catching. Then there was a shout of triumph as four more figures broke from the burning building, running low after Phemie, their carbines in their hands; and firing as they came, but they could not see what they were shooting at. They must have known how small a chance they had, but they would have had none at all in any other way. And maybe they were thinking, if they had time for thinking, that a bullet is a better way out than burning, as a good many have thought before them.

They were clear targets against the flamelight, and the men crouching among the thorn scrub dropped them in their tracks. The first two and the last went down with no more than a choking gasp or a scream that ended halfway; but the third, him with no carbine, and small in his grey coat, twitched about and cried out for his mother; and someone went over to him and finished the work. I recognised Grandfather's pistol first; and then Alan that held it; and there was no shred of pity on his face, nothing but a kind of savage satisfaction as he turned away.

And then, not knowing how I came there, I was out of cover and staring down at the drummer laddie. He was no more than a year or two older than myself, maybe a year or two younger than Alan; and there was a surprised sort of look on his face, and a neat round hole in his forehead where the pistol ball had gone in, and blood already spreading from the back of it – a ball makes more mess coming out than it does going in, but I did not know that at the time. Where he'd been shot in the first place I never saw.

It was all over, and they were stripping the dead of their carbines and anything else that might come in handy. In the leaping flamelight and the confusion no one seemed to notice me. Only the drummer laddie seemed to be looking at me; him with the hole in his head, that had cried for his mother. And the cold black vomit rose in me, and I blundered away into the ditch under the thorn trees, and crouched there, throwing up all that was in me, and sobbing and shivering the while.

I mind falling forward into a great darkness that was more than the darkness of the ditch. And for a while there was nothing more.

2

Two Loyalties

Presently there was jagged light, thrusting at me with bright, sharp fingers; and someone had a hand twisted in my hair and was forcing my head up, and, blinking against the dazzle, I saw that there were men all around me. Men in grey uniform coats, their hard and angry faces lit by the flames of the bit of burning timber that one of them held high.

'Here's one that hasna got clear,' said the man gripping my hair.

'Too busy puking in the ditch,' said another. 'Och, he's naught but a laddie.'

'Not so much younger than Johnnie, I reckon,' said a third, coldly savage.

All of what had gone before had come back to me by that time, and I knew that Johnnie would be the drummer laddie, and the sickness heaved in me again. I gagged, but I'd nothing left to throw up. I crouched there staring up at them, and waiting for them to kill me.

'Looks fair daft to me. But mebbe there's some sense to be got out of him with a pistol butt. Best have him up to the Colonel,' said the first man.

And him that held me by the hair gave a twisting heave that all but had me screaming. 'Up, you.'

Somehow, with the world and the flamelight swirling round me, I managed to clamber to my feet and out of the ditch.

They twisted my arms behind me, and hauled me

back through the thorn-brake, past a man standing by with their horses who spat at me as I staggered by. The alehouse was burned through, and the flames beginning to sink. But there was light enough to see the bodies that had been fetched round from where they fell and lay roughly side by side in what had been old Phemie's kale plot; and light enough also to see the man who wheeled his tall sorrel horse as my captors hauled me towards him.

'We've got one of them, sir,' said the soldier with the torch.

The man on the horse sat looking down at me. 'So I see. A something small one.' His voice was cool and clipped.

'Mebbe he can tell us the who and where of the others, sir.'

'Maybe.'

Memory is an odd and kittle thing. It seems to me now, looking back, that I must have seen then what I came to see and know later: the cool arrogant face well matched to the voice, that could yet kindle into eagerness and quirk swiftly into laughter, the slight, tense figure, even the thin strong hands, nervous, sensitive, horseman's hands inside the riding gloves. But truth to tell I saw only a man on a tall red horse, whose face seemed to hover over me as a hawk hovers over some terrified small creature in the grass.

I began to babble. 'I didna do it! I didna do any of it! I only followed the others to see . . .'

'What others?' The cool voice cut me off between word and word.

I heard the crackle of the sinking flames, and the wind hushing up over the moors in the dark, in the silence between the man and me; that and the racing drub of my own heart. In another instant it would be too late. The merciless grip on my arms tightened so that I must have yelped, but that the terror I was in was more than the pain. And then memory came to my aid – one of the soldiers saying, 'Looks fair daft to me.' Maybe if I could act that way! The memory of Daft Eckie who I had seen once or twice at Lochinloch market straggled into my mind; though indeed I must have looked daft enough already with the shock and fear of that night's doings, and I scarcely had to act at all.

'What others?' said the man again, with a kind of deadly patience that was more fearful than any spoken threat.

And the man who held my arms began to shake me to and fro. I let my head loll sideways, indeed it felt like to part company with my shoulders, and gasped out, 'Just folk. I saw the fire an' I thought mebbe 'twas a wake, and there'd be food an' drink an' – an' an' a fiddler if the minister wasn't there —'

'It was a wake, sure enough,' said the man on the red horse. And then, speaking slow and clear, to reach any understanding there might be in my addled wits, 'These folks, who were they? Did you know any of them?'

I swung to and fro blubbering in the hands of the man behind me. 'I didna ken them. When I got close they was all running away – 'cept them as winna run no more. I'm thinking they was witches – and there werena any food or drink, an' there werena any fiddler, and I was feart —'

'Let me try what a pistol butt will do, sir,' said one of the soldiers who seemed to be chief among the rest.

But the man on the red horse shook his head. 'There's no sense to be got out of that one, I'm thinking, with a pistol butt or any other way. Let him go.'

18

'But, sir —'

'Let him go, Corporal.'

'Sir,' said the one he called Corporal.

The shaking stopped, and the agonising grip on my back-twisted arms slacked off, and I was free.

'Now be away home with you,' said the man on the red horse.

And I turned and ran, darting and swerving like a hare with the dogs after it. But I had just enough sense left to know even then that one of them would like enough to be coming after me to see where I went. I've never known whether or not there was, but I took no chances, and led any that might come off in the wrong direction at the start, and a fine dance through bushes and briars until I was sure that I'd shaken him off, before I turned myself back towards Wauprigg.

I would not be knowing how far I had gone out of my way, nor how long was the road home; time and distance seemed little to do with it, as they are little to do with the hampered and confused journeys of a dream. Broom and brambles clawed at me as though with small, evil, hating hands, and once I fell headlong into a boggy patch; but I came down the driftway at last, and saw the light from the house-place windows that were unshuttered now as though to show all men that they had nothing to hide.

And just as I reached the gate the kitchen door swung wide, and my grandfather came out, flinging his old plaid round his shoulders, and two of the farm men after him. He checked at sight of me, and called back over his shoulder, 'All's well. He's back.' He flung arm and plaid around me as I lurched near, and swept me into the firelit kitchen, slamming the door to behind me, with the farmhands outside.

I mind I staggered back against the door, and stood there, hearing their feet go trudging off to their own lodgings, and looking about me. The neighbourhood-women and their bairns had gone and the place looked much its usual self. Aunt Margaret and Elspeth the maid were sitting at the table with their sewing, the Bible at the other side of it, open for the evening reading, in the light of the tallow dips. Alan stood in the inner doorway; maybe he had just come from putting the old horse pistol back in its usual place. And I mind that just for the one instant our eyes met. Then he turned and strolled across to the hearth and flung himself down on the bench beside it.

Aunt Margaret was the first to break the silence, the frown-line bitten deep between her brows. 'Where have you been?' she demanded. 'Through half the bogs and briars of Ayrshire by the looks of you.'

Maybe there was just a hope in her that I had not been where she knew in her heart that I had been.

'I told you,' said Alan to the ceiling. 'He must have come prying after us.'

I could feel the currents washing to and fro in that room, under the surface quietness of it. Hate and fear and triumph and anger – and shame. The shame was Grandfather's, mixed with the anger.

'I did go after you,' I said, 'and I saw what there was to see – and then the soldiers came.'

'Did they see you? Did they see you?' Grandfather rounded on me as he slipped the old plaid from his shoulders.

'Aye,' I said, 'they caught me and hauled me up before a man on a red horse —'

'What like of man?' demanded Grandfather.

'A man wi' a quiet way with him that was worse than shouting.'

'That will be Colonel Graham of Claverhouse.'

And Aunt Margaret drew the thread through her sewing, and said, 'Bloody Claver'se.'

'What did you tell him?' said Grandfather.

'Nothing. I made out I was like Daft Eckie over to Lochinloch market; and in a bit he let me go.'

Aunt Margaret let her sewing fall and rose from the table. I saw the knuckles on her hands like bare yellow bone where they were gripped together against the dark stuff of her gown. 'Then God help us! They'll have followed you.'

Elspeth was whimpering.

'What matter if they have – now,' said Alan. 'Never fash yourself, Mother, they'll not be finding anything that's no' as it should be.'

And I said, 'They'll not have followed me back, either. I took care of that.'

And Aunt Margaret's hands slowly relaxed. 'Get up to your bed,' she said, and after a moment, 'and forget what you've seen the night.'

'I'll go to my bed,' I said, 'but I doubt I'll forget.'

And I turned and blundered across to the inner door and up the ladder stair.

Lying empty and sick and wakeful on my bed of piled straw in the loft, I pulled the blanket over my head to try to shut out the low terrible roaring coming up from below that was Grandfather giving rein to his anger at last. But I could not shut out the face of the drummer laddie staring at me out of the darkness, with the hole that was like a third eye in the middle of his forehead.

It was still there when despite myself, sobbing and shivering, I dropped off into an uneasy half-sleep. And I never heard feet on the ladder and the rustle of straw;

and when the blanket was pulled down from my head, I thought that it was the drummer laddie. But the hand that clamped over my mouth to cut off my scream was alive, and the voice in my ear was Alan's.

'Hush you,' he said, ''tis only me.'

He was squatting beside me. I could just make out his shape in the faint light from the hole in the thatch that served as a window.

'I'm sorry you saw what you saw the night,' he whispered out of the dark, 'but we need those carbines for the Lord's work, and for the freedom of Scotland. And when bairns go thrusting their noses into the doings of grown men, often enough they get more than they bargained for.'

He was trying to make it all sound quite reasonable. Somehow small. Was that how it seemed to him?

He had taken his hand away from my mouth, and I managed to get out two words, 'Go *away*!'

'I've somewhat to say first,' he said, 'and you'd best listen. The sojers are bound to come asking questions and hunting in the thatch at all the houses round about by morning. Mebbe before morning. And mebbe they'll be the same ones that saw ye back at the alehouse, so mind that ye are still like Daft Eckie over to Lochinloch market! And mind also that I was with Grandfather and his sick cow all evening!' And then suddenly he was bending very close, and his breath was on my face and his hands came up round my neck, quite lightly. 'If ye tell, we shall all hang.' His hands tightened for an instant, making me choke. 'But if we hang, Hugh Herriot, so *will* you!'

He kept his grip for a moment just long enough to be sure I'd got the point, then took his hands away, and got up and turned him to his own sleeping place, leaving me crowing for breath and with a new sense of sick astonishment upon me.

For until he put it into my head, it never for an instant occurred to me to betray my own kinfolk.

It was scarce cock-light when the troopers came. They were not the ones that I had seen the night before, and so I did not have to play Daft Eckie again, which was a merciful thing, for I am no actor, and I doubted my ability to play the part a second time.

'Where were you yestere'en?' demanded the corporal in charge of them.

'And why would you be spiering to know that?' returned my grandfather. 'What was to do yestere'en?'

'Ye've no heard?'

'Heard *what*?'

'Never mind for that.' The corporal came a menacing step forward, but my grandfather never gave back an inch. '*Where were ye?*'

'Most of the evening I was in the byre with a sick cow,' said Grandfather.

The corporal looked round about. 'And the rest of ye?'

'My older grandson was with me, the younger was here in the kitchen with the women. That's so, Hugh?'

'Aye,' I said.

'And I was where all God-fearing bodies should be, at home with my woman and bairns,' put in one of the farmhands, and the rest added their voices to his.

'And for why would ye be seeing to the cow yourself, when ye've farmhands and to spare?' The corporal turned back to Grandfather.

'Because she's a good cow, and dropped a good calf

23

at the evening's end, and I'd not trust her to any care but my own at such a time.'

So it went on. And when the questions were over, they herded us, farmhands and family alike, into the parlour, which had but the one door, and held us there, a man standing in the doorway with his carbine at the ready, while the rest went through the house and out-buildings like terriers rat-hunting in a barn – we missed half the hens afterwards! But they found no sign of stolen carbines or smuggled Dutch muskets; only the ancient fowling-piece which every farm possessed, and my grandfather's pistols in their holsters hanging in their usual place at the head of the big box-bed.

The corporal sniffed at both barrels, but they had been cleaned too well to carry any smell of burned powder, and anyway it was upward of twelve hours since the one had been fired.

When the search was finished, and they had found no sign of anything that was not as it should be, my grand-father asked again, 'Now that you have done turning my house out of doors, will you be telling me the mean-ing of it all, and what happened yestere'en?'

The corporal considered, then shrugged his shoulders. 'Och well, I don't see there's any harm tell-ing ye. For the one thing, three Government issue carbines are gone missing; for the other, the alehouse over at Blackmoor was burned down and the four of our men inside – fools that they were – slaughtered for the sake of those same carbines.'

There was a little silence, and then my grandfather said, 'It's sorry I am to hear it . . . What became of old Phemie that kept the alehouse?'

'Found dead in a ditch this morning,' said the cor-poral. 'Sore burned, she was, and old to be taking a shock the like of that one.'

And he gathered up his men, and in a while they mounted their horses that were waiting in the farmyard and clattered away.

Nobody moved until the last dwindling hoof–beats had quite died into the distance. Then a kind of sigh ran through the little parlour. And I mind a whaup rose crying from the moors behind the house.

And oh, but the grief was on me, for the drummer laddie, and for my own loss of Alan that left me like a stray dog with no heel to follow. My head felt stiff on my shoulders when I forced it round to look at him. He was an odd pearly white, and he was looking at Grandfather. But in a little, as though my looking had reached him like a touch, he turned and answered it with a long cool stare.

Feeling like somebody much older than myself, I said, 'So we'll not be hanging. Not this time, anyway. Bu you be awfu' careful another time, because I'd like to kill you, Alan Armstrong; I'd like to kill you fine.'

I do not know what I meant by it; it was just a bairn's threat, I suppose; though it did not feel like one.

Alan laughed at it. He stood with his head tipped back, and laughed. 'Thanks for the warning, my mannie! I'll mind it – another time!' And that was certainly no bairn's threat.

'Now may God forgive you your wicked words, you ungrateful —' my Aunt Margaret began. But I heard her bitter voice behind me, for I had already turned and was blundering from the room.

I made for the stable and flung myself face down in the straw of old Janot's stall, and bided there a long time, smelling the comforting smell of horses, and hearing their stir and rustle and soft puffing breaths. I wanted no more to do with men and the world of men ever again.

The pull of two loyalties within me was over and done with, and there was some relief in that. I knew now that I was like Montrose: that I was no Covenanter nor ever could be.

But oh, the grief was on me sore.

3

My Lady Jean

A few days later, Grandfather bade me saddle Janot for him, and rode into Lochinloch market.

He got home in a silent mood, and in silence ate the supper that Aunt Margaret had ready for him in the parlour. Dinner in the kitchen with the farmhands, supper in the parlour with just the family; that's the way of it in the big farms and small manor houses of Lowland Scotland. And when he had done, and we had just left the table, Alan and I careful never to catch each other's glance, as we had been ever since the morning that the soldiers came, he called for his clay pipe, and when Aunt Margaret had filled and lit and given it to him, he sat back in his chair and took a long steady pull, and puffed out a blue smoke-garland round his head. (I never knew any man to make more smoke with his pipe than my grandfather did.) And out of the midst of the smoke cloud, said he, 'I was talking wi' Dundonel's factor at the market.'

'It would not be the first time,' said Aunt Margaret, sitting herself down at her spinning-wheel beside the fire.

'About Hugh,' said Grandfather.

The sound of my own name seemed to give me a small jab in my belly, and I stopped playing with Jess's ears, she having her head heavy and warm on my knee; and we all looked at Grandfather.

And Grandfather took another pull at his pipe and spoke out of a fresh cloud of smoke. 'I was telling him that I'd a daughter's son here that I was wishing to find a place in the world for, seeing that I had already a son's son to follow after me here at Wauprigg. And he was telling me that they had room for another laddie in the stables, over to Place of Paisley.'

My Aunt Margaret's foot checked on the treadle, and the thrum of the wheel fell silent. 'And you've struck a bargain with him to take Hugh?'

'Aye,' said Grandfather.

'After all the to-do you made about his getting his book-learning from the dominie?'

'Book-learning will maybe stand him in good stead one day. Meanwhile – he has a way with horses.'

'But to go for a stable laddie!' cried Aunt Margaret. 'An Armstrong of Wauprigg!'

Oh well, I suppose 'twas the disgrace to the family, all over again; and I my mother's son.

I mind getting up so sharply that I all but knocked over my creepy stool, and hearing my voice speaking as 'twere of its own accord. 'But I'm not an Armstrong of Wauprigg, Aunt Margaret, I'm a Herriot of nowhere in particular, and plain enough you ha' made it to me, all this while. And, Grandfather, I would like it well enough, to be a stable laddie for Lord Dundonel.'

Two days later, when the carrier passed by on his weekly way, I was waiting for him at the foot of the driftway, with all that I possessed in the world bundled in an old plaid; a clean shirt and a plumbago pencil and some odd bits and pieces of paper that I could be drawing on, and the like.

Grandfather and I had had a final word under the rowan tree by the gate. 'I'll no' be needing to bid you keep a close mouth on what happened up at old Phemie's,' he'd said. And suddenly he'd been not Armstrong of Wauprigg but just a troubled old man. 'But I'll ask ye not to think of us more hardly than ye can help, Hugh.'

'I'll never think hardly of *you*, Grandfather,' I'd said, with a sudden aching in my throat.

He had put his hand for an instant on my shoulder, then turned back towards the house; and I mind old Jess thrusting her rough muzzle into my hand before she padded after him.

That was my last parting with Wauprigg, that had been my mother's home, though it had never been mine. Then I had picked up my bundle and set out down the driftway to meet the carrier.

I did not look back.

Place of Paisley is a fine great house, and the stable-yard a good enough place to work in, for old Lord Dundonel was one for the keeping and breeding of fine horses. Life was not exactly easy there, not with Willie Sempill in charge of the stables, but there was a goodness to it, all the same.

And so I was part of another Covenanting household, though one that for the most part followed the cause more gently than the last that I had known. Sir John Cochrane, the second son of the house, was refuging in Holland after being caught up in a plot to kill the King; and the first son, who was dead before ever I came to Place of Paisley (they said, praying with his last breath for the death of that same King), had married Lady Catherine Kennedy, of as black a Covenanting family as ever prayed to the Lord, a grim-faced, godly woman who divided her time between Paisley and

29

Auchans, her own house some miles off. And most of their sons and daughters were safely married into families of their own way of thinking, and rearing broods of fledgeling Covenanters in their turn. But old Lord Dundonel, the head of the house, had been made Earl for his loyalty to the first Charles, in the bad days; and I have often thought that there was a likeness between him and my grandfather, and he could have done with a sick cow himself from time to time . . .

And no house could have been quite without light and laughter that held my lady Jean.

Lady Jean Cochrane, youngest daughter to the eldest son and that bleak-faced widow woman he left behind him. Sixteen or seventeen she'd have been, the spring I first saw her; old for a lassie to be still unwed, but I'm thinking she was hard to please, and the old Earl would not force her, though there was talk that her mother would have taken a whip to her if she'd had *her* way. A slight, long-boned lassie, with straight dove-gold hair that she wore at most times tied back with a ribbon as though she were a boy, and a pair of straight grey eyes like a boy's too, and a wide mouth that seemed made for joy. She was in and out of the stable-yard more often than any well-brought-up lady should have been; for she had all her grandfather's love of horses; and wherever my lady Jean wished to be, there she would be, whether or no. And always with her would be her young kinswoman, both henchwoman and friend, and maybe two–three years her junior, a nut-brown lassie with a kind of cool quiet darkness about her, like the coolth of tree-shade on a hot summer's day. In some ways she was like my lady; they were the same shape, and would have had both of them the same grace, but that while my lady Jean met life with a dancing step, the

30

other carried herself always as though she was braced for something. I never knew what, I doubt she did herself; it was something in her, like the strangeness she had as though part of her came from another country . . . Mary, she was mostly called; Mistress Mary Ruthven, but I heard my lady call her Darklis between themselves. Darklis is a gipsy name, a Tinkler name, aye. There were tales of gipsy blood mingled with the Kennedys' – or Kennedy blood with the gipsies', way back . . .

So then, wherever my lady Jean went, there also went Mistress Mary. I mind I envied her, having someone to follow.

But I'm running ahead of myself. My lady was up at Auchans with her mother when I first came to Place of Paisley, and I'd been there two–three weeks when she returned.

She came back in wild April weather; and that same night, as though she had been waiting for her mistress's return, Linnet, her old mare, dropped a fine filly foal. We got the mare into the big loose-box at the doorward end of the stable, where we would have plenty of room to work; and a long hard night we had, all three of us, the mare herself and Willie Sempill and me. Willie had taken a good opinion of me, finding me better skilled with the horses than most of my kind, and showed it by unloading on to me all the extra work about the place, and keeping me out of the warm straw in the loft where the other lads were snoring, to help him get old Linnet through her foaling. But when the light beyond the open stable door was turning green with daybreak and the gold of the big horn lantern fading, all was safely over, and the foal, still damp from its birth, already staggering on to its long legs and thrust blindly around its mother for the warm milk.

And I mind somewhere a lark leapt up into the sky, singing like the morning star.

We gave the mare a warm bran mash with a dash of good ale in it; and then Willie went off to douse his head in the horse-trough and get a bite to eat, leaving me to clean up the loose-box and put down fresh straw, while the world woke and the other stable-hands came down yawning and scratching themselves from the loft.

I had just about finished – working slow and quiet so as not to fret the mare – when I heard a lassie's voice outside, talking to Willie Sempill. 'Why did you not send me word last night, Willie? Ye know how much Linnet means to me.'

'Aye, I ken that fine, my leddy,' said Willie, in the tone of a patient man hard tried, 'and 'twas for that reason I didna send. Where would ha' been the use? Ye would but ha' fretted all night, and that wouldna be helping the mare.'

And next moment, with a sudden dazzle of April sun behind her, and rain sparkling on the shoulders of the dark green cloak that she had flung on crooked in the by-going, was my lady Jean, and behind her the nut-brown lassie that at that time I scarce noticed at all.

Coming in out of the April dazzle, I do not think she saw me at first in the brown shadows of the loose-box; and indeed I would have slipped out, knowing that she and the mare were well acquainted and there would be no risk of old Linnet becoming scared and unchancy, as can happen to a mare with a new foal when strangers come too close; but my lady and her henchwoman, and Willie Sempill hovering behind, were all across the doorway, and I could not well push past them, so I bided where I was.

She gave her first attention to the mare, fondling her

muzzle and crest, and speaking the small soft words of love and pride into her twitching ear, in the broadest of the Lowland tongue, while Linnet slobbered on her shoulder. And then she turned her to the foal, kneeling down in the straw – mercifully it was the clean straw, but indeed I do not think she would have noticed whether it was or no – and putting her arms round the little creature's neck to drop a kiss on the white star upon its forehead.

'There's a kiss for welcome,' said she. 'Eh, my bonnie, my bonnie wee burd, what will we be calling ye? Wi' the star on your forehead an' all.'

'There was a laverock singing like the morning star when she was but just born,' said I, not thinking till I heard my own voice.

My lady looked up then and saw me standing there. 'Were you here when she was born?' said she.

'Aye, Master Sempill and me, we spent the night wi' her.'

'You must be tired,' said she; and then, looking at me more closely, 'You're new-come while I have been from home.'

'Aye, my leddy.'

'And what do they call you?'

'Hugh,' said I, 'Hugh Herriot.'

She gave the foal a gentle hug, and then got to her feet as it went back to its mother and the warm milk, its squirrel tail a'wag behind its little doddering rump. And we watched it together, and laughed. And said she, 'Then thank you, Hugh Herriot, for your night's work; she's a credit to you and Willie Sempill. And as to her name – Laverock will suit her just fine.'

She gave me her lilting smile for the first time, and turned away; and Willie Sempill must have got his share of it, too, for I saw his face creak into an answering grin. 'Willie, I forgive you,' said she, 'because it's April and I'm home again. If ye'll just remember from time to time, dear man, that I'm old enough to fret if I choose, and not just the bairn I was when you set me on my first pony.'

And she was gone; and behind her the nut-brown lassie who had spoken never a word all the while.

After that, my lady Jean was never in the stable-yard but she would have a word with me in the by-going – which was well enough save that Andy Burns, another of the stable laddies, was inclined to jealousy, and took it upon himself to see that this did not swell my head for me.

For a while, chiefly because he was bigger than I was, I put up with having my head held down in the horse-trough until I was half-drowned, with finding evil things in my sleeping straw and being called ill names. But the day came – I'd not be knowing why it was that day and no other – when he called me a wee boot-licking, snivelling bastard just the once too often, and I hit him.

I took him by surprise and he went sprawling into the muck-heap. So, I had the one moment of triumph. But as I plunged yelling after him, bent upon the avenging of many insults, he came up to meet me, fists flailing, and the next thing I knew was a kind of star-burst in my right eye that made the stable-yard spin for a moment. It was a bonnie fight while it lasted; and not just a laddies' tussle, for both of us were out to kill the other if that might be; but in the end he hooked my legs from under me, and there I was, flat on my back, with Andy on top of me, his big bony hands round my neck, and him set to banging the senses out of my head of the cobbles. But between one crack and the next I jabbed a knee up into his groin, and half-choked as I was, contrived to force my head down till my mouth found his wrist, and I bit into it and hung on like a dog at the bear-baiting.

I mind the salt-sweet taste of blood between my teeth, and he yelled and let go of my throat, and began to jab away at me with his other hand, trying to get free, and howling all the while for help.

Aye, that was a good moment, too. As good as the moment when I had made the sketch of Laverock in the home paddock, and looked at it when it was done, and saw that it was Laverock, and not just any other foal at all.

But then came running feet and shouting, and suddenly a pailful of cold water sluicing over us both, and two of the grooms had us apart and hauled to our feet, shivering and gasping. 'Yon's the way to stop a dog fight,' one of the men said, giving me a good hard shake, and there was a laugh; and as the red mist cleared from my head, I realised that Willie Sempill, lord of the stable, was on the scene. Aye, and so was Dundonel and my lady Jean!

The laughter stopped, and a stillness came over the stable-yard, save for the pigeons that we had startled, still circling overhead.

'That's a bonnie black eye ye have there,' said Dundonel to me, with a kind of detached interest, 'and a bloody mouth. You should learn to keep your guard higher.'

'Most of it's no' mine,' said I, rubbing the back of my hand across the juicy mess.

The groom holding Andy gave a startled curse, and

dragged forward the lad's arm with the marks of my teeth in it. And Andy just stood there, white as buttermilk and bubbling through his bleeding nose and saying nothing at all.

'So, a dog fight indeed,' said Dundonel, 'what was it about?'

'What pup could ever tell you what a fight was about, my lord?' said Willie Sempill. 'Best you take my leddy away and leave these two to me.'

'I will so, in a while,' said Dundonel as man to man. Then turning back to me with his shaggy grey brows quirked up, 'Why did ye bite him?'

I shook my head, trying to clear it as much as anything. 'Because he's bigger than me.' And, my brain flinging up an old memory, I added, 'Alcibiades, him they called the Lion of Athens, bit the chiel he was fighting, when he was a laddie. He said if he was a lion he'd fight like one.'

Lord Dundonel nodded. 'So he did, so he did. But who told you about Alcibiades?'

'My father,' I said, and then for good measure, 'He said 'twas no' a very gentlemanly thing to do, but Alcibiades was an aristocrat, which is a different thing altogether.'

'Hugh Herriot—' began Master Sempill, outraged.

But Dundonel gave a bark of laughter. 'Nevertheless, I seem to remember that Alcibiades was beaten for it,' said he. And with a nod to Willie Sempill he turned and strolled away. And my lady with him, she glancing back anxiously as they went.

Oh aye, I had my beating, and Andy also. Willie himself saw to that. He always kept the strap in his own hands, and never allowed the grooms to administer more than a stray cuff in passing. But scarcely was it

36

over, and us washing the blood off each other's backs at the well – no one else would have done it for us, and it's not easy to wash the blood off your own back – than Mistress Mary came running into the stable-yard, with a pot of some herb-smelling salve in one hand, and a lump of juicy raw beef in the other.

'My lady says that you should always salve a lion bite. And there's enough there for the stripes as well,' said she, and set the pot down on the rim of the well. Then to me, 'Bide still,' as she clapped the chunk of raw meat none too gently on my eye. 'There. Hold it there for a while, and 'twill draw out the evil humours.'

And those were the first words ever she spoke to me. And she turned and kilted up her skirts and ran light-foot back the way she had come.

4

John Graham of Claverhouse

Spring turned to summer and the summer went by, and the great old house backed against the ruins of Paisley Abbey became the familiar centre of my life. I cannot say that Andy and I became friends, but I have often noticed that a fight and a little blood-letting can act like the bursting of a boil, and after that blood-letting of ours we got on well enough together; and my lady went on talking to me, for the shared interest that we had in Laverock as she grew to be a fine filly alongside her mother in the home paddock.

News drifted in from the outside world. The Covenanters had quieted for the while, and Colonel Graham of Claverhouse was busy on the Borders, keeping watch for fugitives from the round-up of the plot to kill the King, the Ryehouse Plot, they called it, as they came fleeing north to friends in Scotland. There was a good deal of coming and going after dark that we in the stable-yard, tending half-foundered horses by lantern light, were well aware of; for the Border patrols could not be everywhere at once, and old Dundonel had ever a soft spot for a fugitive, him with his own son fled overseas and all . . .

There was another kind of coming and going as well, for Dundonel kept open house and a welcome for all, even those who came wearing the King's uniform. And among those was Lord Ross, my lady's cousin, and a certain Captain William Livingstone, a dark, quiet man who had been at Saint Andrew's University with her eldest brother. Seeing those two together, you would have thought that *they* were brother and sister, for the closeness that they had to each other; though it was in my mind even then that Captain Livingstone would gladly have been something else to her if she had looked at him in another way.

But she never did. It was clear that he was a friend to her, and nothing more; and he accepted the place in her life that she gave him.

Towards the end of that winter, the troubles that had quieted for a while began to flare up again in the South West; and again the Government sent cavalry to re-inforce the dragoons that were already there, and again in command of them came Colonel Graham of Claverhouse, back to his old hunting-grounds.

Paisley town was full of troops. Claverhouse's own troopers, His Majesty's Regiment of Horse, to give them their full and proper name, were quartered in the long gatehouse by Abbey Bridge that had once been the guest-house of the Cluniac monastery; there were horse lines in the home park; and when there began to be wounded for tending, as there did soon enough, they were lodged in the Place itself.

It was care for his wounded that brought Claverhouse up to the house in the first place. And for the first few times I saw no more of him than a big sorrel charger with a military saddle on him being walked up and down before the main door, and once a distant glimpse of a slight man in buff and steel, too far off to tell if my grandfather had been right in his guess that he was the man I had seen at the burning of old Phemie's alehouse. I knew more about him now than the stories of bloody persecution that I had gathered in the old days at Wauprigg. I knew that he had started his soldiering with the Scottish Brigade in the Low Countries, serving under William of Orange. There was a tale that he had saved William's life in battle by bringing him off on his own horse when the Stadtholder's charger was shot under him, but maybe there was no truth in it; either that or William was not the rewarding kind, for a couple of years later, so said Willie Sempill, the promotion that should have come to Claverhouse went instead to a Highlander called MacKay. And Claverhouse left the Scots Brigade and returned to England; yet with much praise and personal recommendation from Orange William to the Duke of York whose daughter he – William – had lately wed. And it was the Duke of York, now become a friend, who had made Lieutenant John Graham of Claverhouse captain of a troop of horses, and sent him to deal with the Covenanters the first time ever he came down into Ayrshire and Galloway, years ago.

It was a story that woke and held my interest, so that I watched out for the man whenever he came up to Place of Paisley. But I took good care that he should not see me, lest my grandfather had been right, and by some unlikely chance he should remember me in the flamelight of the burning alehouse.

That was until one wild March evening with wisps of straw eddying in the wind all across the cobbles, and the sky flying the gold and saffron cloud-banners of a stormy sunset overhead, when he came clattering into the stable-yard before I knew it, and called to me – being the nearest – in that cool pleasant voice of his, to come and take his horse.

There was no help for it; and I dropped the yard broom and went to hold the sorrel as he dismounted.

If I kept my head down . . .

But I could not keep my head down; something stronger than my own will, a kind of terrible fascination, forced it back on my neck, to gaze fearfully up at him. He had come straight off the moors by the looks of him, and was as weather-worn and weary as his horse, but his face was cool and arrogant though none too clean in the shadow of his battered hat with its sodden and drooping plume.

And my grandfather had been right.

For one hideous moment the fiery sunset sky became the flames of the burning alehouse behind him; and at my feet the drummer laddie lay staring up at me with that hole like a third eye in the middle of his forehead.

For that moment cold shock seemed to stop my breath, and panic whimpered somewhere in the midst of me. Then Colonel Graham swung his leg over and dropped somewhat stiffly to the cobbles. And I mind him looking at me, quick and concerned. 'What's amiss, laddie? You look as though you'd seen a ghost.'

I shook my head. I saw he did not know me – why should he? – and my breath was coming back, though the feeling of icy shock remained. 'Och, 'tis nothing, Colonel Graham, sir; I was thinking of something else.'

'Whatever it was, I'd not be thinking of it too often,' said he; and then, 'So you know who I am.'

'I ken your horse, sir,' I said, 'I've walked him up and down for you more than once while you were in the house.'

His somewhat stern face lit into a smile – if I was writing of a lassie, I would have said that it was a smile of uncommon sweetness. At all events it was not the smile that you would have expected from Colonel John Graham of Claverhouse. Nor from Bloody Claver'se. No.

'Ah, that explains why Hector looks to you as a friend,' for the big charger had swung his head round and was slobbering at my shoulder. 'It seems you've a way with horses. See to him well for me, I'll be a while inside.'

And he turned and went off towards the arched entrance of the stable-yard. And I mind that, for all he held himself so straight, his steps behind the jaunty silver jingle of his spurs had a weary sound on the cobbles. And watching his flat back and slight, braced shoulders, I thought that if he was a horse I'd say he was on too tight a rein.

I turned myself to Hector, and led him towards the stable to off-saddle him and rub him down.

I was still shaking with shock, but Claverhouse's face in my mind was not as I'd seen it against the flames. He had looked at me as I took his horse, in a way that nobody had ever looked at me before. I had yet to learn that any man Claverhouse looked at knew himself to be the only man that Claverhouse was looking at in all the world. It was one of the things that gave him his power to lead men. But I knew that something had happened in my life that could not unhappen again, though I did not at that time know what it was.

Colonel Graham went on coming up to the house, to see how it fared with his wounded troopers. But as the spring drew on, he began to come up in another way, with a cock to his hat, and his uniform brushed and spruced up.

'Och, I ken the look when a chiel comes courtin',' said Willie Sempill, who was as much of a gossip as any old grannie. There was not much happened in the great house that we did not know about in the stable-yard.

But I had another idea in my head that took up most

42

of my thinking about that time. The idea that by and by, when I had seen a few more summers, I might go for a soldier. Maybe you will think that a strange and unlikely thing. Maybe you will picture me torn between two loyalties. But you will mind that I had been dragged up by a father who cared more for the picture taking life under his hand, for its trueness of colour and line, than ever he did for King or Covenant; and my time at Wauprigg had done little to bind me to the Covenanting cause. There was the time when I had been torn, between Alan with the freedom-fire in his eyes and Grandfather with his sick cow. And Alan himself had slashed through that tangle for me.

So now I was free to think long thoughts to myself about finding my way into Claverhouse's Horse (which was no easy thing in itself!) and wearing a fine uniform coat, and maybe ending up myself with a third eye in the middle of my forehead, at the hands of my own people . . .

It was not easy for a stable laddie in a big house to get much time to himself, nor anywhere to get away by his lone, when he would have solitude for his thinking; and most of my fellows seemed not to feel the need. I felt the need; and after a while I had found a place where I could betake me when I would be free of my own kind. It was in the ruins of the Abbey, no distance at all from the house, but yet as it might be a world away; a narrow space between the remains of the chancel wall and a crumbling table-tomb. It was difficult to swing a scythe in so narrow a place, and so the grass there grew as it would, and a briar rose out of the broken top of the tomb itself. The place had no fears for me, but a friendly feel to it, and I kept my bits of drawing stuff that my lady had given me when she found the fondness that I had that way inside the broken corner among the roots of the briar rose.

One evening well into the spring, I was lying up there like a fox in its earth, for I had an hour to myself and a mind to try drawing the clump of little wild daffodils that grew there, as they did in all the green corners of the Abbey ruins where the scythe could not reach them. But daffodils are of all flowers the most difficult to catch, to my way of thinking; and after a while I gave up the attempt, and returned my bits and pieces to their hiding-place, and just lay there with my head on my arm. It was drawing on to dusk, the sky shadowing to the colour of a fading harebell, and half a moon hanging in it clear and pale – pale as the wind-stirred daffodils which seem always, in a spring gloaming, to turn starry and shine with a faint light of their own.

And as I lay there, I heard steps brushing over the turf, and a murmur of voices. Clearly, to two other people than myself the old, kind Abbey ruins meant refuge. They came nearer, and I would have slipped away if I could, but they were close upon me, and if I stirred I should betray my own hiding-place. Nearer and nearer; I heard the silken frowing of long skirts through the grass, and the jingle of a man's spurs. I could not look out; but when the man spoke again, I knew his voice.

'My bonnie love,' said Claverhouse, 'are you sure? Sure beyond all doubting? I am almost twice your age.'

'Thirty-five,' said my lady Jean, with a soft bubble of laughter, 'How very shocking!'

And right beside the broken tomb they halted. I froze like a wild thing. There was naught else that I could do.

When she spoke again, the laughter had gone and

left her grave. 'I am sure past all doubting, John, and there is only one fear in me, that our marriage will harm your career.'

'Harm my career?' Claverhouse echoed her words as though he did not understand them; but I'm thinking he did.

'And you a soldier before you're aught else,' said she. 'Oh, John, John. Colonel John Graham of His Majesty's Regiment of Horse, to be carrying off a bride from the rebel house of Cochrane!'

He laughed, softly. 'I'm thinking my career is firm enough set to stand steady under a little musket fire of *that* kind. Truth to tell, I am more concerned that I have done things amiss by speaking to you as I have done, before asking leave of your grandfather.'

'Why, as to that,' said my lady, 'when a marriage is made for the joining of two great estates, or the combining of birth with silver – a business contract—'

'As the custom most often is.'

'As the custom most often is – then it is maybe a sensible arrangement that the lassie's father or grandfather or whatever should be asked first. But when 'tis between two people as it is between you and me, John, then I'm thinking 'tis another matter. If you're such a timid sojer, my Johnnie, when you go to Grandfather tomorrow, where's the need to tell him that you asked me first?'

'How if he refuses his consent?'

'He'll not,' said my lady. 'Or if he does at first, he'll soon come round when I've worked on him a little.'

'And your mother?'

There was a little silence and then my lady said, 'Not my mother. No.'

'Oh, my Jenny, Jean,' said he, the words muffled a

little as though maybe he was speaking into her hair. 'And that will hurt you, and because of me.'

'Aye – though not so sore as 'twould hurt me if ye didna ask me to go with you.'

'You'll not let her make you change your mind?' he asked in quick anxiety.

'No,' she said, 'never that,' and then suddenly between weeping and laughter, 'All my life ye'll have but to whistle, and I'll kilt my petticoats to the knee and follow you the length and breadth of Scotland, wi' the heart in me singing like a lintie in a hawthorn bush.'

He had her in his arms by then. Oh, I could not see, and I'd not yet had a lassie of my own, but there were them in the stable-yard that had, and 'twas not the first time I'd heard a girl whispering into a man's shoulder, with the breath half crushed out of her.

'There'll be so many times you cannot follow,' he said. 'So many times ye'll need to bide home and wait, maybe for news that doesn't come.'

Aye, and I'd heard a man whispering into the top of a lassie's head, too; but never with the kind of aching tenderness that Claverhouse's voice had in it that evening.

'Are you sure, heart of my heart?'

'How many times will you ask that?' said she. 'I am more sure than ever I have been of anything in all my life.'

'So be it then. Tomorrow I will go to your grandfather.'

She laughed softly, and I heard her pulling away from him. 'And then we shall not be our own people any more; we shall belong to our families and the churchmen and the lawyers, and there will be documents to be signed and new fine clothes to be bought, and maybe a wedding portrait to be painted, and we shall scarce be alone together again until after we are wed. Are you not glad that you asked me first, and we have had this one quiet twilight to ourselves?'

They had begun to move on again, their whispering voices growing fainter. Once I heard his quiet laugh; and then all sound of them was gone into the evening sounds of the place; and the white owl that lived in the ruins of the side-chapel swept on velvet-silent wings down the length of the roofless nave. I lay where I was a little longer, until I was sure that it was safe to move, and then slithered out of my hiding-place and slipped away after the white owl, heading for the old cloister, which was the way back to the house and the stable-yard.

At the far end of it, as I passed, a shadow shook itself free of the other crowding shadows, and my heart jumped into my throat as it swirled across my path. But the hands that gripped my arm were small and hard and urgent, and above all, human; and 'twas only a lassie in a dark cloak, after all; and her face, gleaming pale in the darkness of her hood, was the face of Mistress Mary Ruthven.

'And what might you be doing back there?' demanded she.

'I've secrets of my own, and the need to be by myself, whiles and whiles,' said I. 'Did they leave you on watch here?'

'Aye, and it's the bad sentry I've been, so it seems.'

'None so bad,' I told her. 'I was in-by already, a long while before they came.'

Her hands were still on my arm, and her face turned up to mine, beseeching, the eyes in the whiteness of it wide and shadowy like holes with the dusk shining through. 'Ye'll not tell?' said she. 'Hugh Herriot, ye'll not tell on my lady?'

'Is it likely?' said I. 'Ach away, lassie, do ye think I'm the telling kind?'

And I never have told, not until this day, when it is an old, old story, and will not be mattering to either of them any more.

5

The Dutch Painter

I carried a sore heart with me to my sleeping place in
the loft that night, for it seemed that I was soon to be
losing all that made Paisley a bonnie place to me. My
lady, and like enough Laverock and the old mare, for I
made no doubt that if my lady went to her man she
would take those two with her. And with his wife somewhere the other side of Scotland (for I knew that his
home was somewhere Dundee way) it was not likely
that Claverhouse would be much at Paisley, save in
time of dealing with the 'Saints'. And it would be another year at least, maybe two, before I could be going
for a soldier. Oh, I could have 'listed as a drummer boy
if I had had the skill, but I had not, and in any case that
would not have got me where I would be, since it was
the cavalry I had set my heart on, and they do not take
laddies for the kettle-drums.

Lying awake that night, staring into the dark, I knew
for the first time that it was not so much the soldiering
my heart was set on, as that I would be following Claverhouse.

There is no knowing how much pleading my lady Jean
had to do with her grandfather, but I think not much
(Claverhouse's superiors set their faces dead against it
for a while, but that was another matter), for before
long it was known throughout the household, and
among the troops and over all the country round, that
she and Colonel Graham were betrothed. And after

that I saw what she had meant when she said that once it was out, they would never be alone to each other again until after they were wed.

The coming and the going that there was! The notaries and the silk-merchants and seamstresses, and the great folk visiting from all around! There was a painter coming, too; a Dutch painter who was in Edinburgh at the time, coming to paint a wedding portrait. And that made me prick up my ears, for I had not seen brush laid to canvas since my father died; though indeed it was not much of the painting I'd be seeing, it going up in the great house, and me down in the stable-yard.

And meanwhile Claverhouse came and went about his business of peacekeeping all across Ayrshire and the South West; and many's the time I saw him walking to and fro, waiting until my lady should be free of her dressmakers and her grandmother, until often he could wait no more but must call for his horse and be off back to his headquarters at Stranraer without ever seeing her at all.

She never had time to come down to the stable-yard, either, nor to go riding in the early mornings as she had been used to do; so he was not the only one that missed her.

And then there came a day – the swallows had arrived and the cuckoo was calling in the woods across the river – when three things happened all within a few hours of each other. It was one of those days when a little wind rises and changes the life one woke to in the morning, so that by nightfall one is travelling by a different way.

The first of the three things came with the carrier, who brought me word that my grandfather was dead.

Not word from Aunt Margaret, you will understand. The carrier, who was always the bearer of news, as well as goods and gear, picked up the word at Wauprigg and dropped it again in the stable-yard at Place of Paisley, knowing that I was there.

I had heard from the old man two–three times since I had left, but that was all; and I had no thought ever to see him again; but the news fetched me a buffet under the heart, all the same.

'How did he come to die?' I asked.

The carrier shook his head. 'Seems like he just grew old an' weary an' his heart stopping beating. He was in the byre seeing to a sick cow, an' 'twas there they found him in the morning.'

So my last link with Wauprigg was cut behind me. All the life I had now was here in Place of Paisley stable-yard. But before that day was over, I had something else to think about; for a while later, when I was currying Dundonel's big grey, a shadow darkened the doorway of the loose-box, and when I looked up, it was Willie Sempill himself. 'Ye can leave that,' said he, 'my lady Jean wants ye in the privy garden.'

And as I looked doubtfully at the curry-comb in my hand, he took it from me. 'Off wi' ye now, my mannie, would ye keep herself waiting all day?'

And he fell to, hissing away between his teeth, on the grey's coat.

I spared a moment for my face and hands at the horse-trough, and went, just as I was, for the day was warm and I had left my jacket in the loft, pulling down my shirtsleeves as I went, and raking wet fingers through my hair.

The privy garden was the bonniest place, with knot-beds full of pinks and heartsease, and tall clipped hedges to keep out the rest of the world; and that day the tall flamed and feathered Low Countries' tulips were coming into flower, and the first buds swelling on the little white briar roses against the old sun-warmed house walls, and a thrush was singing in the mulberry tree that was the heart of the place. And on the turf seat under the mulberry tree my lady Jean was sitting; and she half lost in the billows of some wonderful embroidered stuff that she was working at; one edge of it drawn over her knees, and white sheets spread all about her on the grass to save the wonderful thing, whatever it was, from getting stained or muddied. There was a creepy stool with no one sitting on it now, and a gay tangle of silks and wools beside it, facing her as it were, across the beautiful stuff spread between them like a peacock's train; from which I guessed that whatever she was at, Mistress Ruthven had been sharing the labour with her but a little while before.

She did not look up, but went on stitching carefully, frowning at the stitches as she drew the long rose-coloured thread in and out. I walked nearer, until I came right beside the creepy stool; and then I saw that the great piece of green velvet was worked with the figure of a naked man and woman standing hand in hand beneath an apple tree, and wee bright birds fluttering among the branches, and all about them leafy bushes and flowering plants, and beasties – a silent running of beasties; a deer under the leaves, and rabbits and a little lap-dog and a lion. And twisted about the trunk, with its head coming out from among the apple branches, a wicked jewel-bright serpent.

And then I understood. I had never seen such a thing before, but I knew that Adam and Eve in the Garden was the proper pattern for the coverlid of a wedding bed. This one was old, old and faded; my, but it was bonnie; and in places the stitching of the fine embroidery was gone, and in places there showed the brighter colours of new silks where the damage had been made good. It was one such place, the breast of a chaffinch, that my lady was stitching at that moment, the stitches, truth to tell, somewhat larger than those round about it. She pulled through a last stitch, and looked with a sigh, and smiled at me, somewhat ruefully.

'Oh, Hugh,' said she, 'I shall never be the needle-woman my grandmother was in her day.'

'It's bonnie,' I said. 'Did my lady your grandmother make it, then?'

'Och, no. It was old even when she was young; but she mended it when she brought it with her, and again for every wedding that has been among us since, and ye cannot see where her mending is. I do not think you can see so well where Mistress Mary has been helping me, either – but ye can see where I have been at it, all too plain.'

'Where would be the use,' said I staunchly, 'taking all that trouble, and no one to see where the work was done?'

She laughed, 'Oh, Hugh Herriot, you're the leal friend! But 'twas not to be discussing my stitchery that I sent for you this afternoon, it was to ask you something. After the wedding, when I go with my man to his own place – will ye come with me?'

'Come wi' ye?' said I, and for the moment I could think of nothing more to say. I felt stupid with the surprise of it.

And in the silence there came the sound of horses' hooves from beyond the house. Three horses, I thought, my mind being shaped to such things of long

53

habit. And then the distant sounds of bustle from the stable-yard.

My lady noticed my check, and took it for uncertainty or maybe even unwillingness, and she said, 'Mistress Mary comes with me, and old Linnet and Laverock, and it seems to me they'll be wanting someone of their own with them, too. Come with me, Hugh – or will ye be sair to go so far from your own folks?'

I shook my head. 'My grandfather's dead, and there's no one else I'd care to see again.'

'Your grandfather?' she said. 'Ye've spoken of him now and again. I did not know that he was dead.'

'No more did I, until the carrier brought me word, the morn.'

'Oh, Hugh, I'm sorry,' she said, 'and here I am asking you to make your mind up about this, when it's the sore heart ye'll have; and thinking's none so easy with a sore heart. Bide a few days.'

'No,' I said, 'I'd not have been like to see him again in any case; and as for leaving these parts – 'twas in my mind to be 'listing for a sojer anyways, in a year or two.'

She smiled, 'Then come with me for the year or two.'

'I'd like that fine,' I said, 'just fine, my lady.'

She kept me there a while longer, asking about my grandfather and the like; and all the while I could hear the bustle of an arrival in the stable-yard. I did wonder if it was Claverhouse himself, but he came more quietly as a rule. And then just as I was going, Mistress Ruthven came into the garden on flying feet, that pretty soft hair of hers bursting out from under her cap – her caps always seemed too big for her, like huge white cambric columbine flowers half quenching her small brown face. But this time the brownness of her face was flushed with foxglove pink, and her eyes dancing.

'The painter-chiel who is to make your wedding portrait is come,' said she. 'He looks like a wee yellow toad perched up on top of the post-horse, and him with a great curled red peruke on the top, fine enough for a six-foot gentleman! Do you suppose he's a prince in disguise?'

And I heard their laughter skirling behind me as I went out and back to the stable-yard.

And though I did not know it at the time, that, the coming of the Dutch painter, was the third of the three things that were to play a part in the shaping of my life.

Mynheer Cornelius van Meere, that was his name, did indeed look somewhat like a toad under the monstrous curled red peruke; and as long and lean as he was short and squat, was Johannes his apprentice, a wey-faced sulky-seeming callant, with the red rash on his cheeks and chin that plagues some of us when our beards first begin to sprout; aye, an odd looking couple. They were both still in the stable-yard when I got back to it, the apprentice unloading the bundles and cases of painting gear from the pack pony that carried it, while the master stood by to see it done, for clearly he would trust none of the grooms to touch it.

The two post-horses were already being rubbed down, and the pack pony fell to my lot when the weary little brute was finally unloaded. And meanwhile both the newcomers were swept away by the steward, and that was the last we saw of them for a while.

But we heard. As I have said, we heard most things in the stable-yard.

Cornelius van Meere had taken over the Little Dining-room for his workshop. I had never seen it, of course, but I had heard it was a bonnie room, with walls covered in tooled and gilded leather; and I could see in my mind's eye how that would cast warm reflected lights on to my lady's face, whether from the sun or from the candles. And I could see in my mind's eye also how that long spotty apprentice would be tacking the primed canvas over the four stretcher bars, and driving in the corner wedges until the tightened canvas sounded like a drum under the flat of his hand, and how he would be setting out the boiled oil and working up the rough-ground pigments. And all the old memories of my years with my father woke in me, and I fair itched to be in that little chamber and setting a hand to the work.

And then the painting started, and of course my lady Jean had less time than ever for the stables or the garden. At first, seemingly, it had been intended that it should be a great wedding portrait, with the groom in it as well as the bride, and him in his fine new scarlet coat – for the Government had lately ordered red coats to replace the old hodden grey for the Scottish regiments, all save the Dragoons. But the countryside was still not at its quietest, and Claverhouse had no time for the sittings, and so it was just my lady Jean.

So it went on for two–three days; and then Mynheer had the need for a fresh supply of black oil. As you know well enough, the black oil does not keep for long, whether it be oil of poppy-seed such as I myself use now, along with most painters here in the Low Countries, or linseed and walnut boiled together; and so a travelling painter will carry with him only enough to start the work, and bid his monkey – his apprentice – to boil up more for him as it is needed. And as you will know also, for I have warned you often enough, the boiling is a dangerous process, and never if possible to be undertaken within doors.

Between the kitchen quarters and a postern door to the stable-yard was a small well-court which seemed finely suited to the purpose; and there the small charcoal fire was made and the iron pot set over it, and Johannes got to work with the raw linseed and walnut oil.

I contrived to have some horse gear to polish, so that I could wander out to the door of the tack-room as I worked, and catch a glimpse of the doings in the well-court; for I was fair fascinated; drawn to what was going forward as by a kind of homesickness.

Johannes was feeding the little charcoal fire with care, piece by piece, peering the while into the fire-darkened pot; but it seemed to me, even so, that he had too much attention to spare also for the world about him. The black oil when it passes the boil and draws on towards flaming point is kittle stuff, and not to be left unwatched for a single whisper of time. My father had taught me that before I was ten years old.

Well, I never did see just what happened, for I had my own work to do as well; but kind of out of the top of my head I was aware that one of the kitchen lassies had come out to draw water from the well, and there was a chit-chat of voices; and I am thinking that Johannes (did I not say his beard was sprouting?) took his attention from the black oil at just the wrong moment, to give it to the lassie.

Next instant there was a terrified yell, and the lassie screeching and the clatter of the pot lid, and the black oil going up in a belch of flame, and Johannes staggering back from it, crying out like a lassie himself and with his hands clapped to his face.

I flung aside the headstall I was polishing, and ran. Folks were running from all over. Someone had

Johannes on the ground and was beating out his hair that was on fire; and someone else – I never saw who – had snatched up the full bucket of water and was making to throw it over the blazing oil. I shouted 'Leave be! I ken what to do!' and fended him off with the flat of my hand in his face as one fends off an opponent at hurley, and caught up the pot lid from where Johannes had dropped it. I mind the savage blast of heat, and the oil-smoke choking me, and then I had the lid slammed on, and the flame and stink cut off; and I swung the pot aside from the charcoal fire.

Johannes was groaning and sobbing; and indeed the pain must have been sore, for his eyebrows and front hair were clean burned off, and when I saw his hands later – well, I reckon I would have been bawling like a bull calf for its dam, if it had been me. Myself, I had no more than a scorch-mark on one wrist. And Willie Sempill was there, and telling me 'twas well done, and to leave it for all was safe now.

I shook my head, 'If 'tis left now, 'tis good oil ruined and mebbe no more to spare. It needs to be brought to flame-point twice more.'

I suppose I had the air of knowing what I was talking about, for they let me be, and I – I took my attention away from all of them to give it to the oil in the pot.

I made the proper count, then lifted the lid. The oil lay there dark and still faintly stirring. I let the air get to it until the last stirring and dimpling was stilled, then took up the skimming spoon and cleared the sooty scum that had risen to the surface, and left it again for the time of three paternosters said within my head. Aye, I should have counted it off, but my father had taught me the old way; and come to that, I'm thinking there's a good few even here in the Protestant Low

58

Countries that still use the old Popish prayers when they need an accurate timing too short for the clock or the sandglass – swordsmiths and apothecaries and such – then swung it back over the fire and fed a bit more charcoal to the flames and stood by with the lid, watching . . .

The dark surface began to dimple again. I stared down at it as the movement changed to a rolling boil and then fell away into stillness; and above the stillness came the faint blue haze that comes a lick of time before flash-point. In the instant, as the flame began, I slammed the lid back on, and again swung the pot clear of the fire, and again betook me to my paternosters and the skimming spoon.

Once more the whole thing had to be gone through; and then, with the lid slammed on again and the pot swung clear and the last skimming done, I straightened up and fetched a long breath, as though it was the first breath I had fetched since it all started, and drew the back of my forearm across my sweaty face.

And the outside world came to me again.

Johannes had been hauled off somewhere to have his hurts tended, there were folks all about me in the well-court, and amongst them the squat round figure in the preposterous curled peruke of Mynheer Cornelius van Meere himself. And him looking at me somewhat oddly, so that I realised he had been watching me most of the while.

'And where did you learn how to boil the black oil?' said he, speaking our tongue well enough, though with the broad thick accent of the Low Countries.

'My father taught me,' I told him.

'Ach, so – he was a painter, this father?'

'Aye.'

'And you were his apprentice?'

'I was but eleven when he died,' I said, 'but he'd no other help, so I'm thinking I'd learned as well as most apprentices, how to boil the black oil and a size a canvas and grind the colours, and clean his brushes after him.'

'So-o,' said Mynheer thoughtfully, nodding so that I thought his great peruke would over-balance him. 'Then will you finish the task that you have so well begun, and when the oil is cooled, pour it into this flask and bring it to me in the Little Dining-room?'

'Aye,' I said, 'if Master Sempill—' I looked round and caught the head groom's eye on me.

He nodded, 'But mind the kitchen lassies dinna keep you from your proper work.'

And Mynheer turned and trotted away, and for the moment that was all.

But by and by, when the oil was cooled and safely in its flask, I took it into the Little Dining-room, one of those same kitchen lassies showing me the way, for I'd never set foot beyond the great smoky kitchens before. And the place was as bonnie as I'd imagined it, with the tooled and gilded leather on its walls catching the candlelight, for the day was fading, and the tall easel set up and covered with a white cloth, and the familiar smell of oil and paint . . . And Mynheer standing by the table, rubbing his hands on an oily rag.

'Ah, Hugh,' he greeted me, 'that is your name? It seems that Johannes my apprentice will be small use to me for the next few days until his hands are healed. Therefore I have asked Milord Dundonel that he lend you to me in his place meanwhile – if you like?'

'I'd like fine,' I said, feeling a little as though I was in a dream.

'*Goot*!' he said. 'Then clean up all these brushes.'

6

Portrait of a Dream

For the while, then, I became Mynheer van Meere's
monkey; and the centre of my daily world which for
more than a year had been the stable-yard, was the
Little Dining-room, where my lady Jean came every
day to sit in the big carved chair cushioned in faded
golden cut-velvet, for Mynheer to paint her wedding
portrait.

For those sittings she wore a gown of blue damask,
much grander than anything I had ever seen her wear
before, and had her side hair curled into bunches of
ringlets hanging over her ears. 'Confidantes' they were
called, the height of fashion at the time so I was told.
And altogether she did not look at all like the Lady
Jean I knew. But even so, it seemed she lit up the room
with her coming, as thought she brought the sunlight
and the scent of the high heather moors in with her;
aye, and the linnets singing bonnie among the broom.

Most times Mistress Darklis would be there too, just
for company, for Mynheer was not one for chit-chat
while he was painting. (I always thought of her by her
real name, her gipsy name, now, for though we had seldom spoken with each other since the evening in the
Abbey ruins, the shared secret seemed to have made a
kind of bond between us.) And whiles, she would bring
her lute, and sing to it the old songs of the Border
country; *The Twa Sisters* and *The Gay Goshawk*, and
the like; for listening to them, he said, gave my lady's
face the right look to it.

I listened too, and looked on, and thought that I would like fine to be painting the brown lassie with the lute in her lap, and the way her hands caught the light against the dark stuff of her gown.

Once she sang *The Ballad of Johnnie Faa*:

'The Gipsies cam to our gude lord's yett,
  And oh but they sang sweetly;
They sang sae sweet and sae very complete,
  That down cam our fair Lady.

And she cam tripping down the stair,
  And all her maids before her;
And sune as they saw her weel-favr'd face,
  They cast the glamourie ower her.

"Oh come with me," says Johnnie Faa;
  "Oh come with me my dearie;
For I vow and I swear by the hilt of my sword
  That your Lord shall nae mair come near ye! . . ."

And when our Lord cam hame at e'en
  And speired for his fair lady,
The tane she cried, and the other replied,
  "She's away wi' the Gipsy Laddie."

"Gae saddle to me my black, black steed,
  Gae saddle and mak him ready;
Before that I either eat or sleep
  I'll gae seek my fair lady . . ."

And we were fifteen weel made men,
  Although we were na' bonnie;
And we were a' put down for ane,

A fair young wanton lady.'

She sang it very softly, and I mind the glance that brushed between her and my lady, towards the end, guessed that the singing of that song, and the listening to it must have been a small shared rebellion to lift the boredom of the long portrait sittings.

Mynheer worked me hard, at mixing the oils and grinding the colours and clearing up after him, but much of that was done when we were alone, while he himself worked on at the background, or the posy of pansies and briar roses on the table, or even the folds of the stiff blue gown laid across the empty chair with no Lady Jean in it at all. But anyway grinding paint does not take all one's mind, and one can listen well enough at the same time. I seemed always to be grinding the blue called ultramarine which he needed for that gown, for it was a deep blue and he painted thickly; and he would have only small amounts ground and oil-mixed at a time, lest any should be wasted, that colour, which the old church masters used for the Virgin's mantle, being the most costly of all pigments, ground from pure lapis lazuli.

I watched the painting grow from the rough sketches, and its first outline in the warm black-brown ingres, while form and colour took shape. And if not the Lady Jean I knew, then at least this new lady in the fine stiff gown and the 'Confidantes' ringlets bound with silver ribbons over her ears, began to grow out of the canvas. It was all like returning to a familiar but long-forgotten world to me; and I began to itch in my fingers and in some place deep inside myself to an odd bit of board and a brush and a dap of ingres of my own, such as my father had whiles and whiles allowed me.

Then one evening Mynheer, going off for his supper, left me to grind some more ultramarine before I went off to mine, for he would be needing it to put the finishing touches to my lady's slashed and ruffled sleeves in the morning.

When the door shut behind him, I set to work, first with the pestle and mortar, and then when the rough grinding was done, adding the oil drop by drop and working the pigment up on the marble grinding slab until it came smooth as curd and deeply blue as fresh-opened cornflowers. Finally I scraped off with the palette knife and put it into its wee pot, making sure that not one speck was wasted. I had been in a hurry at first, wanting my own supper. But when it was finished – och, I don't know; it was the first time I had ever been left alone in the Little Dining-room, and there was the canvas standing up on its easel, with its veil of fine linen flung over it to keep off the dust while the paint was damp, and plenty of daylight left, for the room faced westward and we were almost into June. And the wish was on me to take a good look while I was on my own with no one by to call me to this task or that. I lifted back the cloth, and there it was, the bonniest thing, even though the Lady Jean looking back at me was not just the Lady Jean I knew. And I thought it was a sad thing that it was just her on her lone, and not a proper wedding portrait with Claverhouse in it, too. But then I wondered how would the man look, dressed up and stiff as she was, with fine new point-lace at his throat and wrists, and maybe his own hair cut off close, and a fine fashionable peruke the like of Mynheer's? And I thought of him as I'd come to know him, riding into the stable-yard with his uniform often enough wet and mired with the moorland ways, and sometimes that quick quiet smile of his, and sometimes his eyes red-rimmed and weary in his head . . .

There were a couple of bits of board on the deep windowsill, all ready sized; the kind that Mynheer used for making sketches, and the window was very near. I had only to reach out my hand . . .

I'll never know what possessed me. I reached out, not really knowing what I did. And I found a small brush and the crock of ingres; and I was settled on the windowsill with the board on my knee.

I began to paint.

And having begun, I went on. I was scarcely aware of finishing with the ingres and calmly helping myself to the colours I wanted and setting out my palette as I had set it out so often for my father and now for Mynheer. I worked at top speed, seeking to catch all that was left of the daylight, utterly absorbed in what I did.

I have become a skilled and, as I think, a bonnie painter in the years since then, though alas, never the great one, the master that every painter dreams of becoming when he sets out. I have had joy of my painting, aye, as well as the hard work and the times when I would have liked fine to throw the whole thing at some fat sitter's head. But I do not think that I have ever had such joy of it again as I had in that hour. I am thinking that as with many other things, love, aye, and friendship among them, so it is with painting and the making of songs and the like, we have a first time, a virginity to lose, and the hour that we lose it is not just like any other hour in all our lives.

But I am wandering from my story. When I came back to myself the painting light was almost gone, and there were footsteps and voices outside the door; and the door opened and in came Mynheer himself, carrying a great three-branched silver candlestick, and behind him Lord Dundonel and her old ladyship and two–three more that must have been supping with them, and my lady Jean – and Colonel Graham.

I sat where I was, frozen, not so much with any sense of guilt or fear that I would be getting into trouble, but because I had not had time to come fully back from one world to another, and was somewhat dazed.

Mynheer van Meere saw the portrait on its easel, uncovered, and then myself in the window embrasure, and he let out something startled in Dutch sounding like a small explosion, and came quickly across the room, the candle flames trailing in the draught of his coming, and next instant he was standing over me, peering down at the bit of board on my knee.

I looked, too, seeing what I had done spring out at me in the new light of the candles. Claverhouse's head and shoulders in his shabby buff coat as I had so often seen him in the stable-yard; and under the slim black brows his eyes looking so directly into mine that for the moment it came almost as a shock.

It was a crude enough bit of work, mind you; I was not yet fifteen, and I had had no teaching save the little that my father had given me when I was too young to profit much by it. But I have always had the knack of catching a likeness from memory.

Mynheer was silent so long that I grew afraid that he was angry after all. But then he said, 'It seems we have another portrait painter here among us.'

And he was not mocking; not mocking at all.

And then everyone came crowding round exclaiming, my lady's portrait that they had come to see all unnoticed for the moment, while I had not even the presence of mind to get up but just went on perching in the windowsill with the bit of board tipped sideways on

66

my knee to show them since it seemed that they wanted to see. Old Lady Dundonel was clucking like a hen just off the nest; and Lord Dundonel said suddenly, as though in surprise, 'John, I never knew you had a look of your famous kinsman!'

'What kinsman would that be?' Claverhouse said.

'Montrose.'

'Montrose,' Claverhouse echoed the name quiet-like, but with something in his voice that made me look round at him. 'I was but two years old when he – died, and I never saw him, but I should be glad to think that I had a look of him.'

He was looking at the little sketch, and I was looking at him, and in that moment I learned something about Claverhouse. I learned that despite his thirty-five years and his hardness with the Covenanters, he had a lad-die's gift for hero-worship in him still; and I knew who the hero was.

As though he felt my gaze on him, he looked from the picture to my face, and our eyes met. As before in the stable-yard I had the feeling that he was seeing me, directly and clearly and consciously, as few men see the people they look at. Maybe he, too, was learning some-thing – that he had a follower for life, though at that time just a follower the like of many others . . .

'It is strange, I have found it before,' said Mynheer, 'how family likenesses will appear in a painting that lie concealed in life; and of a certainty the boy has caught the likeness of Colonel Graham. The work is crude, of course – untaught—'

'But it's bonnie for all that,' Lady Jean put in softly. 'And it *is* like.' And ah, but she was bonnie herself, with the candles making the bright hair shine round her head. 'And for a soldier's wife who must often go lonely with her man not beside her, it would be a fine thing to have such a likeness.' She fell silent a moment, and then speaking still more softly, said to me, 'Hugh, may I have your picture?'

That was the first time I knew the sorrow of a painter, that when he has painted something and set a bit of his own heart in it, folks want to take it from him – oh, maybe they give him gold and silver in its place, but never his painting with the bit of his own heart in it, back again. But it was not for that reason that I hesitated.

'The paint and the board are no' mine,' I said, doubtfully.

'It is not the paint nor yet the board that makes the picture,' said Mynheer, 'it is yours to do as you will with.'

'Then when 'tis dry, my lady, 'tis yours for a wedding gift.'

And that was the first time I knew the joy of the painter, in having such a great thing to give.

'Thank you for my wedding gift, Hugh,' said my lady.

I got up, remembering at last that I should not be sitting in the presence of my betters, and propped the little picture carefully in the window recess.

Mynheer was still looking at it, and rubbing his nose in the way that he had when he was thinking hard. 'Boy,' he said suddenly, as one making up his mind, 'you are a bad painter, but with teaching you could be a goot one, which is more than can be said for Johannes, who vill never be goot for aught but to stretch canvases and grind pigments. If you come with me as my second apprentice – I have room for two at home in Utrecht – I will make of you one day a better painter than I am myself.'

For the moment, as I stood silent, temptations tugged at me sore. But something else pulled more strongly the other way.

'I am thinking Johannes would knife me,' I said, 'and beside then, when my lady is wed, I go with – ' I almost said 'with Claverhouse', but I turned the words in time – 'with her to her new home.'

'And so you will be a groom all your life?' said Mynheer. He said other things, too, but I did not hear them, for Colonel Graham had turned that clear hard gaze of his on to me again, and meeting it, I knew – I scarce know how to put it – it was as though he had heard what I had not said, and understood, and accepted, gravely, like a liege lord accepting the fealty of his newest knight. Och, it sounds daft, I know, but for that moment even my lady Jean was not there. Just the two of us. And I was no longer a lost dog without a heel to follow.

'And now,' Mynheer was saying, 'allow me to show you vat ve came to see – how it goes with my portrait of Lady Jean.'

A few days later, when the portrait was finished, and dry enough to be safely set in its frame, Mynheer Cornelius van Meere rode away, Johannes with him. The apprentice's hands were not yet fully healed, and so I helped him to load up the pack beast. And when all was done, and the fat little man already perched aloft on his horse, he bent down and set a hand on my shoulder. 'If ever you change your mind,' he said, 'ask for me at the third house beyond the kirk in Silver Spur Street – Silveren Spoor Straat – in Utrecht. Look for the two swans carved on the gable. My wife will take you in if I am on my travels.'

7

Wedding Favours

On the ninth day of June in the year of Our Lord 1684, Colonel John Graham and my lady Jean Cochrane signed their marriage contract. There was a fine gathering to see it done; Lord Cochrane that was my lady's brother and Lord Ross and many more; and Captain Livingstone quiet in the background as usual. But my lady's mother bided in her own house, hard black Covenanting woman that she was. And later I heard that old Lady Dundonel had signed the contract in her place.

Ach well, it is all long ago.

Next day, the Tuesday that would be, was the wedding. A soft day of skim-milk skies and hazy sunshine, and the scent of the first elder-blossom drifting from the bushes in the Abbey ruins to mingle with the faint smell of thunder brewing. All morning the great folks that were not already there were arriving from all the country round; and we were kept busy in the stable-yard with the horses and coaches to be seen to, until all the Place was awash with eager voices and the bright colours sweeping to and fro. The men of Claver-house's own troop were there, spruced up in their new red coats that had been hurried through for the occasion, the white ribbons fluttering on each man's left arm as they made their own horse lines in the park. Towards noon, Claverhouse arrived, very fine in dark blue velvet and point-lace – almost the first time ever I had seen him out of uniform – and with him Lord Ross and Captain Livingstone, each with the white and silver

70

wedding ribbons flittering from his left sleeves. We all had wedding favours, guests and household alike; I kept mine for years.

I went to take the bridle of Claverhouse's horse; and he smiled at me as he swung down from the saddle. 'All packed and ready?'

My few belongings had been bundled in a cloak for days. I nodded. 'All ready, sir.'

'Wish me happiness, Painter Hugh,' said he. And then he was gone with the others towards the house.

The Episcopalian minister arrived. It must have gone hard with some in that house to see him come. I had been watching all the while for the Auchans carriage to arrive; hoping against hope; for it seemed a sorry thing that my lady Jean should be wed with no kindness nor support from her mother. But after the minister came, I knew that it was too late to be watching any more.

And then it was noon, and we knew that in the Great Hall of the house, my lady would have come down from her chamber on Dundonel's arm, and Claverhouse would be waiting for her . . . I would have liked fine to be within doors to see it done. But our turn would come later. The long trestle tables had been set up under the linden trees below the terrace, and the grass scythed close for dancing clear down to the river, for my lady was set upon having not just the gentry but all her people close about her on that day that she was wed. And even while we knew that the wedding was still going forward in the house, we began to drift away.

The troopers were there already, ranged up on either side of the terrace steps under command of their lieutenant. Waiting, as we were all waiting, but motionless save for white ribbons stirring on their sleeves.

Then at last they came, the wedding party; the grand

folk, and the bride's lassies like a flock of bright birds, and old Dundonel and his lady stepping stately in the lead, and behind them Claverhouse and my lady Jean. The troopers were tossing up their hats and cheering, we were all cheering. I had managed to push my way through to the forefront of the crowd, and they came right by me from the foot of the terrace steps. And eh, but my lady was the bonniest thing, in a gown of silky stuff the colour of new milk and worked all over with little golden roses, and the white briar roses in her hair, and old Lady Dundonel's diamonds in her ears; but her eyes were brighter than the diamonds, and her cheeks flushed to the colour of hedge-side rose-campions. And Claverhouse beside her looking the proud and happy man. There was a kind of shine to them, a kind of bloom of light that gave a shimmer to the air around them; and I mind thinking that two people should not look just like that, for there was a danger in it . . .

Then there was a deal of kissing and laughing and weeping, and by and by the grand folks sat down to the highest of the tables under the linden trees; and the rest of us, household and Redcoats together, gathered to the lower tables or took our food and drink and settled in clumps and clusters on the grass. And there was feasting and health-drinking and speeches made that I would not be remembering one word of. And I was sitting on my heels with my back against the old sun-warmed wall of the orchard, sharing a jack of ale and a vast mutton pasty with one of the troopers, a long-legged, sandy-headed man, who told me his name was Tam Johnston. A friendly soul, and one that enjoyed the good things of life. I mind how he took a great bite out of the pasty and leaned back against the wall and thrust his long legs even further out in front of him, slacking off his belt with a sigh of content. 'We should marry our Colonel off more frequent. This is the life that suits me fine. Better than stravaigling up and down the high moors after those accursed bog-trotting "Saints" as they ca' themselves, and mebbe a bullet from behind any bush o' broom.'

'But the countryside's quiet enough these past few weeks, is it no'?' said I.

He nodded, 'Aye. That's always the way o't. When Ayrshire an' the South West gets beyond any other man's handling, they send Colonel Graham an' His Majesty's Scottish Horse down to deal wi' it. And the shriek goes up again about Bloody Claver'se and his butcher's ways wi' the poor folk that seek only the freedom to worship God in their own fashion. And no one thinks to mention the poor de'il of a trooper shot in the back wi' a smuggled Dutch musket.'

I saw in my mind's eye the flames of the burning alehouse, and the drummer laddie staring up at me with the third eye in the middle of his forehead; and I pushed the memory away, for it was no fit memory for such a day as this.

And Tam Johnston took a swig of the ale jack. 'Och well, 'tis Glasgow way that's got the trouble this time, an' no concern of ours.'

'Is there trouble that way?' said I, more to keep the conversation going than for aught else.

He wiped the back of his hand across his mouth, and pushed the great leather jack towards me. 'Aye, the Dragoons have been out from Glasgow chasing the Godly rebels since Saturday, so the story runs.'

I took the jack and had a swallow myself, and the talk turned to other things.

Groups broke up and drifted to form fresh groups,

and the food and drink went round, and the shadows of the lime trees shifted in the hazy sunshine over the grass; and it was time for dancing. But just as the fiddlers were being parted from the last of the food, and starting in to tune their fiddles, there came the sound of a horse hard-ridden on the road that came from the Abbey bridge.

Everybody looked that way, for a rider coming at that speed would not be just a late-arriving guest. I had my legs ready under me, thinking there might be a call for me in the stable-yard. But there was a flicker of scarlet beyond the lime trees, and the trooper swung aside from the drive and headed across the grass towards us, slackening his pace as he came. The chatter and the laughter and the sad squeal of the tuning fiddles were silent; and everyone craned to watch as the man dropped from the saddle, tossing his bridle to another trooper who had come running to take it from him, and came striding across to the top table, where Claverhouse was already rising from his place, my lady Jean beside him, to open the dancing.

The young lieutenant got up quickly, and the trooper spoke to him, and was passed on to the Colonel, pulling off his beaver hat in salute. 'From General Dalyell, sir,' I heard him say, handing over a packet.

Claverhouse took it and broke the seal and read it, a frown drawing together those black brows of his. 'I think they might have left me Tuesday,' he said.

I was none so far from him, and in the quiet and the heavy air I could hear every word.

He bowed to Dundonel; a stiff bow, and his voice sounded wooden. 'My lord, my troop is recalled to the King's service. Pray your lordship and all this company excuse the bridegroom from the wedding feast.'

He gave an order, and the troop bugler put the bugle to his lips, and almost before the first notes of 'Boots and Saddles' cut the uneasy summer quiet, the Redcoats were up and gathering from all over the pleasance, heading for their horse lines. Beside me, Tam Johnston drew his long legs under him and came to foot, tightening his loosened belt. 'Och well, 'twas good while it lasted,' said he, and was gone to join the rest. Lord Ross and Captain Livingstone bowed hurriedly over Lady Dundonel's hand and then over Lady Jean's, and turned to be on their way; and in the midst of it all, Claverhouse pulled my lady into his arms and kissed her hard and loving, and openly before us all as though he would be setting his seal on her in the eyes of the world. And she, she kissed him back, but with her hands stiff at her side. I think now that maybe she was afraid to touch him lest she should start to cling, and not be able to let go.

Then he was gone with the other two who had turned to wait for him, and already as he went he was pulling the wedding favour from his sleeve, thrusting it into the breast of his coat. 'I think they might have let Tuesday go by,' he said again, as they strode past me. 'Ah well, back to the Red Lion and get out of these geegaws.'

And they were gone, leaving a low, startled, distressful murmuring behind them.

Then old Dundonel stood up and bade the dancing go forward, for Colonel Graham would never forgive us if we allowed his absence to mar such a day. 'The bride is with us yet,' said he, 'and bids us still to take joy in her wedding.'

So my lady Jean stepped out from among her lassies that had come flocking around her, to lead the first dance with Lord Cochrane, her brother. And her head was up – aye, she was a valiant lassie, and a proud one – and her face the same milk white as her gown; and she smiling fit to make your heart ache within you.

The fiddles struck up and the dancing began. And behind it all the while we heard the ordered bustle of ready-making for the march. We were dancing *The Flowers of Edinburgh* when the bugle sounded again; aye *Monte Caballo*, and then the drumming of horses' hooves, and we knew that they were gone. And the bride danced on down the long line without losing the rhythm of the fiddle-tune.

But for all Dundonel's brave words, the heart was gone from the merrymaking; and by and by the thunder clouds began to back up behind the Abbey ruins; and the great folk who lived near-hand and were not sleeping at Place of Paisley began to take their leave and call for their horses and carriages, so that we were kept busy back in the stable-yard.

Word had drifted round, and by then we all knew that Tom Johnston's Glasgow Covenanters had crossed the Clyde and were into Renfrewshire, and calling others to join them; and it was for that that Claverhouse had been summoned from his wedding feast. And that night I lay in my bed of warm straw, and listened to the thunder, and the rain beating on the stable roof, and the fitful wind that came and went squalling by, and thought about the man spending his wedding night on the high drenching moors over Clydesdale way. And I wondered if my lady Jean too was listening to the voices of the storm, lying awake and weeping, maybe, by her lee-lone in the great bed under the beautiful broidered coverlid worked with Adam and Eve in the Garden. Or whether Darklis Ruthven was there to keep her company. I hope that was the way of it.

76

8

The Dark Lady's Looking-glass

It was the best part of a week before Claverhouse got back out of the wilderness, mired and weary from a long marsh-light hunt after revels who had simply melted away into country where horses could not follow them. And at last we were off and away from Paisley, my lady riding Linnet at the Colonel's side – she was always seasick in a coach, and on the rough cross-country ways riding was an easier thing in any case, though most women still rode pillion on a journey in those days, not solo using a side-saddle as my lady did. Mistress Darklis followed her, riding in the same way; myself with Laverock on a leading rein coming after, a groom with the baggage horses bringing up the rear, and part of the Colonel's own troop by way of escort.

Three days we were on the journey; long June days with the hills shimmering in the heat, before we came at last in the long damp sweet-smelling dusk to Glenogilvie.

The great house of Dudhope was the true end of our journey; Claverhouse's new-bought home hard by Dundee. But I am thinking that he was fain to bring my lady first to the old home where he had been born and where he had been a laddie. And I am thinking that in his place I would have done the same.

For it was a happy place, the glen winding lazy down the north slopes of the Skiddaws and opening towards the misty blue lowlands of Angus. The old house and its outbuildings sitting low-roofed among orchards sloping to the burn, and the swallows busy under the eaves; and old servants waiting, and old friends to come visiting . . .

Among those same friends was a distant kinsman of the Grahams, James Philip of Amryclose, who truth to tell seemed almost to live at the house during the week or so that we were there.

If I had read Cervantes at that time, I would have thought him a Don Quixote of a man, but at that time my only books were the Bible and the *Iliad*, and I knew only that he had the long uncontrolled legs of a crane-fly, and a pair of great eyes aglow with dreams in his long, drooping face; that he had a fine knowledge of the Highlands, though himself he was a Lowlander like the rest of us, and as fine a knowledge of the classics and the faery world, a strong feeling for heroes and lost causes, and a certain skill with the bagpipes. He had a fine carrying voice and was for ever talking, and no one could be within hearing of him or his pipes without knowing all that after the first day or so.

I have aye remembered those days at Glenogilvie, there was a peace to them, a feeling of sanctuary that set them apart from ordinary life. Backwater days, you might say. But they passed, until there were but two–three of them left before we rose on the last ten miles to Dundee and Dudhope. (Claverhouse was made Constable of Dundee around that time. Did I say?) And it was Midsummer's Eve.

I had an idea in my head, not an over-important one, but new, that it would be pleasant to take out to think about in peace and quiet. So that evening when my work in the stables was finished, I wandered off down through the lower orchard to the burn; and followed

78

the water down towards the old cattle-ford midway between the house and the clachan, where an ancient elder tree split into two limbs only a few feet from the ground, and one of them, leaning out over the water, made a good place for sitting. It was a soft heavy-scented gloaming, and when I looked back I could see the taper light dimly apricot in the windows of the bower, where the shutters had been left wide; and when I looked forward again the cream curds of elder-blossom were beginning to shine to themselves among the dark of their leaves, in the way of pale flowers at dusk. But when I came down the bank, there was someone, something, sitting there already in the crotch where the two limbs parted. A girl in a gown that was pale almost as the elder flowers and yet seemed made of webbed and dappled shadows.

For an instant my heart lurched within me, for was it not Midsummer's Eve, and the tree an eldern tree . . .

Then I saw that it was Darklis, wearing a gown of print stuff with little flower sprigs all over the whiteness of it – calico they call it for it comes from Calicut in India – that I had seen her wearing often enough in the daytime.

'Would you be one of the People of Peace, then?' I said, speaking the first thing that came into my head, and using the name that I had heard Amryclose use for the Faery Kind. 'You perched up there in an eldern tree on Saint John's Eve and all?'

She laughed at that. 'I'll no' disappear back into the tree, Hugh Herriot. But have ye no' heard that all Ruthvens, whether they be of the Tinkler kind or the Earl of Gowrie himself, have a streak of the witch blood in them? All of us kin to the Fair Folk?'

'That's but an old story, mistress,' said I, firmly

79

changing my tune, 'and 'tis dangerous to talk so,' for to speak of the People of Peace half in jest was one thing, but to claim witch blood quite another. The duckings and burnings were too real a hazard.

'That depends on who you talk to,' said she. 'But I'm thinking you'll have come here for much the same reason as myself. And I found it first, and I'll not give up to you my bonnie secret place; but I'll share it wi' ye a while. Sit ye down on the grass.'

And whether it was the time or the place or – nay, I'd not be knowing. We had had few enough dealings with each other, save for that one shared secret, in all the year and more since I came to Place of Paisley, and she was my lady's kinswoman and I but a laddie out of the stable, but I sat down with my back against the deep-fissured tree trunk and her feet swinging within a hand's span of my shoulder, as though the meeting had been long fixed between us and the most natural thing in the world.

'So it is from your Tinkler kin that you have your name, Mistress Darklis Ruthven,' said I.

'And how do you know my name?' said she.

'I have heard my lady call you by it, whiles and whiles.'

'Aye, here am I, kin to the Tinklers and kin to the fine stiff-backed Covenanting Cochranes; and there's a daft way to be! Did ye ken that Jean's great-grand-mother – oh, not on the Cochrane side, her Casselis great-grandmother it would be – fell in love wi' a Tink-ler laddie that came wi' his fiddle to play beneath her window, and ran away wi' him from her rightful lord?'

'That's *The Ballad of Johnnie Faa*. You were singing it that time in the Little Dining-room. And her lord hunted them down and hanged her bonnie Tinkler lad-die before his castle gates.'

'Aye, so the song tells. But it doesna tell that nine months later when her hedgerow-bairn was born it was put out to foster, while the lady bore her lord his right-ful brood until she dies o' the last of them.'

In the silence between us, a fish jumped, close in to the bank.

'Then why is your name no' Faa, Mistress Darklis Ruthven?' said I in a while. No question of why would it not be Casselis.

'Because the hedgerow-bairn was a lassie, and mar-ried out of the royal tribe of Faa into the witch tribe of Ruthven. And her son, my father, left the black tents of his own people to settle down and become falconer to the last Lord Casselis all for the love of a white-skinned lassie. He was killed taking an eyas from the nest. They say he was drunk at the time, an' rock climbing's no ploy for a drunk man. And my mother died when I was born, and so—'

'And so here you are wi' the stiff-backed Covenant-ing Cochranes.'

'That was unjust,' she said after a moment. 'Here I am with my kinswoman Jean, and that's a different thing altogether.' And then on a note of surprise, 'Why am I telling a' this to you, Hugh Herriot?'

'Mebbe because you were feeling lonely,' I said, after giving the matter careful thought.

She denied it quickly. 'Why would I be feeling lonely?'

I could not think of a reason, but I had enough sense to know that it was best not spoken. 'Och, I dinna ken. It's awfu' quiet out here in the glen, after Paisley,' I said vaguely, 'quiet enough to make a body feel lonely, most of all in the gloaming.'

'I like the quiet of it,' she said softly now, as though she were listening to it.

And for a while it seemed that neither of us had any more to say. We just sat there, listening to the voice of the burn together. It was that evening I found for the first time the goodness of silence shared between companions who do not need always to be talking.

It was Darklis who broke the stillness at last. 'What are you thinking of, Hugh Herriot?'

I said – for I felt that it was but fair, after she had told so much to me, though I would not have spoken of it in the ordinary way of things – 'I was thinking that when we come to Dundee, and there are merchants to be found, I will spend some of the wedding siller that Claverhouse gave me on more paper and crayons and maybe some good sepia ink.' And then I wished I had not told her, and was afraid that she might laugh; and I looked up quickly, and realised how long we must have sat there, for the gloaming was almost deepened into the dark – such dark as there is in the North at Midsummer – and I could scarce make out her face among the elder branches, though the flower-curds still glimmered pale.

'No paints?' she said. And she was not laughing.

'I'd have no time for the grinding, nor for boiling the oil. The paper and the rest will do.'

'You should have taken Mynheer van Meere's offer,' said she, gravely, as it might be my mother offering me good advice.

'So you know about that.'

'Aye, Jean showed me the picture of himself. She keeps it among her private things.'

Pleasure shot through me. But I shook my head. 'No; I've another plan in my mind.'

'Not to bide in the stable-yard all your life?'

'No. In a year or two, I'm minded to go for a sojer.'

'Aye,' she said, 'Jean said somewhat of that, too.' And then, with a kind of softness in her voice, 'That would be in Claverhouse's troop?'

I found my hands were clenched on my knees, and I unclenched them carefully. 'It's daft. I ken that.'

'It's no' daft,' said she, 'it's no' daft to seek to follow where your heart's away before ye.'

And the quiet settled between us again, filled with the faint suckle of water under the bank, and an owl crying somewhere in the glen woods.

That time it was I that broke it, and with a blundering question. 'And you? What will you do, mistress?'

'Now that Jean will not be needing me as she used to do, you mean?'

'She'll always be needing you,' I said stoutly, though that was what I had meant.

She gave a little breathless laugh, and came sliding out of the tree in a froth of pale skirts, and the next instant was kneeling among the flowering sedges on the very margin of the water. 'Mebbe I'll wed wi' a prince. Mebbe I'll go back to my own people – och, not the People of Peace, the Tinkler folk – who kens what the future has waiting for any of us?'

The burn made a pool, still and dark, just there above the ford, and she leaned forward, gazing down into the darkness of it. 'Mebbe if I look – very hard—'

'Don't,' I said quickly, ''tis unchancy to play such games.'

But I do not think she even heard me; for that was when the strangeness began; and suddenly I knew that she was listening to something else, something that I could not hear.

'I have a tune running in my head,' she said after a few moments. 'All the while I have been here this e'en

– and 'tis no' just like any tune that ever I heard before . . .'

She began to hum very softly. And listening, I knew that it was no tune that I had ever heard, either. If I had heard it, I would not have been forgetting it. I never have forgotten it, I could whistle it to you now. But I will not . . .

A strange, haunting tune, with broken double notes in it that made me think of Amryclose and his pipes; but it was no tune that I had heard him play, and the hairs rose a little on the back of my neck.

Darklis broke off in her humming, then hummed a few more notes, and broke off again. She was leaning further over the water, staring down. 'Dark, down there,' she said, half whispering, in a small frozen voice that was not like her own. 'Black-dark, death-dark . . .'

'Come back,' I said, 'you'll fall in.' I wanted to catch hold of her, but something held me from the movement.

She only leaned the closer, as though something in the black secret heart of the pool was drawing her. 'Black – and torches – and the world falling – falling –' Her voice was becoming a wail, taking on the note that I have heard since in women keening for the dead. 'All things falling – no air to breathe – Jean! Jean, I am coming—'

Somehow I broke through the thing that held me, and flung forward to catch and drag her back from the terrible place that she was being drawn away to. And in the same instant, out of the stillness of the evening, a sudden flurry of wind came up the glen, shattering the still darkness of the pool, and flinging the flower-curdled elder branches up and over like a breaking wave.

Darklis flung out her hands as though to fend something off, and twisted sideways, crying out to me in terror, 'Hugh! *Hugh!*' as though I were the natural one in the world for her to call to.

'I'm here,' I said; and my arms were fast round her, while she clung to me, drawing her breath in great shuddering gasps. 'All's well now. Hold close to me, lassie, I have ye safe.'

Slowly, I felt her come back in to herself. She sat up and drew back out of my arms, gentle like. 'Did I fall asleep? I seemed to be dreaming.'

'Aye,' I said, 'and near enough went into the water.'

'And you caught me back.' She shook her head as though to clear it. The faery wind had died away as quickly as it had come. Already the moment was past, and she was forgetting whatever there was to forget. At least, I thought that she was forgetting. In after time I was none so sure.

''Tis getting late,' I said, 'will I take you back to the house?'

She got up and shook out her skirts, and we went back up the burnside. The night had returned to its proper self, a dog barked down-glen from the clachan, and the sky was like green crystal, with just the faint echo of light in the north from the sunset that would linger on there to join hands with the sunrise.

And I did not even know that we were walking with her hand in mine, until we reached the gate of the stable-yard, and parted clasp there without another word.

I waited in the archway to watch her safe to the side door of the house. The door stood open, and old Leezie, the housekeeper, her that was nurse to Claverhouse when he was a bairn, came bouncing through to meet her, scolding shrill as a Leith fishwife. 'Where hae ye been, ye bad lassie, out this late – '

'Only down by the ford,' said Darklis.

And the old crone let out a wail, 'No' under the eldern tree – and on Midsummer's Eve?'

'Why Leezie, where's the harm?' Darklis returned, half laughing. 'Ye can see the People of Peace havena carried me away.'

'Harm? Harm is it? Dinna ye ken yon eldern tree is ca'd the Dark Lady, an' the pool below her the Dark Lady's Looking-glass? An' dinna ye ken why?'

The door slammed shut behind her skirling.

9

Hard Riding!

So we came to Dudhope.

A bonnie place is Dudhope, part castle, part manor house, of warm rose-grey stone, sitting close among its gardens and its stands of oak and sycamore trees, on the slopes of Dundee Law above the old town with its narrow winding streets and crow-stepped gables and the broad bright waters of the Tay.

A good place to be starting a new life in, I thought, as we clattered through the gate arch into the wide court-yard on that first evening; a warm and welcoming place to become home to my lady and Darklis, aye, and me. But it is little enough the new master of Dudhope saw of his home through the rest of that summer, and the autumn that followed after.

The West was up in flames again, following a new leader, James Renwick, lately come from Holland. Notices appeared, fixed to the market crosses up and down the Lowlands, declaring war on the King and disowning all authority depending on him, proclaiming that every soldier or magistrate or ordinary man who lifted a hand against the Saints was an enemy of God and the Covenant and would suffer their just vengeance accordingly.

The Government answered by issuing an oath to be put to any suspect, disowning the declaration. Refusal to take the oath was to be taken as self-confessed proof of treason, and punished by death. Then Master Renwick and his mob marched on Kirkcudbright, murdering Peter Pierson, a parish minister, on the way, and tearing the country to pieces, far and wide. And Claverhouse and his troops were sent down to deal with the mess.

And when he was not dealing with that, he had another matter to handle – a small enough thing it seemed – for some privates of the Foot Guards had complained to the Privy Council, no less, that Colonel Douglas, him that was brother to the Duke of Queensberry, and therefore an uncomfortably powerful man, had dismissed them and used their arrears of pay to put fine new uniforms on his own company. Claverhouse was one of the Council, and took their part, and was to and fro to Edinburgh on their behalf when he might have had the chance to get back to his wife and home. Once, when he knew that he must go from Edinburgh straight back to Ayrshire again without even a glimpse of his home, he took me with him, that I might carry a letter back to my lady when he left the one for the other. And that was a thing that took a hand in the shaping of my life afterwards.

This was the way of it. On a wild evening and rain not far short of August's end, when Claverhouse was in Edinburgh yet again, my lady twisted her heel coming down the great stair, and fell the last half flight. Darklis and the other women gathered her up and put her into her bed, and at first it seemed that there was not much harm done. But in the mid-part of that night one of the grooms was routed out and sent galloping to bring Dr Anstruther up from the town, for my lady had done herself some kind of sore hurt inside.

Dr Anstruther came, and stayed a long time – an uncommon long time.

The whole stable-yard was awake and waiting by

then, and I mind the odd kind of hush under the wuthering of the storm. And then, with the lanterns scarce lit for the morning's mucking-out to begin, the steward came with word that someone must ride for Edinburgh to fetch the Colonel back, for 'twas like to go hard with my lady.

Archie Grier the head groom was fast in his bed with a flux of the kind that turns a man to a green and shivering wreck, the Colonel's own groom was with him in Edinburgh, and the other two, like the stable laddies, were Dundee-born and bred and had never been a score of miles from home. And that left me, that had ridden the road only a week or so before.

With a sick and heavy-drubbing heart I dashed up to my sleeping place in the loft, found my bonnet and pulled it down to my eyebrows, flung on my thick plaid, for it was like to be a chill ride as well as a long one, and came plunging back, dragging tight the belt that held it in at my waist, as I tumbled myself down the loft ladder.

Kestrel and Folly were saddled up and just being led out of their stalls, their hooves ringing sharp on the cobbles, as I regained the yard; and the web cobbles gleaming like fish-scales in the light of the lanterns; and a great coming and going. 'I'll come down to the ferry wi' ye, an' bring Folly back.' One of the other grooms was already swinging into Kestrel's saddle.

The steward held out to me a wee bag that jinked. 'Here, stow that in your pocket, ye'll need gold for the post-horses.' And as I took it he handed me an old horse pistol. 'And this in your belt. We're not in true Covenanting country, this side of Scotland, but ye'll maybe find a need for it, all the same.'

I took and thrust it into my belt, though I had never

handled such a thing before, and truth to tell, had more faith in the knife that was there already.

I swung up to the saddle; and suddenly there was Darklis at my stirrup, holding up a bulging wallet. 'Bannock and beef and something to keep out the cold,' said she. 'Ye'll have no time for inn meals on your way.'

The lantern light and the first paling of the wild morning splashed together on her face, showing it white and wisht, and her eyes big and aching in the whiteness of it; and I knew in that moment, as I had never quite known before, how much my lady meant to her. 'I'll bring him back before the wind changes,' I said, just for her hearing, and headed for the courtyard and the gate arch. Andy clattered beside me.

The wind was still blowing in long squally gusts, and the rain chill and driving, more like a November dawn than an August one, as we came down into Dundee town; and the waking candles were still blinking in the upper windows of the tall houses as we clattered through the steep streets, making for the quaysides and the ferry. The Tay is a mile wide at Dundee and all travellers to the South start out that way; but the ferryman was not best pleased to be called out so early and on such a morning, and emerged shaking his head as though he had a bee in his bonnet, and cursing. And when he recognised Andy, his temper did not sweeten, for there was always, by long and sacred tradition, something of a feud between Dundee town and its Constable. But the sight of a couple of silver pieces glinting in the light of the lantern above his door put him in a better frame of mind. And when I had dismounted and turned Folly over to Andy to take back, he led the way down to where his boat was beached; and between us we ran her down into the water and climbed aboard.

'Can ye row?' said he, unshipping the oars.

'I never have,' I said, 'but I'll try.' Anything for speed.

He shook his head, 'Nay, ye'd be more trouble than ye're worth.' And he began to swing to the oars.

By God's fortune the tide was at slack water, and so we were able to get across straight from bank to bank. But even so it seemed a weary while before I was scrambling out on the southern shore.

I paid the man off, and headed for the cluster of cottages about the stables where the rich folk of Dundee kept a few horses for the first stage of any southern journey. The place was up and busy, as well it might be; the Dudhope stable had been starting the day an hour and more ago; and the sight of Claverhouse's silver phoenix badge in my bonnet soon produced a horse, and I was away for Edinburgh.

The wind and rain were in my face as I rode hard along the track that follows the southern skirts of the Ochills, and I drove my chin further into the neck folds of my plaid, and settled down into the saddle, the morning coming up grey and sullen out of the Tay estuary behind me.

At Kilmany I changed horses, leaving word with the posting people to have two horses ready for the return journey around tomorrow's noon. That was a wild and maybe over-hopeful guess, but I reckoned it was better they should be on the outlook for us too early than too late. And when I was on my way again, I bethought me of Darklis's wallet, and got it out and ate as I rode, hungrily for I had had no breakfast, but glad when it was done, for I had no pleasure in the food save for the staying of the hunger pangs in my belly.

It was still but ten or so in the morning when I clattered into the stable-yard of the inn at Ferny. At first it seemed that there was no one about save a marigold-coloured cat sitting on the mounting block, who glared at me with a malevolent eye. But my shouts brought forth an ancient hostler, who, since there did indeed seem to be no one else, must take my tired horse before he brought out a fresh one. I mind the peaceful dream in which he moved, like someone moving under water, irked me past all bearing.

'I've no' got all day!' I burst out. 'I should be halfway to Gateside by now – I must be in Inverkeithing before the Forth ferry closes for the night!' And then as he showed no sigh of speeding up, 'Here, man, tell me which horse, an' I'll e'en saddle up for myself!'

He cocked an eye at me then, grumbling, 'Hoots toots, man, will it be a matter o' life an' death, then?'

'It could be just that!' I almost shouted; and seemingly the desperate need that I had for haste got through to him at last. He stopped dead, with the tired beast half in and half out of the stable. 'Weel, ye'll no' be in Inverkeithing before the ferry closes if ye gang round by Gateside an' Loch Leven.'

'What way, then?'

He rubbed his chin. 'Twa miles on the way forks, an' the right-hand road gangs on tae Gateside; but if ye tak the left fork, an' head south through Edensmuir to Leslie an' join the true road again at Cowdenbeath, ye'll knock ten miles or more off the distance, that way.'

'Is the way plain to follow?' I asked. 'I canna risk getting lost.'

He thought for an instant, then nodded. ''Tis your lucky day; old Hammerhead's in the end stall. Leslie's his home stable and he kens his way hame if ever a horse did. Just let him gang his ain gait, an' ye'll not get lost if ye sleep on his back every step o' the way frae here tae Leslie.'

We got old Hammerhead out and saddled up between us; and never was a horse better named, for I never saw an uglier brute in all my days. And at long last, after I'd paid the score and left the same word as I'd left at Kilmany, I was on my way again, and trying to overtake the time I had lost.

Two–three miles on, I came, as the old hostler had said, to a place where the road forked, or rather where the high road, such as it was, ran on towards Gateside and round Loch Leven to Kinross, where we had spent the night when I rode that way with Claverhouse, while on the left a rough track that I had not even noticed that first time went snaking down into lower country, losing itself in scrubby moorland and darkly ragged thorn-woods. There I reined in and sat for a few moments, thinking. The high road was at least clear to follow, while the southward track looked awful untrustworthy. But ten miles was ten miles . . .

Hammerhead was fidgeting under me, eager to turn left into his way home. Finally I gave him his head. 'It's your road,' I told him. 'In God's name keep to it!'

Maybe it was a fool thing to do, and more than once I was cursing myself as we plunged deeper and deeper into the wilds of Edensmuir Forest, following tracks that were mere traces among the heather and did not have the feel of leading to any place in this world at all; and no living creature to be seen save the distant flicker of a roe deer and the curlew and snipe that we startled from the bents as we went drumming by. I have a good sense of direction myself, and can find my way blind about a wolf's belly as well as most, but I take my bonnet off to that old nag; he was as wise as he was ugly;

and not so long past noon, when I had about lost hope of ever winning clear of that black and sodden wilderness, we came to another track that crossed ours running east and west, and a straggling village at the way-crossing, and drew rein before an inn with the Leslie Arms painted on its swinging sign; or rather, Hammerhead came to a halt there of his own accord.

I parted from him with a hurried pat and a word of praise, and having asked my road to Cowdenbeath and again left word for horses to be ready next morning, I took to the wilds again. This time the track was easier to follow; but when we came down into the Rother Glen, the rain in the hills, coming down in brown swirling spate, was over the banks of the burn and had washed the timber bridge away.

With a horse I knew and that knew me, I would have tried swimming him over, myself still in the saddle, but as it was, I dismounted, and keeping an arm through the bridle, took off my plaid – it could not be soaked much wetter by the spate than it was already by the rain, but the weight of it could well drown me if I went under still wearing it – and rolled it into a tight bundle with my pistol in the middle, and made it fast to the saddle with my belt strap.

'Now,' said I, 'in wi' ye, ma laddie!'

The horse laid back his ears and tried to wheel aside; but I had him fast, and somehow I got him snorting and trembling down the torn bank, and we took to the racing water together. My, but the cold of it bit to the bone, August or no, all the chill of the high hills was in it, and the swirling force of it seemed like a live thing trying to carry us away! But somehow, half swimming and half floundering, we got across and found ourselves up the further bank and out on firm ground once more, without, I'm thinking, either of us much idea of how we got there. I know I threw up a surprising amount of burn water, while the horse stood by shivering and watching me – I had the presence of mind not to let go of his bridle the while. When I'd done, I belted on my plaid and the pistol again and, remounting, heeled the poor brute into a gallop without giving him more time to think about it.

The wet and windy day was fading early into a sodden gloaming when we came into Cowdenbeath and pulled up in the inn courtyard. And the hostler asked had we swum Loch Leven.

'We didna come that way; but the bridge is washed away up Rother Glen,' I said. 'Give him a dash of ale in his mash, he's earned it.'

'Ye look as if ye could do wi' something o' the same kind yersel', my young callant,' said the man, kind enough.

'Aye,' I said, and the teeth were chattering in my head. 'But I've no time.' And I was away down the last long stretch to Inverkeithing.

It was long after dark when I came down through the little town, and saw the wind-tossed lantern light among the wharves and jetties, and leaving my horse at the inn, found my way down to the ferry.

The boatman was no better pleased to be called out after dark on such a night than the Dundee man had been to be called out before dawn on such a morning; but he went off, grumbling, his great gawky lad with him and myself hard at their heels. And by and by I was crouched in the stern of the ferry-boat while the lights of Inverkeithing dwindled smaller behind me, and the lights of Queensferry grew out of the blustery darkness ahead. I got out the remains of the food Darklis had given me, and tried to eat, but without much success. I had covered seventy miles and more hard riding since dawn, and I was weary almost beyond eating, and the heart cold within me when I thought what might have happened at Dudhope in the past hours. But I managed to thrust some of it down, and took a swig out of the flask, which made my head swim – unless that was the swing and bounce of the little boat in the choppy waters – I was never much of a sailor. But it put back some of the heart into me; and before long, on the southern shore with a fresh horse under me and a good road to follow, I was off on the last long stage of my ride.

Eh, but I was weary!

There's not much I am minding of that last stage, just the wind and the darkness, and the drumming hooves of the post-horse as the miles reeled out behind me. But it seemed to go on a long, long time, so that I felt it to be far into the darkmost belly of the night before I reached Edinburgh town; and I was vaguely surprised when at last I came clattering up Leith Wynd, to find the glimmer of candles still shining here and there through the cracks in window shutters.

I came out into the Cannongate and swung right-hand towards the Netherbow, and in a few moments more was dropping from the saddle before the tall old house on the third floor of which Claverhouse had his town lodging.

A lantern over the door-arch was swinging in the wind, casting its lights and shadows across the entrance. I hitched the weary post-horse to the ring beside the door, and beat on the timbers until an old woman in a grey wrapper and carrying a candle came and opened it to me. 'Eh?' she said, peering out. 'Wha's there, knocking fit to raise the deid?'

'I must speak with Colonel Graham – ' I began, and then as she tried to shut the door again, 'I'm from Dudhope – from his lady—'

'The Colonel has company,' she said, still trying to shut the door again.

But my foot was safe inside. 'He'll see me,' I said, and thrust the door back on her, then banged it shut behind me.

'Och well,' she shrugged, and holding up the candle, peered at me more closely. 'Dinna I ken ye?'

'Mebbe. I've been here before. Let me up, Grannie.'

'The Colonel will no' be best pleased, I'm warning ye, but that's your affair.' And grumbling to herself still, she shuffled away back to some den of her own in the back regions, taking the candle with her, and leaving the narrow entrance-way in pitch darkness.

I fumbled my way across to the turnpike stair and began to climb, past the doors of the lower landings, feeling with my hands until a faint light began to reach down to me from a wall lantern far overhead. I came to the door of the third landing, and wondered whether it would yet be locked for the night; but when I tirled at the pin, it opened easily under my hand.

The small entrance room was lit by a branch of candles streaming in the draught from a passage-way on the far side, and Claverhouse's gloves lay on a carved chest against one wall, together with a couple of rain-wet riding cloaks. More candlelight and the smell of tobacco smoke spilled out from another door that stood half open, and with it the sound of voices, and Claverhouse's quiet laugh. I turned towards the doorway, and checked in the opening a moment to pull my sodden plaid into more seemly folds.

The booming of the wind had seemingly swallowed

the sounds of my coming, and a screen of gilded leather half-shielded the doorway, and so for a few moments I saw the men in the room before they were aware of me. Lord Ross standing with his shoulder against the mantel as he kicked at a log that had rolled forward out of the fire; and another, a fair-haired man sprawling long legs out from the chair that seemed to have swallowed him, and who I knew, having seen him once or twice before, to be Colin Lindsay, the young Earl of Balcarres; both of them puffing away at their long-stemmed pipes. And in the opposite chair, Claverhouse himself, leaning forward to gaze into the fire, turning his pipe forgotten in his fingers. Indeed he was not one who smoked much, save to keep other men company, and I think he found little pleasure in it.

'Aye well, it's as good as finished with at last,' he was saying. 'Tomorrow to go over matters with the Quartermaster as to supplies and quartering for our own troops, eh, Ross? And with luck I'll be away home by the morn's morn.'

I hesitated to break in on their talk.

It was Balcarres that answered. 'Ye've done a good job for the Foot Guards, and ye've sorted Colonel Douglas, but I'm thinking ye may have done a bad job for yourself.'

'Ye think Colonel Douglas may bear a grudge?' Claverhouse said. 'Man, even if he did, what ill has he the power to do me?'

'The power of being Queensberry's brother,' said Lord Ross, watching the smoke curl upward. 'Ye'll not deny that Queensberry has power in plenty?'

Claverhouse laughed. 'Don't be such an old henwife. Queensberry's by way of being a friend of mine.'

'*By way of being?*' Balcarres shook his head. 'You're

98

too trusting, Johnnie. Queensberry on his way up would be the friend of any man who was friend to the King or York. But Queensberry is no longer on his way up, he's there! He has his dukedom and he doesn't need your good offices any more. Also General Dalyell is an old man and a sick one, and our new duke wants the Commander-in-Chief's place when it falls vacant, for his brother. And I'm thinking he must know you'll get it, unless he can discredit you.'

'All we're saying,' Lord Ross put in, 'is – have a care, Johnnie.'

'And not go spoiling Douglas's little games? Somebody had to see justice done for these poor devils.'

It came to me suddenly that I was eavesdropping, and I made a trampling at the door, and went in round the screen, pulling off my drowned bonnet.

They looked round abruptly, and Claverhouse said, 'Why, Hugh! In God's name what—'

''Tis my lady,' I croaked, 'she fell on the stairs yester-e'en, and this morning—'

Claverhouse was on his feet. 'Is she – how sore is she hurt?'

'Awfu' bad – inside. They sent me to fetch you.'

I heard him catch his breath in between his teeth. Then he spoke, quite calmly to the other two. 'Colin – Ross, you'll have to tidy up things here; I'll be back to the regiment as soon as I can.' He strode past me through the open doorway, shouting for his man-servant, and when the chiel came running, began giving him orders for his horse to be brought round, and for his riding-cloak for he must start back at once for Dudhope. Aye, and orders for me to be dried and fed and put somewhere to sleep.

I cut in on that. 'Sir – my post-horse is still at the

door, and hard ridden; I must get him to his own stable out of this wind.'

'Someone else will see to that,' Claverhouse said. He put his hand on my shoulder. 'I'll thank you as you deserve, Hugh, when there's time. Now away with you and get a good night's sleep.'

I must have shot up like a beanstalk in the past few months, for it was at that moment I noticed, as one notices things when it is no time to be noticing them, that I no longer had to look up at him, for my eyes were on a level with his, and I could look straight into them. 'It's another horse I'll be needing, no' the night's sleep,' I said. 'I'll be riding back with you, sir.'

'That's daft talk,' Claverhouse said, 'ye've ridden close on a hundred miles the day.'

'Ye can knock ten or more off that if ye strike north-east from Cowdenbeath and up through Leslie, 'stead of round by Kinross.' My voice sounded mulish in my own ears. 'Do ye ken that way, sir?'

'I've ridden it as a boy. I daresay I can find it again.'

'It's no' that easy to find. I rode it the day.'

'You'll hold me back—'

'No' if I've a horse to match yours. I'm riding wi' ye, sir.'

His eyes looked back into mine, hard and searching. Then he let go my shoulders and turned to the servant still hovering in the doorway. 'Two horses, Murray, and no bed, but dry clothes and food. Hand him over to Effie.'

And he went clattering off up another turn of the stairs, as I suppose to his own chamber.

In something like a dream, I heard the quick con-cerned voices of his two friends gathering up their own cloaks to depart; the whole place seemed springing to sudden life; and I was in the kitchen, my head suddenly swimming, in the warmth of the fire stripping off my sodden clothes and dragging on dry ones much too wide for me, under the watchful eye (despite all my protests) of a meagre little woman in an enormous night-cap, who assured me, as she set bread and beer and a heel of braxy ham on the table, that she had had brothers of her own.

I had scarcely had time to start on the food when the clatter of hooves sounded outside, and Effie snatched it from me and thrust it into Darklis's wallet which somebody must have rescued and brought in, bidding me drink up, flinging a dry plaid over my shoulder, thrusting me out to go racing down the stairs at Claverhouse's heels.

And almost before I could draw another breath I was in the saddle again, and following Claverhouse up the Cannongate. Mercifully the rain had slacked off, and there was even a late lopsided moon breaking through the ragged clouds, as not much after midnight we left Edinburgh by Leith Wynd and took the road to Queensferry.

I had got a kind of second wind, and I kept going well enough; but truth to tell there's little that I remember about that ride, for when I think of it now, it is like trying to remember a confused dream. It must have been something after two in the morning when we came to Queensferry, and it was in my mind we might have trouble getting across; but ferries that do not ply for the likes of Hugh Herriot ply for the likes of John Graham of Claverhouse, and we made the Forth crossing without trouble; aye, and found all ready for us at Inverkeithing where I had left word, so that we were on

101

horseback again with the least possible delay. And Claverhouse said something to me about having a head on my shoulders that warmed the heart in me, though I have never been too clear what it was.

He made me rise beside him whenever the road was wide enough; I am thinking so that he could keep an eye on me and see that I did not roll out of the saddle in my sleep. I mind the hostler at Cowdenbeath saying that the bridge was down in Rother Glen, and my own voice pointing out that I had come that way yesternoon . . . And unless there had been a lot more rain in the hills . . .

So we took the Leslie road, and I have a dim memory of splashing our way across the still flooded burn, the shock of the cold hill-water waking me somewhat from my dream, and Claverhouse taking the upstream side to come between me and the force of the spate. I mind the Ochills rearing up ahead of us, the heather on their flanks that had been wine-black yesterday turned to hazy amethyst in the late sunlight. I mind the choking taste of spirits that burned my throat like fire being poured into me at the post-house at Ferny and then not much more, not even the Tay crossing, until we were riding into the courtyard at Dudhope in the first dusk.

They must have been keeping a look-out for us, for the lanterns had been lit early, and Dr Anstruther was coming down the steps from the great door even as we reined up. He looked very tired, but there was a half smile lurking somewhere about his face as he came to Claverhouse's stirrup. 'The worst is over,' he said. 'By God's grace your lady will live to bear you many sons.'

Claverhouse dropped from the saddle as I took his bridle from him. 'The sons can wait,' he said. 'I may go to her?'

'Lady Jean is asleep; I have bled her, and now rest is what she needs above all things. But to find you beside her when she wakes will do more for her than any leechcraft of mine.'

Claverhouse took a long step towards the house, then checked and turned a haggard face to look up at me. 'My thanks, Hugh,' he said, and reached up for my hand and gripped and wrung it. Then he went on with the doctor.

I led his horse with my own through into the stable-yard, where other hands took both bridles from me, and there were kindly concerned voices all about me as I half slid, half fell from the saddle, and the cobbles came up to meet me, rocking and dipping under my feet.

I lurched away and somehow clawed my way up the loft ladder, and pitched down on to my straw pallet. Someone pulled the rug over me, but before they had done, I had fallen headlong into sleep with the drum of horses' hooves still beating in my head.

10

Captain Faa

I slept the clock round, and woke aching from head to foot, stiff as a board and hungry as a wolf in a famine winter; but a bowl of steaming porridge and a thick collop of mutton soon set the one to rights, and the rest wore off as the day went by, until by noon I was within sight of being back to my usual self. Aye me, the powers of recovery one has when one is not yet turned sixteen!

Not that any work was expected of me that day. Word as to that had come down from the house. And so I found myself with time on my hands, and yet not quite knowing what to do with it. It was the day of Lady Mary Fair, which as it were ends and crowns the summer in Dundee; and from below came the distant mingling of voices singing, shouting, quarrelling and crying their wares, fiddles and horse hooves and the blare of side-show drums and trumpets that was the voice of the town enjoying itself. I could have gone down to join it: but I did not feel in the mood for noise and crowds and sword-swallowers and gilded gingerbread. At least not yet. Maybe later, when the lanterns were lit and some of the other stable hands would be going down.

Now in one corner of the stable-yard grew an ancient fig tree. Age had robbed it of most of its power to bear fruit, and even its leaves were not so thick and heavy as they must have been in its prime. And time and again, when the light fell in a certain way, striking through what leaves there were, and blotting its shadow velvet dark on the wall behind it (but always at a time when I had work to do), the sight of the old tree had as it were made my drawing hand itch. For the knotted trunk and branches were like some fantastic beast, a dragon maybe, caught in its coilings and turned into a tree.

And that afternoon, as I sat on the edge of the horse-trough and wondered what to do, it caught at my awareness and made my drawing hand itch again. And me with the rest of the day before me empty and un-marked as a leaf of virgin paper.

I fetched down the drawing materials which I had bought with some of my wedding silver and kept in a box under the head of my pallet bed, and settled myself on a convenient mounting block, to the delights of try-ing to capture my vision.

Once or twice as I worked, one of the other grooms or horseboys peered over my shoulder in the by-going, puzzled, and went his way. It had become accepted in the Dudhope stables that I was daft in this one particu-lar; but if I chose to spend my free time scribbling on bits of paper, instead of playing dice or cock-fighting or hanging round the kitchen door after the lassies, there was no harm in it and I would maybe come to more sense as I grew older. Meanwhile, I could make sketches of men or horses or anything else they called for, which amused them from time to time and was maybe none so bad practice for me either.

So I worked on, unmolested, trying to catch the fan-tastic twists and coils, the ugly-beautiful strength of the old tree, the contrasting textures of rough fissured bark and smooth fleshy leaf and ripening fruit with a brown-black crayon on the blank white paper.

It must have been not far short of supper time when

there came a flurry of feet over the cobbles, and I looked up and saw Darklis with a shawl as glowing-red as rowan berries caught round her.

'Hugh,' she said, and crouched down beside me as though to look at the drawing on my knee, 'Hugh, will ye take a message for me into the town? I canna leave Jean, and—'

'We heard this morning that she was better,' I said quickly.

'So she is; but she canna be easy without me beside her, even now that himself is back; and you're the only one I'll trust the thing to—'

'Trust what thing to?' said I, under my breath and still drawing away, for it was clear that whatever the thing was, it was secret. 'Take a deep breath, lassie, an' begin again, an' tell me clear.'

She drew her breath and began again. 'Hugh, 'tis Lady Mary Fair, an' the Tinkler folk will be gathered to it wi' all the rest, and – they're loyal to their own; they have never forgotten that I am of their kin. Always at Paisley at fair-time, one would come up to the house to make sure that all was well wi' me. I thought that mebbe now I have come away all across Scotland . . . But one o' them came up yestere'en, an' I was wi' Jean and didna even know he'd come.'

'An' you're afraid he'll come again?' I said. Not everyone cares for the Tinkler folk anywhere round their house or horses, and Master Gilchrist the steward was of that way of thinking.

She shook her head. 'I'm afraid he may *not* come again. I'm afraid that they'll think me one that breaks wi' my own kin.'

'I'll take whatever message ye give me,' I said.

'Oh Hugh, I knew I could trust you! Ask for Captain

Faa – ye'll find him wherever the horses are. Tell him all is well wi' me, and I'm no' in need of rescuing, and –' She felt inside the berry-bright folds of her shawl and brought out a silver brooch; the bonniest thing fashioned like a sprig of bell-heather, with seven small amethysts set in it where the flowers would be. 'Show him this for a proof that ye do come from me.'

I took it from her, and without another word she was away, running like a deer, back towards the house.

I drew on a wee while longer, then gathered the scatter of pencils and my sketch-paper on its bit of board, and ambled back to my own quarters, taking care not to seem in any kind of hurry. I put my drawing stuff back into the kist, stowed the brooch among the few coins in my purse and, returning to the stable-yard, strolled out by the side door and headed downhill towards the town and the bee-swarming of the fair.

The first lanterns were pricking out here and there though it was still as good as daylight on the slopes of Dundee Law, and in the light of the flares the gaily coloured booths and stalls glowed with a jewel brilliance that hid their raggedness and dirt, making a kind of gaudy fungus-growth all along the dignified south flank of St Mary's Kirk, above which the tower soared upward to cut its own dark-edged shape out of the evening sky. But minding Darklis's directions, I left the bright lights and milling crowds, the tumblers and the gingerbread stalls, the shabby dancing bear and the man in scarlet tights breathing out great gobbets of flame, that had their stands where the lanes of merchants' booths came together; even the savoury-smelling pie stall, though I was hungry for my missed supper; and made for the open space on the western fringes of the fairground where the horse dealing was going on.

The crowds were not so thick there, but thick enough, all the same, and there was a great coming and going; and as I hesitated on the edge of a knot of men who had gathered to watch a bay gelding put through its paces, wondering if the swarthy horse-handler would be a good one to ask for Captain Faa, somebody jostled against me in passing, and all but sent me flying.

Maybe the man was less skilled at his craft than most, or maybe my own thoughts being so much on my purse and the little brooch within it made me aware of what I would otherwise have missed in the general jostling of the crowd. What I felt was the faintest tug at my pocket.

My hand flew down to it and found my purse gone before the small square man who had brushed me by had quite had time to disappear into the shifting throng.

I dived after him with a yell, 'Hi! Gi' me back my purse, ye villain!' and grabbed him by the arm. He writhed like a weazel and was all but gone again leaving his ragged coat empty in my hands, but I managed to hook his feet from under him as he leapt, and he went sprawling full length on the churned muddy grass, with me a' top of him.

'I never touched your purse!' he squealed with his mouth full of mud.

'Then whyfore will ye run?' said I.

And I made to shift my grip for a better one; but he took the instant's chance, and up he came as swift as a weazel indeed, and fetched me a jab on the nose that drew the good red blood.

Folks were pressing in round us to watch, and somewhere in the back of my head (the main part of it was full of the need to hang on to the chiel that had stolen

108

my purse with the precious brooch in it, and get it back from him again) I heard someone laugh, and a voice crying us on as though we were a pair of game-cocks. And then there was another voice, I never heard what it said, but on the instant, hands were hauling me up off my enemy, and the chiel himself stumbling to his feet, whining out protests of his innocence. And I found myself staring up at something that looked at first sight like a very splendid and lordly tatty-bogle – what they call a scarecrow in the South.

A very tall thin man wearing the wreck of a coat that had once been mulberry velvet trimmed on cuffs and pocket-flaps with tarnished silver lace, and a proud, if something weather-worn, bunch of blue-black heron hackles clasped into his battered bonnet by a brooch like a silver targe. Grey hair hung in thick greasy locks to his shoulders, and out of the mane of it looked a long brown-skinned rogue's face with a great hooked nose that could have belonged to a Roman emperor, and a short stump of a blackened pipe that seemed as much a part of it as his nose did, and a pair of yellow eyes – blazing wicked yellow like those of the fish-eagle that the Highlanders call *Iolair-Suil-Na-Greine*, the Bird with the Sunlit Eye.

A scarecrow he might be, but clearly he was a scarecrow in some kind of authority, and I appealed to him. 'Sir, yon de'il stole my purse!'

The wrinkles round the yellow eyes deepened, as though there were amusement somewhere at the back of them, and he jerked his head towards the pickpocket. 'Search him,' he said to the world in general, without moving the pipe in his mouth.

Two men from the gathered crowd set about it, pulling open the man's ragged shirt and delving into his breeches' pockets, while a third went through the pockets of his cast-off coat. But there were tiny glances going to and fro between them all the while, and when a few coins that might have been anybody's and a rabbit snare and a knife and such things had been brought to light, my purse was not among them.

I turned back desperately. 'He did take it, he *did*! He must have passed it on somehow!'

'What was in it, young master?'

'Three siller shillings, and something else – a lassie's geegaw that I was to take wi' a message to Captain Faa.'

Nothing moved behind the yellow eyes, but he gave a slow considering nod. 'See to it,' he said, again seemingly to the world in general, and to me, 'Let ye come wi' me then.'

And he turned and headed away towards the edge of the fairground. I went after him, close as a burr; there seemed nothing else to do. In a little the crowds thinned away, as fine horses and their buyers and sellers were left behind and we were among the tethered ponies and tilt-carts and the humped black tents of the Tinkler camp.

Here and there in front of the tents the light of the cooking fires was beginning to bite, and faces with the queer shuttered look of the gipsy kind wormed out of the shadows and turned a little but never more than a little, to watch us go by. Faces of old grannies, walnut-wrinkled and with pipes as firmly rooted between their blackened teeth as that of the man I followed; hawk faces of men intent on the horse harness or the pots and pans that they were mending; flaunting vivid faces of girls with bright shawls about their heads and shoulders, as I had seen Darklis wear hers only an hour since. The smells that came from the cooking pots brought the soft warm water to my mouth. A man sat on the shaft of a tilt-cart playing softly on a fiddle. Bairns and dogs and once a little pig ran in and out across our path as we went. It was like a strange country, and I mind wondering if the strangeness of it accounted, at least part-way for the strangeness that was in Darklis, too. Darklis's left-hand world that reached out to her sometimes in this right-hand world that was hers now . . .

Close to one of the fires, we passed a knot of bairns and bigger louts amusing themselves by throwing clods and bits of wood and the like at a miserable mongrel pup tied by a piece of cord to the gaily painted wheel of a cart. Every time it tried to get round behind the wheel into some kind of shelter, someone kicked it out again, yelping dismally, and the game went on.

I looked to the man I followed to do something about it, as he had done about my own affair, but he only cast a casual glance that way in the by-going, and ducked into the entrance hole of a big black tent close by. And again I followed him. It was not to be worrying about ill-used puppies that I was there, I told myself.

Inside the tent was very dark with a kind of animal darkness, and closely warm with a faintly animal smell to it. The man struck flint and steel and kindled a horn lantern that hung against the tent pole. And as the tawny light grew and steadied, I saw the place where I was; the few pots and crocks, a three-legged stool, the thick-piled heather of the bed-place with a couple of old rugs flung across it. And save for a pair of fine brindled greyhounds tied to the tent post, the man's lordliness certainly did not seem to include his living-place. Yet lordly the man was, even more so now that I looked at him fully.

111

He sat himself down on the creepy-stool and gestured me towards the piled heather of the bed-place.

But I was not sitting down for a chat. 'It's Captain Faa I'm wanting to speak wi',' I said.

'And it's Captain Faa ye're speaking wi',' he said. 'Sit ye down.'

I think I had known it all along.

So I sat me down on my haunches in the piled heather. 'I am from Mistress Darklis,' I said, 'from Mistress Darklis Ruthven.'

He nodded, 'I was thinking ye might be so. And is it well wi' the Rawni – wi' Mistress Darklis Ruthven?'

'It's well with her,' I said. 'She bade me come because she canna leave my lady Jean while she is ill – an' tell ye that all's well wi' her and she's no' needing to be rescued. She gave me the wee brooch to bring to ye, for proof that 'tis herself that sent me.' And then the thought of what had happened rose in my throat, and the thought of going back and telling her that I had lost her bonnie pin, and I burst out, 'But yon thieving de'il—'

Again the lines deepened at the corners of his strange yellow eyes. 'Bide a wee, and 'twill surely come back to ye. Meanwhile, what like is it, this brooch?'

'Siller,' I said, 'like a heather sprig wi' sparks o' amethyst for the flower bells.'

'And these heather bells, would ye have noticed the number o' them?'

'Seven, I think.'

He knocked out his pipe, and began to refill it from the tobacco box he brought forth from a silver-laced pocket of that once-splendid coat. 'Aye, that would be the number.' And he lit his pipe at the lantern and settled to puffing away, gazing into the shadows beyond the tent pole as though I were not there at all.

'Bide a wee,' he said once again, when in my desperate impatience I began to fidget, and that was all. And as I sat listening to the voices outside, and the shifting of the tethered ponies and all the distant sounds of the fair, until at last somebody ducked in under the tent flap, and gave something into the hand Captain Faa held out for it, and was gone again almost before I knew he had come.

Captain Faa opened the purse – aye, it was my purse, sure enough – and took out the silver pin with the bright flecks of amethyst, holding it to the lantern, on the thin brown palm of his hand. 'Aye, seven it is,' he said, and tossed it to me, and my purse after it. 'It seems ye are a messenger to be trusted. Go back now to the Rawni, and tell her ye have done as she bade ye, and brought her back her bonnie pin again.'

Eh! I was glad to have it back in my hand! But I was looking into my purse before I dropped it back in; and it was empty. 'There were three siller shillings in here when 'twas taken,' said I. 'Where would my three siller shilling be now, Captain?'

He looked at me without a blink. 'Och, well now, that's a different matter. One siller shilling is much like another, and no' so easy to trace as a siller pin wi' seven amethysts in it.'

I gave him back look for look. 'I'm thinking ye could come by them easy enough, gin ye were minded to, Captain.'

'Aye, but then ye see 'twould be a poor-spirited kind o' thing, and going altogether against the customs o' the Tinkler kind, to be handing back good siller that was honestly stolen,' said he blandly. And then he turned thoughtful. 'On the other hand, I myself might well feel that a small recompense for your trouble – aye, and your bloody nose . . .'

113

By that time I was on my feet, and all the stubbornness had set hard within me. 'I'm no' wanting payment for a service done in friendship,' said I, in what you might call a dignified snuffle, for my nose was indeed sadly the worse for wear.

'A stiff-necked young callant,' said Captain Faa, and blew out a cloud of tobacco smoke that curled about his head in the lantern light.

'An' come to that, was Mistress Darklis's siller pin no' honestly stolen, too?'

'Mistress Darklis is one of us,' said he, watching the smoke with one eye narrowed; patient speaking, like one explaining something very simple to a dim-witted bairn.

I knew that he was playing with me, idly, finding some kind of amusement in my utter helplessness to do anything about it.

I stood silent, glaring. I wanted my money back, for silver shillings did not grow on trees, but if I accepted it as a recompense – I knew that I had but to say the word – he would have won his game, and I would have backed down in some way that mattered more than the money did; and if I went back to Dudhope without it, still I would have backed down, though in a different way . . .

And at that moment a shrill shower of yelps rose outside; the piteous yelping of a pup in distress. And into the dark inside of my head flashed the picture of the miserable little creature tied to the cartwheel, and the gleeful tinkler louts gathered round.

And suddenly, that was something more important still. 'I'll take yon pup for my three shillings,' I said, not knowing that I was going to, until the words were out of me.

He brought his gaze back from the wreathing pipe smoke, and looked at me full with those yellow eyes. 'How if I'm no' selling?'

'Ye dinna' seem to set much store by the wee beast.'

'No' much,' he agreed, reaching out a foot to flick the ear of the nearest greyhound. 'How if he's no' mine to sell?'

'I'm thinking that most things hereabouts are yours, gin ye choose to make them so,' I said. 'I'm thinking three siller shillings would be a good price for him.'

He went on looking at me, consideringly; then he gave a kind of laugh, soft at the back of his throat that never broke through into the open; and he came to his feet all in one piece and one fluid movement as a cat does. 'It might be,' he said. 'Aye, it might be that.'

And I knew that he had conceded the game and left my honour safe; and suddenly I was not at all sure what the game had been about, anyway.

So I returned to Dudhope with Darklis's silver pin safe in my pocket again; with a bloody nose and a faintly bewildered mind, and a bedraggled brown and white mongrel pup under my coat, his muzzle puffing warmly into the hollow of my neck.

And when I got back, it was assumed that I had got the bloody nose in fighting somebody for possession of the small beastie. I let it bide that way. The truth was too complicated to try explaining it to anybody. Besides, the thing was between Darklis and me. But I did not tell even Darklis until long after, lest she should think in some way that she had cost me my three silver shillings.

For me, there was never money so well spent, for it brought me Caspar.

I felt strongly that he should have a noble name, for

his front end, with its little flattened muzzle and long silky ears, once he was cleaned up, was like the little soft-bred dogs that I had sometimes seen in the laps of great ladies passing in their coaches along the Edinburgh streets – my father had once had one of them to paint, on a velvet cushion, with a collar of wee silver bells round his neck – though his back legs and long stringy tail seemed to belong to another sort of dog altogether. And I felt also that by rights he should have a gipsy name. Darklis said that Caspar was a gipsy name; and it was also the name of a king. The same of course is true of Balthazaar and Melchior; but neither of those would be so good for shouting. In naming a dog, one should always consider the shouting.

Caspar he became. My dog. A jaunty wee dog when his bruises were mended, and valiant, once the fears and sorrows of his mistreated puppy days were forgotten. I have had four dogs since Caspar, and loved them well, but they do say that however many dogs a man may whistle after him, there is always one that comes closer and stands taller with him than all the rest, and despite the partings that came between us, Caspar was that one to me.

But I am getting ahead of myself again.

11

'Wishful to go for a Sojer'

Lady Jean came down from her room in a while, and after that 'twas only a matter of days before she came out into the stable-yard, looking white and somehow burned out, and muffled close in a great fur cloak with Darklis watchful beside her; but with her old smile coming back again, and wilful-set on having a word with Linnet and Laverock, aye, and thanking me for fetching himself to her when she had sore need of him.

But long before that, Claverhouse was away back to his regiment again.

He was to and fro between Dudhope and Edinburgh and the South West all autumn and into the winter, whether or no the roads were fit for travelling; while at home my lady grew stronger and the house began to be full of its old comings and goings, whether its master was there or not. Sometimes Balcarres or Lord Ross would be with us, or Captain Livingstone in the by-going; sometimes Philip of Amryclose with his stories of Montrose and the Highland legends that he would be telling; and his Greek and Latin, and him marching on his long crane-fly legs up and down the terrace before the house with his pipes under his arm and over his shoulder and the skirl of them floating down to Dundee town.

That winter the bad blood that Balcarres had foretold grew into some kind of open quarrel between Claverhouse and the new-made Duke of Queensberry. Garbled murmurs of it even reached us in the stable-yard. It seemed there was a deal of mischief made at Court, and King Charles, who was already a sick man, listening to lying tales and allowed himself to be pulled this way and that; and at the last, for all that Claverhouse had been friend to him and his brother a' many years, he felt that he must support his Officers of State – that meant Queensberry – and the South West that had been Claverhouse's kale-garth for so long was stripped from him and the military command given to Queensberry's brother, Colonel Douglas, while his powers as a magistrate were given to a certain Lord George Drummond – so now there was two to muddle up between them the job that he had dealt with single-handed well enough.

So all that winter and into the spring Claverhouse was left kicking his heels, the unemployed colonel of an unemployed regiment of horses, while under Douglas and Drummond things went from bad to worse in Ayrshire and Wigtown and Dumfries.

And the chief thing I mind about him in those months is that his patience snapped over-easily and his eyes looked hot in his head.

Early in the spring we heard that the King was dead, and James his brother was king in his stead; and then that Queensberry had been made High Commissioner for Scotland in James's place. And within a few weeks all Scotland – and I suppose all England too – knew that the young Duke of Monmouth, him that was Charles's by-blow son, was ready in Holland to make a try for the English throne, and the Duke of Argyll with him; and I'm thinking that with those two on the doorstep, and the Scottish South West behaving like one of those heath fires that smoulder among the heather roots unseen, and break out in pockets of flame for the wind to carry it where it will, King James must have felt that he could not be doing without the best soldier he had. So he ordered Claverhouse and Queensberry to make up their quarrel (I would have liked fine to see that!) and then – eh! the weakness and shilly-shallying of the man! – he promoted both Colonel Graham and Colonel Douglas to Brigadier, Douglas with just two days' seniority to counterbalance the fact that Claverhouse was Horse and Douglas Foot, and cavalry always counts for just that bit more.

Then Claverhouse was ordered down into the South West again to clean up his old territory.

The night after the order arrived, when a galloper from the Brigadier's own troop who were quartered in Dundee town had been sent off with word to the rest of the regiment in Edinburgh, and the red-coated coming and going in the stable-yard was over, I lay in my sleeping place, staring into the darkness and listening to the spring wind over Dundee Law, and thought long thoughts to myself, with Caspar lying in his usual place with his warm chin across my ankles under the blanket. I had never changed my plan to go for a soldier, but I had yet maybe a year to wait, by my own reckoning, for I was but sixteen as yet, and they did not take raw young callants in Claverhouse's Horse. It had all seemed a comfortable way off, something bright and beckoning on the skyline. But now suddenly the remoteness was gone, and I was being torn two ways.

Part of me, still set on following Claverhouse when the time came, was glad that the time was not yet. Not this time, not down into Ayrshire against my own people, like enough to get my death at their hands. Part of me knew that if I was going to follow Claverhouse at all, it must be anywhere, at any time, against my own

119

kind if need be, facing the wrench of divided loyalties, because that was the only kind of following worthy of the man . . . But to ride down into Ayrshire in a red coat . . . even if Claverhouse would take me; like enough he would not, and all this drama and agonising be to no purpose . . . I tried to laugh at myself, but that did not work, either. My thoughts went round and round inside my head like a squirrel in a cage, and could find no rest as I lay wakeful and staring with hot open eyes into the dark.

At last Caspar, as though sensing my trouble, came crawling up from his usual place to thrust his silky head into the hollow of my shoulder, whimpering softly; and I buried my face in his fur and put my arms round his neck while he licked and licked at my chin. And so at last I fell asleep, with the thing still chasing itself round and round inside me.

But when I woke in the morning, the decision had made itself while I slept. Whether Claverhouse would take me, young as I was, I knew that I was going to try.

I had to speak with my lady Jean before all else, for I was still her riding-groom. So as soon as I could get away from the work in the stable-yard, I went up to the house and contrived to get hold of one of the serving lassies and ask her to take word to my lady that I begged leave to speak with her. She departed, tossing her head and proclaiming that my lady had other things to do, the day, than talk with horseboys; and brought back word that I was to go to my lady in her bower. 'And wipe your feet!' said she, 'for I wasna born to clean up stable-muck tramped all over the house!'

So I wiped off my feet, and followed her up to my lady's bower, where I had never been before; and found her folding shirts and the like and packing them

120

into a pair of scuffed and weather-worn saddle-bags lying on a fine polished table among all the bonnie fallals of a lady's chamber. She looked as though she had maybe not slept so well, either, and there were bruise-coloured shadows under her eyes, but her smile came as quick as ever when she saw me.

'Hugh,' she said, 'come in, and don't be standing in the doorway turning your bonnet round and round!'

I had not known that I was doing that, and I stopped, carefully, and came in. 'My lady,' I swallowed. 'My lady, I am for leaving your service.'

She put down the shirt she was folding, and looked at me, her eyes widening and seeming to darken. 'Oh, Hugh, why? Are you not happy with us?'

'Very happy,' I said, 'an' the heart is sore within me at the thought of leaving; but I am wishful to go for a sojer.'

'You always had that thought, did ye not?' she said gently. 'One day. But – now, Hugh? You're so young.'

'I am sixteen,' I said, 'there's others go at sixteen.'

'Into Claverhouse's Horse.'

I nodded. There was a lump in my throat that made it not that easy to speak. 'If Claverhouse will take me,' I said huskily.

'We shall miss you sore, if he does,' she said, and then, 'Would you have me to speak to him for you?'

I shook my head violently, 'No, my lady, please no; 'tis – 'tis between me and himself.'

I mind the silence there was then, and the wuthering of the springtime wind, and a sharp spatter of rain against the windows, and my lady Jean and I standing there looking at each other.

'Of course,' she said at last, 'that was foolish of me.'

Before I could answer, Darklis came in through another door with some more linen in her hands. She

121

checked at sight of me standing there; and my lady turned to her and said, 'Darklis, here's our Hugh come to tell us he's minded to go for a soldier.'

'Is he so?' said Darklis, and without giving me another look, she dumped the linen on the table, and turned with a whisk of her skirts and disappeared again through the inner door.

I stood there looking after her, feeling a wee thing hurt. I had thought Darklis might show some interest, that she might even care if I was going away.

Lady Jean looked after her too, a moment, and then turned back to me. 'I am thinking you had best go now and find himself, for there's not so much time to spare. You'll find him in his study, like enough. I never kenned how much of paperwork there was to being a soldier until I came to be a soldier's wife!' She was half laughing, but the weeping was none so far away – or would have been in a less proud lassie.

I knew where the study was, for I'd been there more than once, to report on a sick horse or the like. But when I came down the stair from the end of the Long Gallery, the study door at the foot of it was opening, and Claverhouse came out, hitching at his sword-belt as he came. He looked to be in a sore hurry, and I all but let him go. But not quite. 'Sir,' I said, and he turned and looked at me, those dark brows of his quirking up in the way he had.

'Sir – can I have a word wi' ye?'

'Will it wait, Hugh?' I knew well enough how little time he had to spare.

'Sir – it canna wait – I'll no' keep ye but a minute—'

He checked a moment, then turned back to his study. 'Come, then.'

I followed him in, and he propped himself against his

big writing-table and looked at me. 'One minute, you said, Hugh; so – what is it?'

'It has been in mind for a while back that I am wishful, when the time comes, to go for a sojer,' I told him, somewhat breathless. 'I waited, because I was feart that ye would mebbe think me over young. But now—'

I hesitated. Suddenly it seemed a big thing that I was asking.

'I still think you over young,' he said, and then, 'Have you said anything of this to my lady?'

'I dinna forget that I am her riding-groom. I am from my lady now.'

'It's serious then,' he said, with a trace of a smile. 'Do I flatter myself or am I right in supposing that it's Claverhouse's Horse you would be joining?'

I nodded, 'Sir.'

'Why *now*, Hugh? You are but one day older than you were yesterday. In a few weeks, you will be older still.'

'It's the right time,' I said. 'But first, there's a thing I have to tell ye.'

'Tell it, then.' He was sitting sideways on the writing-table by then. He had taken up his riding-gloves and was stripping them between his fingers, but that was the only sign he gave that he had not all day to spare.

And standing there, with my eyes on the panelling just above his head, I told him of the night I had first seen him, and him me. Only I did not tell him even then aught that might betray Alan; seeing that he was a soldier with a soldier's duties to carry out.

I had not known until I came into the room that I was going to tell him of that night, but suddenly I understood that it had to be told, and told now.

When it was done, I pulled my gaze back from the

panelling, and looked him in the face, nerving myself for the anger or disgust that I must surely see there. But there was no anger, no disgust, only that same alert, listening look of one giving his whole attention to whatever or whoever it was he looked at.

'I have wondered sometimes, how long it would be before you told me,' he said.

'You – you knew all the time?'

'Oh, yes.'

'But you – you said nothing at Place of Paisley – an' you took me into your service –' I was stammering like a July cuckoo.

'I saw no reason why I should do aught else . . . How many nights have you dreamed of yon drummer laddie?'

I did not answer. He did not expect me to; but we looked at each other and there was no more to be said on that matter. Then Claverhouse said, 'You'll have to learn your soldiering on the hoof, Hugh.'

'Then ye'll take me?'

He tossed aside the gloves he had been playing with, and reached for a sheet of paper from the stack on the table. 'I've need of a new galloper since Anderson went sick – you have already given proof of your abilities in that direction . . .' He had taken up his quill and dipped it in the big silver ink-well; and leaning sideways on the table he began to write. When he had finished – it was but a few lines – he sanded the sheet, folded it, and sealed it with the big signet-ring he wore, then held it out to me. 'Take this down to Major Crawford. 'Tis to tell him that you are joining the troop as my galloper. When they have kitted you out, come back to me. The Brigadier's galloper stays within whistle of the Brigadier.'

*

So with Claverhouse's note in my hand, down I went into Dundee town, first to Major Crawford, by whom I was handed over to Captain Livingstone – he being captain of the Brigadier's own troop – who in turn handed me over to his senior corporal, Pate Paterson by name, to be kitted out from the Quartermaster's Stores. And in a while and a while I was heading back for Dudhope, wearing the red coat laced with blue, the hard-topped riding-boots and black beaver hat of a trooper of Claverhouse's Horse, and carrying a greasy and weather-stained buff coat under one arm, everything except the hat and boots a good deal too wide for me. 'Ye'll grow to them if ye live that long,' Pate Paterson had said encouragingly.

Eh, but I was the proud one, with a cavalry sword belted round my waist, and a pair of horse pistols bundled in my buff coat, and the stiff black stock tipping up my chin for me.

I was greeted as though I was some kind of raree show, the lassies for the most part admiring, the stable folk jeering. Even Caspar, whom I had left lying on guard over my bed, that being the only way of keeping him from following me, sniffed me over as though he had to make sure who I was. And truth to tell, I was none too sure who I was myself just then.

There is something unreal about that day in my memory, even now. The day before, I had been Lady Jean's riding-groom; the day after, when I rode away behind Claverhouse, I was a trooper of His Majesty's Regiment of Horse, and the Brigadier's galloper, but that day I was between lives. Once, Claverhouse sent me down into the town to Major Crawford again, with further orders for tomorrow's march. But for the most part I hung about the stable-yard which I did not belong to any more, not sure what to do with myself, and wondering how I was to get word with Darklis.

For I could not leave without bidding her goodbye, even though she did not seem to care that I was going. Besides, care or not, I had to ask her to take charge of Caspar for me. Just as it had had to be me that took that message for her to Captain Faa, so it had to be Darklis with whom I left Caspar.

As it turned out, I need not have worried – about getting word with her, I mean – for that evening as I squatted beside my bed, packing my few belongings, a clean shirt and the like, into my saddle-bag by the light of a lantern, with the voices of the grooms playing cards in the harness room coming up through the floorboards, there was a quick light flurry of feet and petticoats on the loft ladder, and there she was, with her skirts tucked up round her knees, and something white and neatly folded in her hands.

'Jean sends you these twa' shirts,' she said, a little breathlessly. 'She was thinking ye'd be needing clean linen as well as himself.' And as I got up, she dumped the carefully folded bundle. I mind that it smelled of herbs from the linen press, rosemary, and southernwood that they call lad's love.

My box of drawing things was beside the saddle-bag lying there; and she looked down at it, and the rolled-up study of the fig tree that had sprung open.

'You are taking your drawing gear with you, then?'

'No,' I said. 'One thing at a time; an' it's no' the time for making pictures. I was going to ask you, would you be taking care of the things for me, while I am away?'

'I'll do that,' she said, with her face still turned away; and then she turned and looked full at me in the lantern light, and I saw that she did care about my going, after all.

126

'Oh, Hugh,' she said, 'and you so grand and tall in that red coat, wi' your chin cocked up and the fine cruel sword at your side. But I'm thinking, ye'll make a better painter than ever ye will a sojer, when all's said an' done.'

'I'm thinking the same, mebbe,' I told her, 'But I'll just have to be the best sojer I can. For I must be following Claverhouse.'

'Aye, you're good followers, both of you,' she said. 'Caspar, too.'

And at the sound of his name Caspar, who was sitting beside me, looked up and thumped his disreputable plume of a tail behind him.

'Caspar was the other thing,' I said. 'I was coming to find ye if ye hadna come to find me. Will ye be keeping Caspar for me too?'

'Will ye no' be taking him, either?' she said – for often the troops marched with a rag-tag of dogs among the baggage train, that came in handy for poaching.

'No,' I said, reaching down to fondle the soft places behind his ears. 'He's no' the sort, not wi' his little legs an' all. An' I couldna bear it if – if harm came to him.'

Darklis squatted down in the midst of her flouncy petticoats, and held out her hands to him. They had been good friends since the night I bought him back from Lady Mary Fair. 'Caspar,' she said softly, 'will ye bide wi' me, and we'll wait together till the bonnie lad comes back from his bonnie war?'

And Caspar put out his long frilled tongue and licked her hand.

So I knew that I need have no fears for Caspar.

'I'll leave him to guard my bed.'

Somewhere in Caspar's fantastically mingled ancestry there must have been a cattle dog. We always had to keep him tied up when the drovers came by, or he would be off to lend a hand to their dogs, which might not be over well received. Failing cattle, he would round up anything that came his way, ducklings, maybe, or even a bed of tulips, and the best way of keeping him from following me when I had to leave him behind was to set him to guard my bed. There he would lie nose on paws, putting the power of his eye on the piled straw and the rough folded rug, as the best sheep and cattle dogs do, to make sure that it did not scatter but stayed where I had left it.

She shook her head. 'No; if you do that he'll maybe no' come away for me. I'll come for him tomorrow, before you ride away.'

She got up and shook out her skirts, and it seemed as though she was going. But then she checked, and her eyes had a shadowy look to them in the lantern light. 'Twill be hard for you, among your own hills,' she said.

'I know,' I told her. 'That is why I have to go now, an' not wait for an easier time.'

'I said you were a good follower.' She reached up and took my face between her hands and drew it down and kissed me. The first time ever.

'God be with ye, Hugh Herriot,' she said. And she turned and gathered her skirts and went much too fast down the steep loft stair.

12

The Killing Time

So I rode down into Ayrshire, with King James's red coat on my back; into the rolling hills and the boggy moors of my mother's country, in the stormy sun-shot April weather. And I learned my soldiering on the hoof, as Claverhouse had said. I had always been able to ride anything on four legs, and I knew the bugle calls by heart and the pattern of camp and quarters life that I had picked up in the time since Colonel Graham and his troops came to Paisley. Also I knew something of the country; so though I had never until that time handled sword or pistol, I am thinking that I pulled my weight in the troop none so ill. Also the horse I rode, a raw-boned Galloway gelding with a streak of Spanish blood in him – Jock, his name was – was a trained cavalry mount and knew the job even when I did not. So between us we managed well enough. I was a raw enough recruit when we rose south westward, but I learned; aye, I learned . . .

From merchants and Scottish sea captains I have heard over the past few years that in Scotland the time that followed is now often enough called 'The Killing Time', and Claverhouse named 'Bloody Claver'se' for his part in it. But raw recruit though I was, I rode with the man through those weeks, and I will set it down here and now, that maybe two score of men were killed in a couple of skirmishes we had, and half of those were our own fellows or the dragoons that worked with us, killed in those same skirmishes or picked off by snipers' musket balls from behind a peat stack or a bush of broom; and over and above there, one of the 'Saints' was executed by firing squad at Claverhouse's orders. And I will tell you the way of it:

As soon as he was King in his brother's place, James offered a pardon to all rebels and fugitives, if they would take an oath of allegiance to himself and disown the bits of paper that I was telling you of – Renwick's bits of paper declaring war on the King and Parliament – or failing that, promise to leave the kingdom within two months. If a man refused, he was a traitor and liable to be executed as such, then and there, by a commissioned officer and before two witnesses. That was the law. And you will mind that the whole South West was under martial law by that time. (Most of the prisoners *I* saw, took the oath or promised to get out. But how many of them kept their promise is of course another question; another question altogether.)

Well, so we followed Claverhouse down into Ayrshire and Galloway, to deal with them that would neither swear to their loyalty nor take their disloyalty elsewhere. If he had known that he was taking his life in his hands the first time he rode that way, five years before, I'm thinking he must have known it with uncommon clearness this last time of all.

We had scarce got there when several prisoners at New Mills, waiting to be sent to Edinburgh for trial, were broken out of gaol by a bunch of their own kind, and we were up and away on the hunt for prisoners and rescuers who had all of them melted into the heather, leaving the New Mills dragoons mostly dead behind them. So when, among the hills Douglas way, we came upon two chiels that ran like hares at sight of us, Claverhouse, having learned as you might say to have a

130

suspicious mind, gave orders to be after them. (Innocent men seldom run at sight of a buff coat.) They took to the mosses, being clearly men well used to those parts, where horses would be hard put to follow them; so the best runners amongst us dragged off our boots and went after them on foot, and after a hard chase contrived to run them down.

And when we got them back, Corporal Paterson who had ridden those hills before, looked at the elder of the two, a big powerful man with eyes like hot coals in his head, and said he, 'That's John Brown, him they call "The Christian Carrier".'

Now carrying is a trade that makes good cover for the passing of secret letters and the like; and a good few of the Lowland carriers were in Dutch William's pay by then, what with Monmouth and Argyll in the Low Countries waiting for the tide. And when we had searched them and found no arms, we took them back to John Brown's house, the Corporal knowing where he lived, no more than a mile further down the dale.

And there, while some of us stood guard at the doors and windows and the rest of us searched the place, the goodwife standing by to watch with her knuckles crushed against her shaking mouth, Claverhouse asked the older man would he take the oath of allegiance to the King. The man refused, saying that he owned no king, and gave allegiance to God alone. Nor would he deny that he had been among those who freed the prisoners at New Mills. Aye, he was a brave man, and I will not forget his face; for it was the face of a man who will kill, and face death himself, for the thing he believes in, sure in either case that his God is bidding him to it.

And while Claverhouse was yet seeking to reason

with him, one of the troopers from the search party came in, and reported that they had found an underground room, the entrance hidden under the stored hay in the barn, well stocked with weapons, and with stores and space to shelter a dozen men.

Claverhouse bade Major Crawford to take over from him in the house, and strode out back with the trooper. I mind the stillness after his going, and the sound of the carrier's horses shifting in the stable across the yard. Even the woman, who had kept up a kind of low muffled keening all the while, fell silent. In a while, Claverhouse came back; he had papers in his hand, and a cold face the like of which I had not seen on him before.

'John Brown,' said he, 'you will scarcely plead ignorance of a hideout under your stable, well stocked with fire-arms, powder and ball and, above all – these.' And he flicked the papers in his hand. 'Treasonable letters from Holland, enough to bring a man to the death penalty five times over. Have you any defence to make?'

'None that I will make to you, who have slaughtered so many of my brethren for the following of God's word and the Covenant,' said the man.

Claverhouse went a wee thing white under the wind-tan of his face. 'Very well, then, I shall now slaughter yet another,' he said; and to Pate Paterson, 'Corporal, make ready a four-man firing squad.'

Pate began picking out his men. I was sweating lest I be one of them, but I need have had no fear of that, having too little skill with a carbine as yet for such sorry service. Claverhouse said quickly to the Lieutenant, who had come in after us, 'Keep the woman inside, Barclay.' And two of our troopers who had been holding John Brown between them turned him to the door.

He walked between them as steady as a rock, and the firing squad followed after. Claverhouse went out last of all, Major Crawford with him. The woman shrieked and made to rush after them, but I grabbed a hold of her, and Rob Rutherford, the biggest man in the troop, strode in front of the door and slammed it shut.

'No, mistress, better not,' Lieutenant Barclay said. I let go of her, now that the door was safely shut, and glad enough to do so; and she backed into a corner and began to rave at us, pulling down her hair and clawing at her own face.

I tried to listen to her raving, because that would be better than listening to what went on outside. But I heard what went on outside, all the same. The ordered tramp of feet, and then the clatter of carbines being un-slung, and the hoarse fervent sound that was John Brown praying to his God. My mouth felt very dry. Then the praying stopped. I heard a snapped-out order, and then the sharp rattle of the carbines. Four shots almost together, but not quite.

In a little, Claverhouse came back, and the Major with him. The woman rushed past them through the open door, none offering her let or hindrance, now; and we heard her wailing and sobbing and cursing us over her man's body outside.

'Leave her be,' Dundonel said, 'she is like enough as guilty as he, but it is her right to be alone with him now.'

Then he turned to the younger man, who all this while had been slumped on a creepy-stool, staring at the ground and sweating. You could smell the sweat on him, the rank smell of fear. The troopers on either side of him hauled him to his feet, and he stood there, his mouth slack and trembling, and his eyes wide and dull with terror.

Claverhouse demanded his name, and he replied, so well as he could for the fear in his throat, that he also was John Brown, and the other was his uncle. When the oath of allegiance was read to him, he took it eagerly, but when he was asked if he too had been at New Mills, he fell over his words, and contradicted himself, and at last said that he had, but only because his uncle had bidden him.

Claverhouse stood and watched him the while, with more a kind of contemptuous pity than aught else in his face. He said, 'I am divided in my mind whether or not to deal with you as I have dealt with your uncle. But indeed I think that you are scarce worth the powder and ball. Therefore I will give you a chance to save your skin. Tell me the names of the men who were at New Mills, and I will delay your execution, and send you instead to General Drummond for trial, as though there were indeed some doubt of your guilt; and I will make the plea for you that you are young and were under your uncle's hand in what you did.'

My, but his mouth looked as though there were a sick taste in it, as he spoke the words.

And indeed young John Brown was not the man that old John Brown had been, for he yelped it all out like a beaten puppy; names and names and names, as many as he could remember; there were close on sixty, he said, in all. Then, all unasked, he began on an account of a great conventicle held by Renwick himself, beyond Cairntable, where there had been upward of three hundred mustered and exercising with their weapons. And again he gave names and yet more names. Man, it was pitiful. Indecent.

Well, Claverhouse kept his promise. I know, because

134

later that day, in the sanded parlour of the inn at Douglas where he had made his quarters, when young John Brown had already been sent off under escort to General Drummond, I stood by while he wrote the letter. And when it was written and sanded and sealed, Major Crawford, standing beside the empty fireplace, asked, 'Do you think that will save him? If, of course, he's worth saving.'

And Claverhouse said, 'Every man is worth saving if it can be done. As to whether this will save him or not, God knows. I've done my best, David.'

And he gave the letter to me for carrying to His Grace of Queensberry, in Edinburgh.

13

Encounter Beyond Douglasdale

When I got back to the troop some five evenings later, news had come in of another of James Renwick's conventicles, called for next day on the high moors north of Douglasdale – aye, we had our friends in that countryside, too. And next morning the bugles sounding the 'Stand to Horse' gathered us from the houses where we were quartered, almost before daylight. The horses were fed and made ready, and with our breakfast bannock still in our throats, and the sun scarce clear of the hills eastward, we were off and away up Douglasdale, the Brigadier's troop of Claverhouse's Horse, and a company of dragoons, heading for James Renwick's latest gathering.

It was a bonnie morning, with the pools among the moorland heather and bilberry reflecting back a blue sky and high-sailing clouds, and the whaups skirling fit to break a man's heart with the sweetness of it, and just enough wind in our faces, together with the wind of our own going, to lift the troop standard back from its lance and let the silver Graham phoenix spread wing on its blue silken folds. I could hear the soft heavy wing-flap of it, for I rode close up behind the cornet and his colour escort, my job being, as usual, to keep as close as might be to Claverhouse himself.

It must have been close on noon when we came to the foot of the last long moorland ridge, and knew that the chosen village of the conventicle lay beyond it. We set the horses' heads to the rough track that snaked upward. We rode two by two, the track being not wide enough for more, dropping gradually from a trot to a foot-pace as the slope grew steeper towards the crest; for whatever was waiting for us over the skyline, it would be as well not to meet it on blown horses.

Just on the crest, somewhat to the right of the track, a spinney of wind-frayed fir trees broke the skyline; and following Claverhouse and the blue-and-silver glint of the colours, we turned aside into the shelter of the trees. Most of us were old hands at this game, and even I, who had been at it only a few weeks, knew about the dangers of getting skylined. So we came down through the trees, and broke into the open again well below the crest on the far side.

From our feet the hillside dropped away gently through rough pasture and little plots of ploughland where the young barley was silken green, to a narrow burn looping its way between hawthorn bushes milky-flecked with their first blossom. And where the track came down to cross the burn, a sizeable clachan huddled close under its roof of heather thatch.

Across the burn was open pasture, coarse grazing dotted with more may trees and green broom, and then the hills rising again to heather beyond. And on the open pasture land was gathered a great crowd of people, a dark multitude spreading up even over the lower slopes of the hillside beyond. And now that we were over our crest, the little wind through the rough grass brought up to us the sound of singing:

> 'I to the hills lift mine eyes,
> From whence doth come mine aid.
> My safety cometh from the Lord,
> Who Heaven and earth hath made . . .'

Next instant a shot cracked the Sabbath quiet of the hills, and away on our right, well out of range, a dark figure sprang out of the scrub, and went hurtling down the hill towards the burn and the congregation beyond it.

'They have kept their eyes on the hills, all right, but 'tis no' exactly their aid that's coming this way,' said the trooper beside me out of the corner of his mouth.

Then Claverhouse's arm rose and swept forward in the signal to advance, and we were heading downhill ourselves on the heels of his raking sorrel, fanning out as we went.

We passed by the cottages of the clachan, empty save for a few scratching hens and a cow, and came down to the burn. On the far side the conventicle folk were still at their psalm-singing, but a faint movement had begun on the outer fringes of the great crowd, men rising from their knees, and here and there the spring sunlight glinting on a musket barrel or the slim new-moon curve of a billhook.

On the near bank, we drew rein. The burn was only a few feet wide and maybe a foot deep, lost altogether in places where the elders and hawthorn bushes leaned together over it, but none the less it seemed to form a frontier of some kind, a barricade with the Covenanters massing to defend it on one side, and ourselves tensed for the attack on the other.

The chanting came to an end, and the ripple of movement was spreading in from the fringes to the heart of the crowd; the solid mass of country folk's hodden grey hackled with the black streaks of the preachers' gowns, the glint of weapons that seemed to spring up in hand after hand, as though kindling one from another like torch flames; the faces all turned towards us. That was

138

when I first noticed that there were no women among them, no bairns, no old men.

Claverhouse urged his horse forward to the very brink of the water, and shouted to them. He was a quiet-spoken man, but his war-shout was a clarion, that could carry from one end of a battlefield to the other. 'This is an unlawful gathering! Lay down your arms in the King's name; yield up your leaders; and the rest of you may depart quietly to your homes.'

A kind of low angry snarl that was the voice of the crowd made him answer; and in the midst of the gathering, a tall man in black with the white flash of Geneva bands at his throat – like enough it was Renwick himself, certainly he seemed to be the leader among them – stood with arms upraised, his grey hair blowing about his face, and shouted back, 'In the name of God be gone from us, ye sons of Belial! For we own no king save God himself and no law save His Covenant. Unbelievers! Boot-lickers and tame butchers to a papist so-called king and his hell-spawned bishops! Get you gone and leave the righteous to their peaceful prayers!'

'It seems that the righteous are well armed, for these same peaceful prayers!' Claverhouse returned. 'I bid you once more to lay down your weapons and deliver up those who have led you into this revolt!'

They stood and looked at us, each man with his weapon, sword or pike or pitchfork, ancient flintlock or new Dutch musket, ready in his hand. They must have outnumbered us by upward of three to one, and eh, but they looked so ugly. Then in the midst of them, close beside the leader, somebody put his musket to his shoulder, and a ball sang past my ear.

'Right,' said Claverhouse, while the puff of smoke drifted away. He gave an order to the dragoon officer behind him. Further to our right, the dragoons had already dismounted and turned their horses over to their horse-holders, and stood ready with carbines unslung. There was a barking of orders, and they dropped to their knees and fired their first volley over the heads of the crowd.

Across the burn there was a great shouting and crying out, and the crowd scattered at the edges and gave back, while at the same instant a ragged burst of firing answered the dragoons.

Claverhouse's arm went up and swept forward in the gesture to advance.

'This is it. This is us!' said something within me; skirmishing I had seen before, but this was my first set-piece action, and my mouth was uncomfortably dry as, with the rest following the blue and silver standard, I urged my horse forward. The burn was nothing in the crossing; some of us jumped it, some just walked our horses through; I am not sure which I did, I seemed to have too many other things to think about, just then.

I found myself on the far side and still close to Claverhouse, and the feeling was in me of having passed a frontier, pushed across some kind of defence line into the enemy stronghold. Aye, and I mind the whole lot of them coming in a great sudden surge towards us, and someone shouting above the tumult, 'Death and damnation to the enemies of the Covenant! On them in the Lord's name, and *kill*, brothers!' And they came pounding on, seeming unaware of carbine fire that was no longer aimed in the air.

I fired my right-hand pistol, and slammed it back into the holster; I had no thought for the left-hand one, there was no time; no time for dragoons or troopers to reload; and as the blood-thirsting mob, yelling 'Kill!

Kill! No quarter!' hurled themselves upon us with their hideous mix of weapons – you have never seen the wounds that can be made by a bill hook on a pole, and you can thank God for it! – we of the troop betook us to our swords, while the dragoons for the most part reversed their carbines and used them as clubs.

I mind the kind of surprised half-unbelief in me, at the sight of men with hate-filled yelling faces surging about my horse, and the slashing and thrusting weapons in their hands, and knowing that they were going to kill me if they could, if I did not first kill them. Raw as I was, I doubt if I killed any, for all that. I mind a man coming at me with a snickie, one of the curved blades they used to cut the bridles and make the horses unmanageable, and sending him reeling back with a hand dripping red that maybe lacked a finger or two. I mind an ancient firelock going off at close quarters, and the sight of a dragoon with his head half blown away and some of his brains spattering my knee . . .

How long it lasted, I'd not be knowing. It could have been half-a-dozen heart-beats of time; it could have been from sunrise to sunset of a summer day. Now that I have seen more of fighting, I should guess that it was maybe something over a quarter of an hour. Then there began to be a change, a lessening of the thrust against us, a different note to the uproar that was made of shouts and weapon-ring and the scream of stricken horses. The Covenanters had had numbers to make up for their lack of soldierhood, and for a while it had been a near thing, but now the fine balance of the fight was tipping against them; they were beginning to give back, then to stream away, breaking from their solid mass into desperate pockets.

But away to the right they were holding still, among the hawthorn bushes around an old sheep fold.

Claverhouse swung his sorrel and headed that way. And I, having only the one thought, to keep close to him, went after him as close as a man's shadow follows him into the sun.

A short sharp struggle among the may trees broke the last of the resistance, and it crumbled into running figures making for the heather and a few fallen left behind him. Claverhouse rose in his stirrups, his arm up in the familiar signal, 'After them! Take Renwick!' and we were off again. And at that moment three things happened, so quick together that there was no saying which of them came first.

Hector stumbled, and Claverhouse pitched forward in the saddle gathering him from a fall; and from the hawthorn brake on our right came the whip-crack of a pistol shot, and again something whined past my ear, and this time knicked the white plume from his hat. If his horse had not stumbled, his head would have been just there.

He held straight on. Maybe he was not even aware of the escape he'd had. But hardly knowing what I did, I wrenched Jock's head round and plunged into the thicket. I think it was in my mind that a pistol is most often one of a pair; or maybe there was nothing in my mind at all . . . I ducked low under the branches and thrust Jock forward.

There, crouched against the trunk of an age-snarled hawthorn, was a young man in weather-stained homespun, with bright red-gold hair tumbling about his head. A pistol lay before him on the ground, a faint wisp of smoke still curling from the mouth of the barrel. My grandfather's silver-mounted pistol. And even as I recognised it, its fellow seemed to come of its own accord from his belt into his hand.

Time, that had been wide-spread and without shape, became suddenly slow and narrow, fragile somehow like a strand of spider's silk. In the long-drawn stillness of it, I had a sharp awareness of things; the first creamy knots of blossom on the hawthorn sprays, aye, and the scent of them too, the milky sweetness, and the dark under-scent that one catches only with the back of the nose, a little like the smell of blood; the sun-spots dappling his figure and the rough bark behind his head; the light bright familiar devil-dance at the back of the man's eyes. All about us, fading now, but still walling us in, rose the hideous tumult of fighting still fouling the spring noontide; but it was very quiet within the hawthorn tangle.

'The De'il's greeting to you, Hughie lad; here's turning your coat with a vengeance!' said Alan.

And his pistol hand came up . . .

The queer moment of stillness was over. It was him or me, and the sword was still naked in my hand. I flung forward in the saddle and used the point on him as though it had been a rapier.

The point went in through the loose end of his neck-cloth just below the collar-bone. I felt it grate on bone. He arched back against the hawthorn trunk with a short-cut bubbling kind of cry, and his pistol hand flew wide with the pistol still in it.

I tried to drag my point out again, but it was jammed in the shoulder-blade and would not come. No time to dismount and set my foot on his chest and drag it out that way. I abandoned it there, and swung Jock out from the thicket, and headed after the standard.

I came up with Claverhouse again in a little, and rode on after the fleeing Covenanters. But the country ahead was boggy, and they knew the ways of it while it was strange to us; it was clear that most of them would get away. And anyway it was only the leaders that Claverhouse wanted. We got a couple. Later, they took the oath or promised to quit the country, and were let go. James Renwick, as I heard later, got clean away.

In a while Claverhouse called off the chase, and ordered us back to the ground we had fought over. I had learned from the older hands by that time the unwisdom of leaving the wounded too long unguarded when the women of a conventicle might be near-hand.

So we got back to the open pasture by the clachan, weary men dropping from weary horses. There were a good few bodies lying across the level ground between the burn and the heather, red coats and dragoons' grey among them. Women had appeared from somewhere, and were moving among their own wounded. They took little notice of us when we went in to bring off our own.

Now it so happened that Claverhouse came in again almost over his own tracks, close beside the sheepcote and the hawthorn thicket, and drew rein there to eye the fighting-ground. And it was only then that I, sitting my weary Jock a little behind him, saw the blood-trail leading in among the may trees, for it was on the far side from where I had gone in. Two other troopers saw it in the same instant, and went in like a couple of terriers.

They hauled out Alan's body, with my blade still fast below his collar-bone.

'Somebody's lost his sword,' one of them said, and set his foot on Alan's shoulder and wrenched it out.

Corporal Paterson stooped and twisted the pistol from the rigid grip he still had on it, broke and glanced inside. 'Not loaded,' he said, and snapped it shut again and thrust it into his belt. All captured weapons would be handed in later.

One of Alan's feet hung crooked, below the red pulp of his ankle where a carbine ball had smashed the bone. I remembered how he had been crouched against the hawthorn trunk. I had not seen his feet at all.

'Must have got a hit in the ankle, and hauled himself in there to take cover while he reloaded,' said the corporal. 'But cover wasna quite good enough.'

I looked from Alan's smashed ankle to his face. A faint fierce mockery had set on it like a mask, and out of the mask he seemed to be staring up at me. But he had only two eyes to stare with, not like the drummer laddie.

The trooper who had pulled out my sword looked doubtfully from the blooded blade to Corporal Pate, and then to Claverhouse who still sat on his horse looking on. 'What shall I do with this, sir?

I cut in before himself could answer, which was almost a hanging matter as you might say, but I was not thinking of such things just then. 'Give it here, Alec, 'tis mine.'

And Claverhouse looked round at me quickly, but said no word.

Alec Geddes handed over my sword; and I took it and made to return it to its sheath. I had not felt anything when I killed Alan, just the stillness and the two of us together in it; but now suddenly I was deadly cold. I could scarcely get the point into the mouth of the scabbard for I was shaking as though with an ague, and I had to clench my teeth until the muscles of my cheeks and jaw went rigid, to keep them from chattering in my head.

The next thing I knew, Claverhouse had sent me off

145

with some message for the Captain of the Dragoons at the clachan end of the field. By the time I reached him, I had got myself somewhat pulled together; and for the rest of the day I was kept too busy to have much time for thinking of what had happened under the may trees that noon.

That evening back in quarters in Douglas, the Brigadier sent for me when I was halfway through my supper of oatmeal porridge and pickled herring. I pushed the platter away thankfully, for I had small stomach for food just then, and went to answer the summons.

Rain had come on at the daylight's fading, and I mind looking up through the chill whisper of it on my face, and seeing the regimental colours hanging out above the inn doorway, just catching the light from within, for the door stood open for the usual comings and goings of headquarters. Inside, there was a smell of blood and hot pitch, for the place, being the largest building in Douglas save for the kirk, was also serving as a hospital. I went up the narrow stairs, to the room over the front door where Claverhouse sat writing the usual dispatch by the light of a couple of tallow dips.

He glanced up at my coming, and made a small gesture with the hand that held the pen, acknowledging my presence and bidding me wait; and went on writing. There were but a few lines left. He finished and signed them, then looked up.

'Was he a friend of yours?' he said.

I think I caught my breath a bit, but I'd no need to ask his meaning.

'Aye,' I said, 'it was my cousin Alan.' And then, 'But ye never saw his face that night, sir? When they burned the alehouse?'

'I doubt I'd have remembered it, if I had,' he said. 'I saw yours, today, when you claimed your sword back.'

The rushlights guttered in the wet breeze from the window, which stood ajar to let through the shafts of the colours propped across the sill. And we looked at each other in the unsteady light.

'I didna ken that he was wounded,' I said.

'No.'

'And I thought it was him or me; I didna ken his pistol was empty.'

'It would not have been, if he had had time to reload.'

Claverhouse laid down his pen, and carefully sanded the dispatch and began to fold it.

'But he *was* wounded,' I said, desperately, 'and his pistol was empty – and I killed him.' I was staring down at my own hand as though it were somebody else's, seeing it clenched until the knuckles shone waxen yellow like bare bone.

'Hugh,' said Claverhouse, 'look at me when I am speaking to you.' And I looked up, and found his eyes waiting for me coolly compelling in the taper light. 'You wear the King's coat. Today you were in action against the King's enemies. War is not sport, and it is not governed by the rules of fair and unfair that govern sport; and its honour, if it has any, is of another kind.' Suddenly his face gentled into its rare swift smile. 'Do not be adding a new nightmare to the old one that you suffer already.'

'No, sir,' I said, and unclenched my hand carefully; later I found the red marks of my nails on my own palm; and as he sealed the dispatch, I moved forward to take it.

He shook his head, 'No, Hugh, not this time.'

'I am your galloper, sir,' I said.

'But Kerr can take this as well as you can. Word has

come in that the Duke of Monmouth has landed in England – a place called Lyme – and His Grace of Argyll on his own coast. The Whigs are sending Highland irregulars into the West against him, and we are ordered down into the Borders, lest trouble come up from the South. I shall need my galloper with me.'

Next day we marched for the Borders.

I have wondered whether Claverhouse had any thought as we rode out from Douglas that early summer morning that he was leaving the South West that had seen so much of his soldiering and become his own kale-garth, for the last time; the last time of all.

Eh well, there we were, waiting in the Borders with our pistols cocked; but in England the rebellion petered out in a few weeks; and even Covenanting Scotland did not rise for Argyll, as he must have thought they would. He was, after all, not a man to follow to the death, as they say that young Monmouth was. So the both of them were taken and Monmouth went to the block, and Argyll to the gallows in Edinburgh, as better men than he had gone before him.

And we went back to Dundee.

As the Brigadier's galloper, I was among those of the troop to be billeted in Dudhope itself. And Caspar was the first to greet me when we rode in; Caspar with ears and tail flying, and his short legs scarce showing save as a blur beneath him as he came, almost before I was out of the saddle, to fling himself into my arms and lick my face from ear to ear, singing like a kettle, and send my hat spinning in his joy. And hard behind Caspar, Darklis came from the stillrooms, with her skirts kilted and spread like wings in either hands, calling 'Caspar! Caspar, ye wicked wee dog!'

But at sight of me, she checked. 'I might have known that it was yourself, when he ran like that.'

Hector was being brought round from the courtyard, where Claverhouse had dismounted; and the other troopers were swinging down from their saddles, and the stable folk had enough to do without watching Darklis and Caspar and me under the broad-leaved summer branches of the old fig tree, and me with my arm still through Jock's bridle, so that he bulked between us and the rest of the world. Darklis took my face between her hands as she had done on the night before I went away; and so her face was close to mine.

'Thank you for taking such good care of Caspar,' I said, feeling the wee dog's forepaws scrabbling at my knee, because suddenly I could not say any of the things I was fain to say to her.

'I have taken good care of your painting gear, too,' said she, half mocking me. But then the mockery flickered out, and she held me off a little, looking at me like – it sounds daft – like somebody looking for familiar landmarks in a strange country. 'Oh, Hugh, Hugh, you were such a laddie when you went away. I felt so much older than you – and now you're not a laddie any more. Did the sojering do that to you?'

'Aye,' I said, 'just the sojering.'

But when I would have put my free arm around her, she shook her head, and took her hands away without giving me the kiss that I had looked for, and turned and ran.

14

Two Kings

After the Monmouth and Argyll rebellion, Scotland had upward of three years of what looked on the surface like peace. The King was so relieved that the danger had come and gone that he rewarded his people with a Declaration of Indulgence, making it lawful for all men to go to conventicles. That fair infuriated everybody – the Loyalists and Moderates who had suffered at the hands of the Saints, and even the Saints themselves, for I suppose there was little point to such gatherings now that they were tamely within the law; and a kind of spice must have gone out of life.

My lady's grandfather and old General Dalyell died within a few weeks of each other, early on in that time. And in Dalyell's place General Drummond was made Commander-in-Chief. And Claverhouse? He was promoted General, again two days behind Douglas. He was Provost of Dundee now, as well as Constable, and still a Privy Councillor; and was for ever riding between Dundee and Edinburgh on business of the Council and the affairs of His Majesty's Regiment of Horse. Once, he took my lady Jean to court. They were gone all summer, and when they came back, Darklis gave me fine accounts of sending Lady Jean off to court balls and masques, all in aurora-coloured damask with pearls in her hair.

Dudhope was as full of comings and goings as ever it had been; Balcarres and Lord Ross, and Major Livingstone who had transferred into the Scots Dragoons in search of promotion (there is only one major to a regiment, and so there could be no way beyond captain in Claverhouse's Horse until Major Crawford transferred or retired or stopped a bullet) and Philip of Amryclose, with his pipes and his hero tales; never many of my lady's kinsfolk, though.

So taking it all in all, you might have thought that life was full and rich enough for Claverhouse, let alone that he had my lady Jean for his wife. But the man was a soldier before all else. He had hoped once to be Commander-in-Chief in old Dalyell's place (he should never have allowed his liking for justice to get him on the wrong side of Queensberry, that time) and under all the to-ing and fro-ing he was the out-of-work commander of an out-of-work regiment again; and there was a restlessness about him, and times, again, when his eyes looked hot in his head.

And I was still the General's galloper, and to and fro between Dundee and Edinburgh, also; and learning my formal soldiering that there had been no time for when I rode down into the South West at his heels. There were things I learned under the eye of authority, such as the proper use of pistol and sabre and carbine, and how to make a horse charge straight and stand firm under fire. Eh, those practices on the level ground below Dundee Law, the horses almost dancing to the canter-tune of bugle and kettle-drum; and the oneness linking myself and Jock between my knees! There were other things learned not under the eye of authority at all, such as the secret way up the hidden side of Edinburgh Castle Rock, known to most men who have ever been quartered there and needed to get back from the town after Lights Out!

During the first part of that time, too, I was finding

my way into the troop; for the troop was a strange world to me. Oh, I knew most of the men by sight, even to talk with in the by-going; but to become one of them, that was another matter. You might think the matter simple enough; you join a troop, and having joined, you are part of it. But the General's troop of His Majesty's Regiment of Horse was not just like any other troop of any other regiment. It was not, strictly speaking, what is called a Gentleman's Troop, but it was an oddly mixed and mingled one. There were veterans among us, even a few who had served under Claverhouse in the Scottish Brigade in Holland; there were men from the plough and the loom and the counting-house, sons of dominies and small lairds and alehouse-keepers, and good men and rogues, such as are to be found in every troop; but among us also were friends and distant kinsfolk of the Grahams; younger brothers and younger sons who had chosen the army as many younger sons do, but chosen to serve as troopers under Claverhouse rather than try for commissions in other regiments or go overseas as he had done himself.

You might have thought that that would make for a loose-knit company easy for anyone to settle into place in. But the truth was quite otherwise, for it was as though, feeling the danger of such a loose mesh, they had closed ranks in some way, interlocking their differences for Claverhouse's sake. On the surface they seemed an easy comradeship, underneath, they – well, I have never met with such a close-knit brotherhood in all my after-years of soldiering. Nobody sought to keep me out, but it was many months before I ceased to think of the General's troops as 'them' and 'me' and found, almost without noticing it, that I was thinking of it as 'us'.

But all that was long past when, on a day of high summer three years later, I sat in the window of the Unicorn's taproom – we were often wont to gather in the Unicorn tavern in off-duty hours – with a jug of ale on the sill at my elbow, and Caspar lying contentedly at my feet. The wee dog was often with me when I was in Dundee, and being newly returned yet again from Edinburgh, I had just been up to the house to collect him from Darklis who always took charge of him for me when I was off and away. He seemed happy enough to be left with her, but he was never in any doubt that he was my dog, and would leave her without a backward glance when I whistled. Darklis had seemed glad to see me, too; she always did. But there was a distance between me and Darklis these days, even while she told me about the London gaieties and laughed with me and at me, and mended my shirts. I had been there ever since the spring that I had gone down into Ayrshire with Claverhouse, as though maybe she felt some danger in letting me close to her, now that I was not a laddie any more. And yet I did not think that she liked me any less than she had done before. I hoped not, anyway, for I liked the lassie well; too well, maybe, for my own content . . .

Caspar looked up, whining softly, and thumped his tattybogle tail on the sanded floor behind him, as though he knew the vague trouble that was in me, and sympathised. I stooped and rubbed him behind the ears, and he rolled on to his back, exposing his creamy underparts for the like treatment. But at that moment there came the nearing tramp of feet on the cobbles outside, and Corporal Pate Paterson loomed into the street doorway at the other end of the long taproom. The rest of us gathered there looked up from our ale or our dice, or the kind of casual talk that men share when they are through with the day's work and weary, or waiting to go on duty, and are well used to each other's company. And seeing that it was Pate, we watched him hopefully as he flung himself down on a settle, stretched his long legs out in front of him and shouted for ale.

Pate Paterson was our chief source of news, partly because he had a friend who was a newsletter writer by profession; but also because he was one of those people who have a natural nose for tidings of all kinds – it was long enough, in all conscience – and seem able to sniff news out of the wind, not just rumour, either, before it reaches anybody else.

He had been on three days' leave, too, and so he was greeted on all sides with demands for the latest word of the world outside. He took the ale jack from the pot-boy's hand, and set it down beside him, and waited until we were quiet. Then he said, 'It seems the Queen is to have a bairn around Martinmas.'

You would not think there was anything so earth-shaking in that, and the Queen a young second wife and all; but the words dropped small and hard into our waiting silence like a pebble into a pool, and set the ripples widening. Somebody whistled, and somebody demanded with a startled and sober face, 'Man, is it sure?' though a few more, the young ones, myself amongst them, gave tongue joyfully.

'Have ye no sense?' Pate said to us. 'This is no time to be yammering like hound pups wi' their dinner set before them!' And the bleakness of his face quieted us all.

But I got to my feet and pushed in closer among the rest, Caspar padding at my heels. 'But surely that will be a fine thing for the King?' said I, puzzled, 'especially if 'tis a son—'

''Tis in just that chance that the danger lies,' somebody said.

And Pate shook his head. 'Och, my innocent young Hugh! Has it never dawned on you that Orange William has sat quiet in Holland all this while because King James has no son, and he is wed to James's eldest daughter, and he has but to wait for James's kingdom to come to him through the Princess Mary? If James has a son, William will have to do more for his British kingdom than wait, and wink at a few smuggled muskets!'

I mind there was a kind of jolt inside me, cold but lilting; three years is a long time to spend kicking one's heels on garrison duties and training for the sake of training. 'Then do ye mean – will there be war wi' Holland?'

'No,' said Pate, making a great show of flicking the dust off his boots. 'I'm no' thinking there'll be war wi' Holland.'

And Matt Ferguson, who was something of a student of history, took up the tale. 'James is too much like his father in some ways – so was his brother Charles, but he knew how to get clear wi' it; James has never known how to get clear wi' anything.'

'Aye, he's done some awfu' daft things has James,' someone else said, swirling his ale jack and watching the swirl of it. 'An' he's lost his people – an awfu' lot of his people – just as his father did, more than forty years ago.'

'Not civil war,' Willie Kerr said quickly, 'I'll no' believe it.'

'God knows,' said Pate, 'but the folk – those on both

155

sides of the Border that are thirsty for a change in their royal house – have been waiting too. Though they've done it more quietly in England, they'll know, like William, that they canna wait any longer.'

'But just till the bairn's born,' I said, with the lilt gone from me and only the coldness left. 'Just till the bairn's born –' as though the decision were Pate's and I was urging him. 'Mebbe 'twill be another daughter, after all—'

'Aye, mebbe,' Pate said, still rubbing at the dust on his left boot. 'but if 'tis a son, then 'twill be too late for them to call William over. They darena wait.'

Everyone was silent at that, and again I had the feel of pebbles dropped into a pool; and the ripples spreading . . .

Then young Robin Findlay, who had been sitting in a corner silent all the while, lunged to his feet, with every red hair on his head standing out round his long white laughing face as though it had a life of its own, and said he, 'There's mebbe two words as to that, while Claver'se is for the King, and we are for Claver'se!' He looked round him. 'Och, away! Ye look as though Corporal Pate has brought news of a wake, not a bairn on the way! Let's drink to the King and the King's son and heir, and another bud on the bonnie white briar!'

And so in the end we all came crashing to our feet, ale jacks in hand, as the laughter took us, and drank to King James and his son, Pate with the rest of us, while the snotty-nosed potboy looked on with his mouth open wide enough to catch a cuckoo.

Pate was right. Only a few days later we heard that a group of Whig noblemen had sent to William and the Princess Mary, offering them the Crown.

Looking back, it seems as though all that summer and autumn went by to the beat of distant drums. James had already recalled the British regiments in Dutch service, and the States General had refused to let them go, though leaving each man free to return on his own account if he chose to. Not many of them did. The militia was called out, the castles ammunitioned; and on Dundee Law, aye, and on hilltops all up and down the East Coast, beacons stood watched and ready to pass on in fire the warning of William's coming. The men who were not in the militia formed themselves into companies of volunteers; and that year women and old men from the chimney corner got in the harvest as best they could.

And then, with our late northern harvest scarcely in, the King sent for the Scottish regulars to strengthen his English troops, since by then it seemed sure that William's landing would come in the South.

The Scottish Council were not happy, not happy at all, to be left with one cavalry regiment and the militia and a few companies of volunteers to hold Scotland and the English North. But the King's orders were the King's orders, and so in October, with the rooks on the stubble and the heather dun-dark on the hills, and the berries bright in the wayside tangles, we rode South, His Majesty's Regiment of Horse, and Drummond's Dragoons and Douglas's Footguards, Buchan's Regiment and one troop of Lifeguards, with Claverhouse in command of the cavalry, and Douglas, by right of his two days' seniority, in command over all. Less than three thousand of us, but you would have been hard put to it, I am thinking, to find better troops anywhere in this world; and we with the hearts high within us, going to save James his kingdom.

It was late October when we reached London, and made our camp in the meadows about Chelsea. It was a raw grey evening, with the mist creeping all up across the fields from the river. The campfires made tawny smears on the grey of it, and the sounds of the camp seemed smeared and muffled by it, too. We seemed like a camp of ghosts, I thought, as I came up from the horse lines after seeing to Jock, and headed for the low-browed tavern that for tonight was Cavalry Head-quarters. I had almost reached the open door, threading my way through the coming and going all about it, when I heard the jingle and hoof-beats of a horse being ridden hard; and a sentry's challenge and a muffled reply; and the hoof-beats, which had checked, came on up the cart-track. Horse and rider loomed out of the mist into the light of the open door, and I saw that it was the Earl of Balcarres, who had been sent ahead to tell the King of our coming. A trooper stepped forward saluting, to take his horse as he dropped from the saddle; and I saw his face clear in the door-light. By nature he had a fresh-coloured face, smooth as a lad-die's's that has not yet begun to shave; but now it had a greyish look, and his eyes stared out of it and his mouth was shaking. And at sight of him a little cold fear went through me.

A voice behind me said, 'Colin, what's amiss?' and his blank gaze went past me to the doorway, and I knew that Claverhouse had come out.

'The King has changed his mind,' said Balcarres dully, 'when William lands he intends to make no re-sistance but yield up the crown to his daughter and her husband—'

'Not here, Colin,' Claverhouse said quickly. 'This is for the Commander.' And took him by the arm, and turned him round, and together they disappeared into the mist in the direction of General Douglas's headquarters. And more than ever, it seemed to me as the mist swallowed them, that we were ghosts in a ghost camp.

Indeed it seemed like that even when the river mist was gone, through all the weeks that we spent there, waiting, and none of us sure what we waited for.

Now you will understand that there are parts of this story that I cannot tell of my own knowing, but only by piecing together afterwards, and setting down the general knowledge of the day, and the word of what was going forward that drifted around the camp as it does round all camps. I have wondered sometimes if the officers of a regiment would be surprised how much of their inmost affairs is known to the men round their campfires.

So – we knew that Claverhouse went to wait upon the King next morning. It was said afterwards that he tried to stiffen the man to meet William when he landed, friendliwise, but at the head of his army, and ask for an explanation; or to ride north with his Scottish troops if he was no longer sure of his English ones, and wait in Scotland to see what the next move might be. He went again and again; but whatever it was that he sought to bring about, we saw his face when he came back, and judged that he had had no success.

What had happened to James, there is no knowing to this day; for whatever else he lacked, he had not lacked courage until then. Some say that he had a seizure of some kind, some that it was his heart that was sick, with grief that his daughter Mary should have turned against him, and her sister the Princess Anne with her, so that his own world had crumbled about him and nothing

159

mattered any more. But even when the news came that William had landed in Devon – aye, and the first troops to land with him the Scots and English Brigades – he would do nothing but say it was God's will he should become a king in exile, and he must submit to the will of God.

Almost at the time of William's landing, the Queen's bairn was born. And it was a son. But even that put no heart into him. Early in December he sent his queen and bairn over to France; and next day he made public announcement of his own departure. That day, also, he disbanded the army.

It is an odd feeling, being disbanded, listening to your officers reading out the words that make you cease to exist.

And that day Claverhouse had his last audience with King James, and came back with an odd look on his face, almost as though he had been weeping; and word went round that the King had made him Viscount Dundee.

Next day in soft early-winter rain, the King crossed the river to Vauxhall on his way to France. Aye, and three days later he was back again, brought in by a fisherman who had mistaken him for a smuggler!

'Och, the man canna even manage his own flitting. How in the De'il's name would he manage an army?' said Pate Paterson, when that news reached us, and laughed; but the laughter was of a dreich and dreary kind.

Claverhouse and Balcarres went off to wait on him at once. No doubt they had one last desperate go at the man. But he was firm set for France, and would do no more than promise to return if the people regained their senses and called him back. He promised also to send Balcarres a commission to manage his civil affairs in Scotland, and Claverhouse his commission to command his Scottish troops. Then he was off downriver again; and the very next day, Orange William was in St James's Palace. None of it seemed quite real, I mind, and more and more we felt ourselves to be some kind of ghosts, drifting in limbo.

Orange William would fain have had Claverhouse and Balcarres to be his men. He was some kind of kin by marriage to Colin Lindsey, and as I told you before, Claverhouse (I must try to get into the way now of calling him Dundee, but he remains Claverhouse in my mind) had served under him in his youth. And there was that old story of how he saved William's life one time, bringing him off from the battlefield on his own horse after William's was shot under him. But as to that, I'd not be knowing, I never heard Dundee claim it.

But neither Dundee nor Balcarres would take service with him; Balcarres, so I have heard tell, saying with that kindly, somewhat troubled smile of his that he could have no part in turning out his own king, who had been a good lord to him, though imprudent in many things; and Dundee telling him, 'I carried my sword in your army, but not that I might turn it against my rightful king. If I were to break faith with His Majesty King James, could you ever be sure that I would not break it with you?'

And yet I think they both liked the man. I saw him once, during those days – as Dundee's galloper I went to unlikely places with him – a little dark uncomely man in a black suit, with a cough that seemed to be tearing his lungs to pieces; not the kind to win easy liking from all men, but I could have liked him fine, if the pattern of things had been otherwise. Seemingly he made a good king, too . . .

But not for Dundee, nor for us that followed him.

15

The Lord of Convention

In February we rode north again, with all our high
hopes left behind us. But not all of us had ridden south.
In disbanding the army, James had set us free, and
most of the regiments, some even of Claverhouse's
own, had gone over to William. We called them turn-
coats and traitors at the time, but truly, I do not think
that they were; I think that like most of the kingdom,
they had had enough of Stuart kings and their Popish
ways, and were for a king of their own faith, with a
reputation for sound military leadership; aye, and a
Stuart-born wife to share the rule and keep the thing
from straying too far from home.

Some of the leaders who would not take up arms for
William just turned their backs on what was happening
and went home. Claverhouse could have done that. He
was not young any more, and had soldiered hard for all
the years of his grown manhood. Nobody could have
blamed him if he had thought he had earned some
peace – aye, and him with his new Viscountcy, and
maybe an heir to it on the way, for after all the long
waiting, my lady Jean was carrying a bairn – but that
was not Claverhouse's way.

So here we were, Claverhouse and Balcarres and a
few friends and his own troop – around forty of us all
told – that chose to follow him by way of escort, riding
back up the long road north and over the Border, and
so at last into Edinburgh. And none of us sure of anything save that Claverhouse was still for King James,
and we were for Claverhouse.

Edinburgh was throbbing like a softly tapped drum. The Privy Council had sent a message of welcome to Orange William; and a great Scottish Convention was fixed for March 14. But three weeks before that, my lady's bairn was due. And so out from Edinburgh we rode, under the Castle Rock where the Duke of Gordon was sitting like a moulting eagle on his crag, holding for the Stuart King, and away back to Dudhope for the while.

Dudhope in early spring is a bonnie place, with the rooks busy in the top-most branches of the tall oaks and sycamores that are flushed with rising sap and woolly with the thickening buds that will soon be breaking; and the furze flaming gold on the slopes of the Law, and the late snowdrops in sheltered corners of the garden. And eh, but it was good to be home again after those grey ghost-months in the South!

My old welcome was waiting for me; from my lady Jean, swathed in a great soft velvet wrap the colour of mulberries, and her face seeming all eyes, for I think that she had found Claverhouse's bairn not easy in the carrying; and from Darklis with the same gladness and the same holding back that I had known so long; and from Caspar with all the gladness and no holding back at all, with eyes of liquid amber and his tattered bracken-frond of a tail so hard a'wag behind him that his whole rump must go where it led.

I gave him my cupped hands to thrust his nose into, the way that we had, then picked him up and held him aloft while his frilled pink tongue licked and licked at the air at arm's length from my face. 'Mistress Mary,' said I – for we were in the stable-yard and there were others by – ye've let him grow fat! Eh, but ye're growing to be a leddy's lapdog, ma mannie!'

'Ye're jealous because he hasna pined away for lack of ye,' said Darklis.

But we were only skimming words on the surface of things, for the things beneath the surface, the things that mattered most deep with us, we could not be speaking of at all.

So we settled down to wait, for my lady's bairn and the great council in Edinburgh, and which of the two came first was like to be a close-run thing.

Claverhouse spent a good part of the waiting time walking the hills. Horseman that he was, and lover of horses, there were times when the fret within him seemed to demand that he should leave his horses in the stable and walk, far and fast, as though to outwalk something that he could not outride. Then he would whistle the dogs to heel, and myself also, like as not, and head for the high moors.

So a day came, only two or three before he must leave for Edinburgh again, when he whistled up the dogs and me, and I whistled Caspar – there was an established custom in the thing – and we headed north-ward for the long lift of the Skiddaws. And with the sun beginning to wester, and the cloud shadows drifting across the hills, we sat looking out over the blue levels of Angus, with the first rampart of the Highlands at our backs, and the whaups skirling over their mating-moors, and the dogs sprawled at our feet.

We had scarce spoken all the way; one does not talk much, walking in high hills; and beside, I am thinking that there were times when Claverhouse took me as a walking companion much as he took the dogs, and for the same sort of company. I am not complaining, mind you, we understood each other fine, Claverhouse and me.

But there was a thing I was fain to ask him. It had been nagging at me ever since we came north again.

I looked from picking bits of last year's bracken out of Caspar's long flopping ears, and began, 'Sir—' and then found that I could not go on.

'Hugh?'

I shook my head. 'No, 'twas nothing.'

Claverhouse brought his gaze back from the blue distances of Angus, and turned it on me, intent and deeply focused in the way that he had. 'Something, I think,' he said after a moment.

I swallowed, and began again. 'Sir, the Scots Dragoons were in Edinburgh when we passed through.'

'Aye.'

'And had taken service with William of Orange.'

'Which will be a sore loss to the King's fighting strength in Scotland,' Claverhouse said. And then, as I bided silent, 'But there's more to it than that?'

'And I was hearing that Colonel Livingstone was serving with them still.'

Claverhouse's gaze went back to the soft distances and the cloud-shadows drifting in from the coast.

'Aye,' he said, 'Colonel Livingstone has chosen to bide with them, and I make no doubt that he has his own reasons. And I make no doubt that whatever they are, they will not smirch his honour.' Suddenly he smiled. 'Try to remember, Hugh, that honour is an intensely personal thing. I am one of the fortunate ones; for me, it is for the most part a simple thing, a straight road to be followed. For you, I think, also. For some men it is not simple at all.'

He was a loyal friend to a friend, was Claverhouse, as well as a loyal man to his king.

He drew his legs under him to rise. 'We must be

starting home, for the shadows are lengthening, and I would not that the bairn should be born while I was stravaigling among the Skiddaw mosses.'

We came back to Dudhope in the first of the spring gloaming; the time when it still seems all but daylight out of doors, and yet within doors the candles are lit and the light shines out through the windows in squares of shadowy apricot. There seemed more lights than usual for that time of day in Dudhope windows, and a watch must have been kept for us, for as we came through the postern gate into the garden court, old Leezie the housekeeper, she that had been Claverhouse's nurse when the world was young, came scurrying to meet us.

'Praise be you're back, my lord, my dearie.'

'The bairn—?' said Claverhouse.

'Aye, the bairn.' And as he would have strode past her she shot out a hand and gripped like a cockle-burr on to his arm. 'None so fast, my dearie dear, 'twill be many hours yet. Mistress Mary and the midwife are with her now—'

'Let me go, old nurse,' said Claverhouse, 'I must see her—'

She cackled, 'Aye, and so you shall. But only for the moment, mind, then leave her to the women. There'll be work enough for all us women, my lady most of all, between now and dawn. And for you, just the waiting, my dearie, as many a good man has waited afore ye since the world began.'

That night I could not sleep. In a little room under the eaves of the north wing that had become mine whenever I was at Dudhope, I lay hour after long hour staring at the pale square of the small high window,

167

until the waning moon rose and made a kind of cobweb paleness that showed me my boots in the corner and my sword propped against the clothes kist beside them. I listened for any sound, but heard only the creak of a floorboard as the old house settled, and 'Kee-wik-wik-wik' of a hunting owl. Somewhere in the house Dundee would be listening as I was listening; hearing the silence, pacing up and down, I guessed, up and down; and only the hunting owl to keep him company.

Once I thought I heard a door slam, very far off, and a man's voice; and then just the silence again . . .

At last I gave up all attempt to sleep, and getting up, pulled on my coat – I had lain down in shirt and breeches, as many of us did in our young days – and stole out of my room and down the turnpike stair to the side door giving on to the drying green. I knew fine that there would be no locked door in all Dudhope that night, for there must be nothing to hinder the new life coming, just as there must be nothing to make the passing of an old life harder when the traffic runs the other way.

At the foot of the stair, the doorway was in wolf-dark shadow. I put out a hand and felt for the pin. It lifted easily, and I opened the door and slipped out and across to the stable-yard, Caspar as always pattering behind me. From the second branch of the old fig tree it was possible to see the great central gable of the house, and even catch a sideways squint at the window beneath it that I knew belonged to my lady's chamber. It was full of light; and now and again as I sat watching, with Caspar, disappointed because he had thought we were going ratting, curled up on the ground beneath me, I saw the shadows of people moving in the room pass across the light.

Slowly the sky began to change colour, the faint promise of sunrise that was still far off mingling with the snail-shine of the moon, and the light in my lady's window faded back to dim apricot again. There was a first sleepy stirring and stamping of horses in the stables, and then as though in answer a shimmer of faint birdsong waking among the bushes of the garden.

And then somewhere in the house I heard it, a very small sound caught in the waiting quiet of the morning, like as it might be the bleating of a newborn lamb.

Then for the second time I heard a door slam, somewhere very far off. And the tiny sound was lost behind it, and strain as I would, I could not catch it again.

It seemed a weary long time after that, but in truth I think it was not so long as it seemed, before I heard quick light footfalls speeding from the house, and a shadow came through the arched gateway, a lassie's shadow with skirts gathered and spread on either side like wings that came straight towards the old fig tree.

I dropped from my branch, all but landing on Caspar, and met her on her way. 'Darklis! Is the bairn born? – I thought I heard something. How is it wi' my lady Jean?'

I was drawing her back into the shelter of the fig tree, and she came, lightfoot and breathless. 'The bairn is born,' said she. 'A son – and it is well wi' him and wi' Jean.' A faint laughter shimmered in her voice. 'And wi' Viscount Dundee, from the looks o' the poor man, though we came near to losing him in the night.'

The laughter took me too; if laughter it could be named, for it was not the kind that is called up by a jest, but born of relief after long anxious waiting; and our hands came out to each other in the midst of it, suddenly glad of each other in the way that we used to be in

169

the days before I followed Claverhouse down into Ayr-shire.

'How did ye ken where to find me?' I asked.

And she answered as though it were the simplest thing in the world. 'I knew you would be here. I felt you here, waiting for word; and so I came as soon as I could.'

'This is the brave morning for Dudhope,' I said. 'Listen to the bell-tit and missel-thrush in the garden!'

But even as I spoke, the birdsong fell quiet for a moment, and with a soft whirr of wings a small bird came over the wall into the topmost branches of the fig tree, then fluttered down to a branch only just above our heads and began the strangest little sad-sweet song of its own; a thin trail of single long-drawn notes that had in it somehow the sound of autumn.

Darklis heard it, too, and raised her head to listen, and I saw her face very pale in the growing light, like a face seen under water, and the eyes in it huge, with all the laughter gone from them. 'Listen,' she said, and suddenly she seemed a long way away; further than ever she had been. 'Oh, listen, Hugh, robin's keening!'

'Och away,' I said, ''tis naught to fret you – just fool-ishness. I've often heard him make that sad bit song in the early springtime. Mebbe he's crossed in love.'

But she shook her head and said again, 'Robin's keening.'

And pulled herself away from me and turned and ran back towards the house.

And the robin sat on in the branch of the fig tree, keening, as they say.

Three days later we were back in Edinburgh. But not for long.

On the fourteenth day of March the great Convention sat in the Parliament Hall; gathered there for the fore-chosen purpose, after all the talk was done, of deciding to offer William the Scottish crown. It was a squally day, with the rain and the sunshine darkening and lightening beyond the windows of the ante-chamber where I waited, kicking my heels along with other messengers and the like. There was a great coming and going through the chamber, and from time to time the inner door would open, letting out loud voices that rose to anger as the time went on. And once Colonel Livingstone passed through, and in a while came back with a set face that looked stiff and heavy like his own effigy that had been carved from wood by a none too skilled hand, and he looked straight before him, neither to right nor left, as if he strode through an empty room.

A good while later the inner door opened again and I heard the angry scrape of a chair being thrust back, and somebody crashing to his feet, and Claverhouse's voice, not overloud, but with an edge to it that cut like a Toledo blade. 'My lords, it seems that the Parliament Hall is no longer any place for me; nor this Convention any company in which I would spend another moment of my time. Therefore I bid you goodbye!'

And then his quick step sounded on the polished floor as he came out into the ante-chamber and the door crashed to on the sudden babel of angry voices behind him.

I knew then that the decision had been taken – if it had not been already taken before the Convention sat at all – and the King had lost Scotland.

Claverhouse looked round for me, then strode straight on and out into the street where a fresh shower was pox-dimpling the puddles, with me at his heels.

He walked past the kirk of St Giles and straight on up the High Street as though he knew where he was going, but in truth, I do not think that at that moment he cared, wanting only to be clear of the Parliament House and those within it. He walked until he came to the Grass Market, and then checked and looked around him at the tall many-eyed houses. 'I wonder did the houses stare just this way when my kinsman Montrose came here to the scaffold for *his* king's sake?' he said.

'So 'tis all over for the King?' said I.

'Not yet.' He began stripping his gloves between his hands in the way that he had. I could see how he must have snatched them up from the council table as he came away. And then he looked round at me, and the odd thing is that he was smiling. 'Hugh,' said he, 'you would be knowing the De'il's Turnpike?'

That was the name we gave to the unlawful way down the shielded side of the Castle Rock, which I have spoken of before. I was surprised he knew it.

'Aye,' I said, 'I know it well enough. Is it a message you're wanting taken up to the Castle?'

'No, I must go myself, and not in full view of the town; but my education has been neglected, and I am thinking that I need a guide.'

'If I can find it in the daylight,' said I, 'I'm more used to it in the dark, ye see.'

'As to that—' We were already walking again, this time in the direction of the great rock, and his words came back to me with a kind of reckless laughter over his shoulder. 'I fear I cannot wait for the dark. They have sent poor Livingstone with a trumpeter and an escort to demand the Duke of Gordon's surrender of the Castle. He's to be allowed twenty-four hours' grace, but he may not take it unless I can come to him quickly.'

172

'Ye think he'll listen to ye?' I said.

'Oh aye, he'll listen to me because of the news I bring him – that King James is already landed in Ireland and gathering troops to take back his own!'

Well, so we came to the blind side of the Castle Rock, and we made the climb – Claverhouse was a good enough climber, though, strange to the De'il's Turn-pike as he was, there were times when I had to slip past him to find him a handhold or set his foot on the proper ledge. And we came to the ledge below the sheer black crag of the castle wall at last, and made our way along it to the wee postern gate.

'God!' said Claverhouse, as a raven swept by his face. 'And you came this way at night?'

'Night or day, drunk or sober, it doesna make a' that difference gin ye know the way and have a head for heights,' said I, and I gave the door-timbers the familiar signal rattaplan that the sentry inside would know.

There was a certain amount of explaining to be done, but after the sergeant of the guard had been fetched, and then the captain, they passed him through at last; and I settled down on my perch to wait for his return. The rain had passed, and I mind the evening light and the wind together playing through the tuft of grass on the ledge beside my foot, until the day began to fade into a windy March dusk.

In a while and a while the postern opened again, and the glim of a lantern spilled out across the path and on into empty space; and scrambling to my feet, I saw Cla-verhouse, and with him a tall man wearing trews of the Gordon tartan; I had only a glimpse of his face in the swinging lantern light, but I had seen the Duke of Gordon often enough to know him again.

173

'My thanks,' he said. 'I hope that my answer to the Convention would have remained the same even without the news you bring; but with it, I shall send that answer tomorrow with a lighter heart. And you? What road do you ride now?'

There was a small silence, and then Dundee said very simply, 'I go wherever the spirit of Montrose shall lead me.'

And I saw his face for an instant clear in the lantern light, and wondered suddenly if Montrose had looked like that when he rode out to raise the Highlands for *his* king.

The two of them shook hands and wished each other Godspeed, and Claverhouse came past me over the ledge on to the first drop of the De'il's Turnpike.

Much later that night, after a deal of quiet message-carrying, there was another gathering in the back room of Wedderburn's Coffee House, which had, as you might say, plenty of exits and entrances in case of need. Not a great gathering like that day's Convention in the Parliament Hall, but just four men: Dundee himself, and the Earls of Balcarres and Atholl and Mar that was Governor of Stirling Castle; and myself standing guard over the chamber door, while the Edinburgh caddies in Government pay watched the lodgings of each of them like terriers at empty rat-holes.

I did not listen, you will understand, but I have always had quick hearing, and the door was none so good a fit, which was one reason why I was drinking my bowl of the bitter hot stuff just there to make sure that no one chanced too near. And so from time to time, when the wind fell away into a trough of quiet, I heard something of what passed inside.

''Twas the letter that did it,' Atholl said. 'If His

Majesty had but sent the letter that you and Balcarres drafted for him . . .'

'I could not believe my ears when the President read out the one that he did send—' That was Mar, who had a fretful way of speaking that could not be mistaken. 'Stupid, arrogant, threatening. Could the man not see that it was no time for threats, nor himself in any position to threaten?'

'I must say, I think that Dundee's and mine was better,' said Balcarres. 'Maybe they *might* have been swayed by a more moderate tone.'

And then Dundee's clear incisive voice cut across the rest. 'I doubt it, Colin, I very much doubt it. But be that as it may, the thing is done and the harm wrought. Mulling over it will not help. The question is what is to be done to amend it?'

And then the wind swept back and I could hear no more for a while. And when the next lull came, it seemed that they were making some kind of plan to withdraw to Stirling and summon a convention of their own. And Mar was saying, 'As Governor of the Castle, I can answer for the loyalty of Stirling.'

And Dundee said, 'Aye, and with the Highlands at our backs, and your Highlanders, Atholl, added to my own small band of brothers, we shall be in a very different position. Gentleman, I will not yet believe that the King's cause is lost. If the Highlands stand loyal, this Edinburgh Convention will have no power to offer the crown to William of Orange. And with His Majesty already landed in Ireland and gathering troops, we do but need to play for time.'

So in a while and a while the thing was sorted out and it was arranged that the four of them, each with whatever following they could gather meanwhile, should meet at a certain point beyond the North Loch three days hence, and march for Stirling, and there raise the King's standard.

16

The Lion of Scotland

But on the Monday morning, the agreed day, when we clattered behind Dundee down Leith Wynd and out under Carlton Hill along the shore of the North Loch, to the agreed trysting place on the Stirling road, instead of the gathered troops, we found only Balcarres, sitting his fidgeting horse beside the way. There was a mist that morning, cold and drifting, and it was not until we were almost upon the man that we realised that he was alone.

Dundee reined in sharply, the rest of us behind him, and sat looking at the Earl as he brought his horse out from the side of the track. And said he, 'What means this, Colin? Where are Mar and Atholl?'

Balcarres had a cold, I mind, and he blew his nose, and took a long time stuffing his handkerchief back into the breast of his coat. 'Mar has taken a fever of some kind, and gone to lie up in his own house,' he said at last.

'And Atholl?' Dundee said. 'Has he taken a fever, too?'

'He said he must have one more day to finish summoning his Highlanders.'

And in the silence, beyond the jink and fidget of the waiting horses, I heard lake water lapping in the mist. Then Dundee said, 'Only you and me, then, Colin? But I do not see even your own men behind you.'

Balcarres shook his head miserably. 'No – well – Atholl thinks that to avoid suspicion we should both bide along with him in Edinburgh the one more day while the plan goes forward . . .'

And a bird rose crying through the mist on the water.

And Dundee said, 'Only me then, eh, Colin?'

''Tis just the one day,' Balcarres said beseechingly.

'Is it?' Dundee said, quick and fierce. 'Don't you see – Convention knows us for King James's men. By tomorrow the city gates will be shut to hold us.'

And he drove his heel into Hector's flank.

'John – wait—' Balcarres called after him, as the sorrel started forward snorting from the spur.

'Not another instant,' Dundee cried. 'I have other men to meet upon the way, surer trysts than this one, I hope, to keep upon the road. I'll wait for you at Stirling, Colin; join me there if you can get out of Edinburgh when you've a mind to.'

And we were away down the Stirling road.

We bided in Stirling waiting for them three days, quartered in the town, since troops could not quarter in the castle with its governor not there; but when the three days were up, bringing no sign of any of them, Claverhouse had had enough, and we marched back to Dundee town, to await his commission from the King.

Dudhope was all a'bustle and a'twitter with women making ready for the bairn's christening; and Dundee's brother David arrived the same day as we did, and Amryclose and a good few more, and on the ninth day of April the bairn was christened James, with his Uncle David to stand sponsor for him at the font.

Darklis had made the Long Parlour bonnie with knots of sweet chilly primroses and the year's first wood anemones, though the spring was late that year, and the land still half frozen. And for font there was the big silver cup in which all the Claverhouse Grahams for five generations had been baptised. I mind it all as clear and small and sharp-edged as it was reflected in the curved sides of that cup – and the thin April sunshine and the liquid fluting of a blackbird coming in through the open windows, and the knot of friends and kinsfolk in their bravest coats and gayest gowns. Aye, and wee James with his face screwed up, poppy red and poppy crumpled in the midst of all the frills and fine lace that must have come near to smothering him, bawling like a bull calf at the touch of the cold water. And Darklis – it was she that held him – saying when his mother would have hushed him, 'Och, no, he is letting out the Devil, the wee lamb, let him be.'

And I mind Dundee reaching out to take my lady's hand that came to meet it.

But behind the minister's voice and the bairn's bellowing, there came the sound of horses' hooves in the courtyard, and raised voices at the great door. And I saw how himself's hand tightened over Lady Jean's, and the look they gave each other, as the small ceremony went on. They must have known how short their happiness was to be.

When all was finished in seemly fashion, and we trooped out into the hall, there were three men waiting there; a narrow weazel-faced chiel in a tie wig and a coat of great importance with all the gold lace that was on it; and on either side of him a trumpeter of the Scots Dragoons.

I sensed rather than saw how Dundee checked for an instant, and then put Jean's hand gently from his arm and walked forward to meet them.

'My lord,' began the weazel-faced man, 'are you in the habit of keeping your guests waiting in your hall under guard?' He cast an angry eye at two of Claver-house's henchmen who did indeed look to be standing guard over them.

'Not my guests, no,' said Dundee quietly, and held out his hand. 'Is that letter for me?'

'From the President and Lords of the Convention ye left so unmannerly and without leave,' said the man.

Dundee took the letter and broke the seal. He turned aside to catch the light of the nearest window on the crackling sheet as he opened it; and so I saw his face, and how his brows snapped together and the deep frown line between them as he read. Nobody moved. When he had done, he refolded the letter and turned back to the man who had brought it.

'It seems to me quite extraordinary,' said he, 'that His Grace the Duke of Hamilton should send a herald and trumpeters to summon any man to return to the Convention, which he has a perfect right to leave if he so wishes. Even more extraordinary, to summon him to lay down his arms, when he has not taken them up, but is living peacefully in his own home.'

The man flushed and seemed to have difficulty in swallowing. 'Then you refuse?'

'I refuse to return to the Convention. As I have just said, I have not taken up arms,' Dundee returned, still quietly. He turned from the man, as from something of very little account. 'Davy – Jean – take our guests through to the dining-room. I have a letter to write before I can join you.' He smiled into my lady's tense white face. 'It seems that in one way or another, the Government can never keep from meddling with our private days of joy, sweetheart.'

I minded how he had spent his wedding night on the high moors, and the rain on the roof, and the taper-light shining lonely from my lady's window.

William and Mary were proclaimed King and Queen of James's kingdom two days later, though of course it was a few days more before the news of it reached us. And by that time there had begun to be a different kind of gathering at Dudhope. It was no good waiting any longer for the King's commission to raise troops, for word came only a few hours after the herald and trumpeters that James had indeed sent it, but that it had fallen into the hands of the Whigs. So what had begun as a gathering for a bairn's christening became a gathering to the Stuart cause.

We raised the royal standard for King James on Dundee Law, our hearts high within us, for all the chill of the east wind that was blowing. Aye, I'll not forget how it was that day, if I live to see your sons grown to manhood. The Lion Rampant of Scotland striking out crimson and gold into the wind, held high by Philip of Amryclose who had laid aside his pipes and his legends to become our standard-bearer, and under it, Dundee and his officers sitting their horses bareheaded.

There was around sixty of us, I suppose; David Graham that was Dundee's brother, and a handful of friends that were of his way of thinking, and us, the men of his old troop, under the blue and silver of his personal standard; and a petty chieftain here and there with a tail of half-a-dozen men and a proudly tattered flag. And over all the skirling of the great war pipes, for Amryclose was not the only piper among us. A small enough company we made on the wide steep stretch of Dundee Law; a small company to be setting off to raise the Highlands for the King. But Montrose had done the same thing with a smaller company more than forty years before.

It was a custom, as I have already told you, for Dundee town to be not just on the best of terms with its

181

Constable, but Claverhouse had come to be well enough liked during his term as Provost, and a good few of the townsfolk had come up, if not to wish him well, then at least to see him on his way; and most of the Dudhope folk had come out likewise, my lady Jean of course amongst them; and Darklis.

I wished that she had brought Caspar out with her; but we had said our farewells in private, Caspar and I, and now he was shut up, waiting for Darklis to go and let him out when we were well away.

There were many farewells going on; aye, and I had mine too, for at the very last moment, the lassie caught the hand I held down to her, and set her foot on mine and swung up as light as a bird, across my saddle. 'A stirrup-kiss, for luck,' said she, laughing, and gave it to me before them all. But so quick and light that it was gone almost before I knew I had it, a kiss that would somehow melt like the faery gold that turns to autumn leaves, if I had tried to grasp it. The kind that you would expect from a lassie that heard strange pipe-music under an elder tree on Midsummer's Eve

Then she sprang down, and as her feet touched the ground, the trumpets were sounding for the march.

17

Hare and Hounds

We rode north, the Grampians lifting on our left fiercely dark against a cold harshness of blue sky; and the wind was from the east, laying the moorland grasses over all one way. We crossed the Dee at Kincardine and headed for Huntly country, descending that first night on a wee dour-faced clachan where the welcome was as chill as the wind, and the folk grudged us even the shelter of byres and linhays till they saw the colour of Dundee's silver.

Presently, bearing westward, we came down into the broad vale of the Moray Firth. And after each hard day in the saddle, Dundee would sit far into the night in whatever quarters he had, writing letters to the lairds along the way, to summon them to the King's standard. Quite a few came, amongst them an old friend, Lord Dunfermline, out from Gordon Castle to join us where we crossed the Spey; and with him sixty men of the Atholl country; long-legged Highlanders who could cover the hills on foot at night on the speed of cavalry. And so we were upward of two hundred strong when we came to Elgin.

Aye, and by that time the great Lochiel, Chief of the Camerons, had sent offering his allegiance and that of his clan, and his man MacDonald of Keppoch with a strong force to meet us at Inverness and escort us in to Lochaber.

At Elgin, Dundee made his headquarters for the night in an inn close behind the half-ruined cathedral –

the Lantern of Moray, it used to be called, so I've heard, but that was in the days before most of it stood open to the sky. Eh well, its kirkyard made a good enough place to pen the horses. The private chamber they had given him was over the taproom, and I heard the clatter of the tankards and the high-pitched gaelic voices that broke now and again into song, as I put out his gear and saw about getting him some supper. The man generally forgot to eat when he was on campaign, unless somebody saw to all that for him; and as I have said before, I had come by then to be to him much what a squire was to his knight in olden times.

So I had badgered the surly landlord who wanted nothing to do with Redcoats arriving late at night when Godfearing folk should be a'bed, into providing a rough meal and a bottle of decent wine and a sea-coal fire, for the nights were still cold though it was coming up towards the end of April; ale and a flask of the stuff the Highlanders call the Water of Life, a foul and fiery brew, but better than any wine for warming the heart and belly of a man dead-weary.

And I was helping himself off with his mired boots while he sat on the edge of the box bed, when there came a rapping on the door, and on being told to come in, Amryclose opened and stood with his tall head ducked under the lintel. 'There's a Tinkler chiel would be speaking with ye, Dundee. Says he brings word from Jean – though why my lady should have entrusted such a tattybogle—'

Dundee was on his feet, with one boot off and one still on.

'Send him in, Philip.'

Amryclose sighed, and ducked his head back from under the lintel; and into the room, with the light prowling step of a mountain cat, came Captain Faa.

The splendid wreckage of the mulberry velvet coat was gone; the coat he wore now was the wreckage of mere homespun; there was a filthy rag tied round his neck, and his bonnet sported a knot of wild cherry blossom that hung rakishly over one eye; but having once seen that sly brown face with its glinting humour, and looked into those strange yellow eyes, there could be no mistaking the man.

He pulled off his greasy bonnet and bowed; one great gentleman greeting another. 'Travel-stained I may be, with the speed that I have made to come to your honour,' he said in that odd tongue that was Lowland Scots with a little of something else. 'But as to being a tattybogle, I am a gentleman like yourself, and a chief among my own kind.'

'I would apologise for my friend's mistake, if there was time,' said Dundee with a hint of a smile, holding out his hand. 'You have a letter for me?'

'No letter,' said Captain Faa. 'It seemed best that there should be no letter to be found on me if I were searched. All that I bring you is safe in my head.'

'Then sit you down and tell me the news that you bring.' Dundee sat down again on the edge of the bed, while Captain Faa seated himself on the room's one chair.

'A drop of the Water of Life would not be coming amiss,' he said.

Claverhouse pushed the stone flask across the table to him. 'I apologise on my own behalf. Now your news.'

I would have left the room, but Dundee gestured me to bide, so I bided, and became part of the furniture. One does not spend months and years as a general's galloper without learning how to do that.

Captain Faa took a long pull at the flask, and set it down, drawing the back of his hand across his mouth. 'In the first place, the Earl of Balcarres has been arrested and is held under guard in his own house. They say he made no trouble; no trouble at all, the douce mannie.'

I saw the frown deepen between Dundee's black brows, but that was all.

'In the second place, your lordship has been proclaimed rebel and fugitive at Dundee market cross.'

'That was to be expected. Your news, man!'

'In the third place – six companies of the Scots Dragoons under Colonel Livingstone arrived at Dundee eight days since, sent to arrest yourself.' He took another pull at the flask. 'Och, that warms a man's bones.'

Claverhouse said very quietly, 'Poor William, poor old lad,' and then, 'Where are they now?'

'Still in the town, wi' orders to bide there to keep the peace in these lawless times. And being there, Colonel Livingstone sent up one of his lieutenants – Crichton, by name – to tell your leddy that the Dragoons are yours to a man if you do but whistle for them.'

There was a silence, then, and Dundee was looking at Captain Faa with that odd intent look that went right through into a man's inmost places. I'd not have cared to face it, if I were lying to him. 'And my lady sent you to tell me this? You seem, if I may say so without giving offence, an unlikely choice. I would have thought maybe one of my own grooms . . .'

'One of your own grooms would mebbe not ken the Highlands so well as one of the Tinkler kind,' said Captain Faa, his yellow eyes bright and unblinking. 'The Rawni – Mistress Ruthven – would vouch for me, were she here.' He glanced aside for a moment and met my gaze. 'And so, I think, will yon soldier laddie in the corner, clasping your lordship's left boot to his whame.'

I had not realised that I was still clutching the boot that I had just pulled off when he entered. I gave him back his look, and set down the boot with care. I did not feel called upon to vouch for Captain Faa. Claverhouse made his own judgements in such matters.

Captain Faa was speaking again, softly, on a faintly sing-song note; clearly he had the words off by heart. 'My leddy showed me the letter. It ran this way: "Tell Lord Dundee we are unfailingly at his lordship's service." And then at the foot of the page, it was written, in a hurry as it looked, "Please tell John I am no traitor, and neither torture nor death shall ever make me so."'

And hearing the words, I seemed to hear Colonel Livingstone's own voice, grave and always a little anxious, sounding through the lilting Tinkler tones. It seemed that Dundee heard it, too. 'Aye, that sounds like William Livingstone,' he said. A moment longer he sat looking at the man before him; and then I saw him gather himself for action as a horse gathers itself to take a ditch.

'Food and sleep for you now, my friend,' he said, 'for you must be away again at first light, carrying word to my lady. Nothing written, I think, this time either. Tell her that you have seen me, and bid her get word to Colonel Livingstone to hold his men ready for my whistle, biding in Dundee according to their orders until I can come for them myself.' He smiled. 'And, Captain Faa, my deepest thanks to you in this matter.'

Later, when Captain Faa had departed to be fed and bedded down for what remained of the night, Claverhouse said, 'One thing is sure; if the Scots Dragoons are ordered to bide in Dundee, there will be others ordered up from the South on our trail; and I am thinking our road back to Dundee is like to be less peaceful than our road up here. Ask Lord Dunfermline and Major Crawford to join me here at their earliest convenience.'

'Will it no' do in the morning, sir?' said I, greatly daring. 'Gin ye had a few hours sleep—'

'We march in the morning,' he said. 'Tonight is the time for making plans. May I remind you that you are not old Leezie, my galloper and not my dry nurse, Hugh?'

But as I was making for the door, he checked me a moment, and when I looked back he was half smiling. 'We know now why Colonel Livingstone chose to remain with an Orange brigade.'

So Inverness must wait; and with courteous messages to Lochiel, back we started next day over the long road that we had come, on the chance that we might be able to pick up the Scots Dragoons before other troops from the South could come up with them or us.

Those troops were coming, sure enough; word of them reached us about Cairn-o'-Mount, between Northesk and the Dee. General MacKay, him that had served with Claverhouse in the Low Countries in their young days, was out from Edinburgh with two hundred of the Scots Dragoons and the whole of Colchester's Horse (and four companies of the very Scots Dragoons from Dundee, that we were on the march to pick up – but that was a piece of ill news we did not learn until later). He was at Fettercairn only a few miles off when our scouts picked him up. And, said Claverhouse when they brought in their report, 'At the moment I have more pressing matters on hand than a tangle with

MacKay.' So we took to the hills and left the Government troops to pound around looking for us on an empty road. And that evening – eh, but we were weary – we rode into Huntly, fifty miles away.

We had lost our chance, for that time, of picking up Colonel Livingstone and the Dragoons. But we had got rid of MacKay; and we turned back to the earlier plan, and headed for Inverness.

We rode in four days later, on a fine clear evening with the cloud-feathered hills of Sutherland across the Moray Firth looking near enough to touch; and found Coll MacDonald of Keppoch waiting for us with seven hundred Highlanders to his tail. Leastwise, they were sitting there outside the tumbledown palisade which was all the place had by way of walls, demanding four thousand marks from the burgesses as their price for not sacking the town.

Coll MacDonald of Keppoch! Half a head taller than the tallest of his clansmen, and like them wearing the philibeg under his plaid instead of the trews that any Highland gentleman would be wearing; looking out from a bush of hair and beard as red as fire, with eyes that were the pale pure blue of snow-shadows on a sunny day. More like something out of Amryclose's ancient legends – Finn MacCool, maybe – than any man of the present day. And him filled with honest bewilderment when, the four thousand marks being paid, as seemingly they had to be, Claverhouse was not happy, but went surety for it himself that the money should be returned when the King came to his own again. Inverness was a MacIntosh town, the huge man pointed out, and there was blood feud between the MacIntoshes and the Keppoch MacDonalds; and himself happening to be there and with seven hundred men

189

to his back, surely my lord Dundee could see that 'twas the only reasonable thing to do.

I doubt Dundee saw it as clear as that. But there was no more that he could do about it, and he did see that with seven hundred well-armed clansmen to add to the rest of us, he could turn back on MacKay and finish him once and for all.

It had been fixed with Lochiel that we should meet him in Glen Roy of Lochaber, on May 18, the day that he had appointed for the clan-gathering to begin; and so there was time, if the luck were with us, both for MacKay and for picking up Colonel Livingstone and his Dragoons.

But it was the first time Claverhouse had had to deal with Highlanders; though I am thinking that he must have guessed what might happen, seeing that it had happened to his beloved Montrose, forty years before.

It is quite simple: when a Highlander has his booty, he goes home; and Keppoch had his four thousand marks. He was not interested in marching against MacKay. I doubt he had the smallest interest in King James's cause; or King William's, for that matter. He had been sent to guide Dundee to Lochaber, and if Dundee would not return with him to Lochaber now, then he would return alone. And return he did, with a wee thing of pillaging and cattle-rieving on his way through MacIntosh land. And we must follow him as far as the head of the Spey valley, that, now that we had come as far as Inverness, being the quickest way back to Dundee town and the Scots Dragoons.

'Never did I think to march on the heels of a rabble of bog-trotting cattle thieves,' said Pate Paterson to me as we rode.

What Claverhouse thought, there's no knowing, for

he wore his most shuttered look and spoke no word, unless it were to his horse.

Well, so we left the high hills with the snow still lying in their corries and turned down into the Spey valley. And there our scouts brought us word of an armed band in Dunkeld, collecting taxes – taxes for Orange William, which should by rights have gone to King James.

So we changed direction somewhat, crossed the Grampians and came down more southerly through the hazel woods where the Garry was running green and swift with snow-water; through Blair and by the pass of Killecrankie which was nothing but a break in the hills without special meaning for us as yet; and into Dunkeld, under cover of a good loyalist mist, and took for King James what was rightly his. Weapons, too; we reckoned we had a better use for Dutch muskets than the tax gatherers had.

It was a good morning's work, and we off-saddled to let the horses roll, and ourselves rested in the long river-side grass for a few hours, for we had a busy night ahead of us.

At dusk we took to the road again making for Perth, where a new regiment was being raised for the Orange Government; and in the darkest heel of the night, Claverhouse himself, with twenty of us behind him, got over the town wall – the burgesses having let it fall into disrepair according to their usual custom – and took the gate sentries in the rear. Och, they were a raw lot, and had not yet thought to grow eyes in the backs of their heads. And by noon we were on our way again, with forty fresh horses that had been meant for the new regiment, and a good supply of captured arms and money that had been collected for William of Orange and would now be put to more loyal use.

And on the afternoon of Monday the thirteenth of May, with the first of the hawthorn coming into flower, we were on the high ground above Dundee. There we waited, as the long hours wore by, for Colonel Livingstone and the Dragoons to come out to us.

'They're no' coming,' said Robin Findlay to me, as we sat beside our horses chewing on grass stems to pass the time.

And he was right.

Presently there was a dust-cloud on the road up from Tayside, but it was only a knot of horsemen, only a few of Claverhouse's friends who had not joined him when he raised the royal standard, and had second thoughts and come to join him now.

Aye, and ill news they brought with them, for beside the loss of the Dragoons, Colonel Livingstone was taken, and in gaol in Edinburgh in peril of his life; and most of his officers with him. Who had betrayed him there was no knowing; and so far as I am concerned, there is no knowing to this day. There was a new man, an Orange man, Balfour by name, in command of the remaining Dragoons; and the Provost and bailies of Dundee had had the gates shut and barricaded, allowing no one in or out.

'Do they think I am going to sack the town, with less than two hundred men?' Claverhouse said.

Nevertheless, we waited until dusk. Maybe he had a hope, even then, that the Dragoons would find a way to break out to him. But Colonel Balfour had done his work too well.

18

Meetings and Partings

Late into that night, having left the rest quartered in
and around the village, Claverhouse and I, just the two
of us, came riding into Glenogilvie. He had spoken not
one word all the way, and we rode in silence save for
our horses' hoof-beats and the creak and jingle of saddle leather and accoutrements.

I had wondered earlier that he had made no attempt
before we had left to make for Dudhope and snatch a
glimpse of Lady Jean and the bairn. But when we came
riding up the burnside and saw the glimmer of light
from the unshuttered window of the bower and the
signs of life and movement about the place, the truth
dawned upon me.

When we rode into the narrow courtyard the house
door stood ajar, late as it was, as though the old house
was expecting us. One of the Dudhope grooms came to
take the horses. I heard a sudden frenzied barking
somewhere, and as I dropped from the saddle, Caspar
came with flying ears and tail to meet me.

I began to feel as though I were in some kind of
dream, as I followed Dundee into the hall. There was a
feeling of people nearby, and I caught the smell of
cooking wafting out of the kitchen quarters, that
brought the soft warm hunger-water to my mouth as I
turned after Dundee towards the door of the bower
which also stood open.

In the bower, the tapers burned crocus-flamed on the
mantel and on a table near the window, and there was a

fragrant waft of burning wood from the low fire on the hearth. And in the great cushioned chair beside the hearth sat my lady Jean, her foot on the rocker of the heavy carved wooden cradle at her side. I mind she had a green gown on, like the sun on young beech leaves; and her hair had come out of its fashionable curls – maybe she had let it loose on purpose – and was caught back with a ribbon as she had used to wear it when I first knew her. She looked young, that way; only a lassie still, and like the lassie that had given her word to Colonel John Graham in the Abbey ruins at Paisley, more than five years ago.

And on the rug before the hearth, Darklis sat among the tumble of outflung russet skirts, with her lute lying in her lap. But her hand had fallen away from the strings, as my lady's foot had fallen still on the cradle-rocker, and both of them were looking towards the door, and for that moment not moving at all.

There were no explainings or greetings; it was as though we had all four of us just come by old and sure arrangement to a moment that had been waiting for us for a long time.

Claverhouse did not even speak my lady's name, nor make any move towards her, not at first. He just stood within the doorway, leaning against the jamb as though he were very weary. 'I should not have left the Dragoons to wait for me so long,' he said, 'but I had pressing need to be elsewhere in the King's service. If William hangs, his death will be at my door.'

And my lady said nothing but his name, with an aching tenderness. 'Johnnie, my Johnnie,' and held out her arms to him.

He went to her then, and stumbled to his knees beside her, and put his head in her lap.

And I had not even the sense to look away, until I found that Darklis had set aside her lute and was beside me with her hand in mine, turning me back towards the door. 'Come away now,' she said, ''tis a fair night, and you must be saddle-cramped, a wee stretch to your legs before supper will do you good.'

We did not go down to the pool where the elder trees hung over the burn. Whether she remembered anything of that long-past Midsummer's Eve I would not be knowing; she had never spoken of it since. But I remembered uncomfortably well, and we had never gone back there again. Instead we went up the glen to where the unkempt garden ran out into a few old apple trees, not enough to be called an orchard, where there was a little garden-house.

Darklis was right; it was a fine night, with a young moon tangled in the apple branches; and the dew already falling. You could smell it on the long grass – too long, it should have been scythed, but in a place such as Glenogilvie, that is only woken from its sleep to be lived in now and then, such things get overlooked.

Darklis went ahead, her long skirts trailing through it, and Caspar followed after me, so close that he must dodge from heel to heel behind me as a cattle dog does; and I mind the apple blossom that had lost its daytime coral tips was ghost-pale in the light of the moon.

We came to the little garden-house and ducked in under its moss-cushioned roof. Inside, it smelled dark and earthy; a brown smell; and I could scarcely see Darklis as she sat down on the bench and drew her wide skirts close to make room for me. Caspar jumped up beside me, and lay down half across my thigh, and I felt his long belly-hair cold-wet with the dew when I put my hand round him to draw him close.

I put my other hand out and Darklis's came somehow to find it in the dark.

We sat there talking a little, but mostly in silence a long time, while the young moon, slipping lower in the glimmering sky, began to silver the threshold of the garden-house and make a water paleness among the shadows so that we could see each other again.

'I'm no' just sure whether I'm waking or dreaming,' I said.

'And why would that be?' said she, laughing at me a little.

'Och – because yestere'en – even today the noon – I'd no' thought that tonight I would be sitting here in the garden at Glenogilvie wi' you and Caspar,' I said. 'I wondered why himself didna spare a wee while for Dudhope.'

'When we heard about Colonel Livingstone, Jean got word to Mr Haliburton – he being set to join you—'

'Aye, he joined us this afternoon, wi' a few more.'

'—that now there was nothing more to hold to Dud-hope for, she would be here, the night, if he could come.'

'And tomorrow? Will it be back to Dudhope?'

'I think we will be biding here a while,' said Darklis. 'This place has more the feeling of sanctuary about it than Dudhope has . . . And you? Where is it for himself and you, in the morning?'

'Northward again,' I told her. 'In four days' time we must be in Glen Roy, in Lochaber. Lochiel has offered Claverhouse himself and his clansmen, and Glen Roy for a gathering place; and the gathering of the chiefs is fixed for the eighteenth. The Fiery Cross is already going round.' (I was quoting Amryclose, that bit, half Highlander that he was.)

196

I heard her catch her breath. 'Aye me, that has a brave sound and a fearsome sound to it.'

There was a little shaken silence between us. Caspar turned his head and licked my wrist; and I began to fondle his ears, feeling how the silky dome of his head fitted into the hollow of my hand. And suddenly I was wondering, as I had not quite wondered at any parting-time before, whether I should ever feel the loving warmth of Caspar's head pushing up into the hollow of my hand again.

'Ye'll take care of Caspar for me,' I said.

I had said it so often before, and I knew that there was no need to say it; but as usual the other things, the things that there was an ache in me to say, could not be said.

Darklis slipped her hand out of mine. 'If I am to look after Caspar for ye yet again, then 'tis but fair return that ye should look after something for me,' she said; and when I looked round, she was taking something from the breast of her gown, holding it out to me.

In the faint moon-water light, I saw what it was. Like a heather sprig made of haw-frost in her fingers.

'Darklis, no,' I said, 'not your bonnie pin.'

'Take it.' It was a command, though a whispered one. 'I would have given it ye before – the day ye followed the King's standard from Dundee Law; but there were so many folk all around, and – I think 'twas in my mind that ye would be back before long, anyway.'

'And this time? Mebbe I'll be back before long this time, too.'

'Mebbe,' she said, 'mebbe . . . Take it, all the same.' And this time it was a plea. ''Tisna good for a laddie to go riding off to war, and no keepsake from a lassie to take with him to keep him safe. And 'tisna good – for the lassie left behind.'

197

The last bit she said so quietly that I was scarce sure that she had said the words at all. But I took the brooch, and pinned it inside my shirt, under my buff coat.

And with the feel of it there, warm with her warmth, 'It isna good for a laddie to go riding off to war wi'out a kiss to remember in the cold nights, either,' said I; light enough, as it might be half in jest; and I put my arms round her.

For a moment I had the odd unchancy feeling that she might turn into empty air, as though she were indeed one of the People of Peace; but then she gave a little fluttering sigh, and leaned closer into my hold, and the warmth and life began to spring up in her, and she was of the human kind after all . . .

And I am none so sure what would happen next; but in that instant, down in the house behind the lighted windows, the bairn began to cry. And Darklis slipped free of me without a word, and turned and ran down through the long grass of the ill-kept garden.

And there I was, alone in the garden-house save for Caspar.

And my heart within me drubbing away like a kettle-drum under my breastbone.

In a while I got up, feeling for the silver pin inside my shirt, to make sure that it was still there and had not disappeared with all the rest, and whistled Caspar to heel, and went down towards the house too – and the smell of cooking from the kitchen.

19

Highland March

We rode out from Glenogilvie at first light; a green morning dusk with the cuckoo calling away down the glen. And Caspar as usual shut up until we were well away.

We picked up the troop and the Gordon clansmen, and headed back by yesterday's road, skirting Perth and Dunkeld, to Pitlochry among the outriders of the high hills; and there we made camp for the night.

Pate Paterson and Willie Kerr and I found ourselves warm enough shelter in the last year's hay that yet remained at one end of a tumbledown barn, and when we had picketed and fed and rubbed down the horses, we turned in. And I for one was asleep almost before I had done burrowing into the hay. It was a June crop, I mind, clover-scented.

I dreamed that I heard Caspar barking, and woke with a start and lay listening. There was nothing to hear now; but the dream had been so strong that it was with me still, and I could not find the sleep again. And in the end, just to clear my mind of the thing, I got up, falling over somebody's legs in the dark and being cursed for my pains, and found my way to the rickety door. Something was snuffling under the crack; I could hear it now that I was close by, and as I put my hand on the wooden pin, there was a piteous whine outside, and a frantic scrabbling of paws. I pulled the door open; and a small crouching shape in the darkness flung itself against my legs.

I stooped, scarce believing it, and next instant Caspar was in my arms, sodden wet and shivering from nose to tail; too far spent for any outcry of reunion, but refuging against my shoulder as a weary traveller who has come home.

There was a stirring in the hay behind me, and Pate's voice sleepily demanding to know what the De'il was amiss.

'It's Caspar,' I said, and shut the ramshackle door. I could feel the ragged end of the strap about his neck. 'He's chewed through his leash and come after me.'

We scraped him together some bits of stale bannock and cheese out of the bottoms of our saddle-bags, and he slept the rest of the night in his usual place with his chin across my ankles. And in the morning he marched out with us. There could be no question of getting the wee beast back to Glenogilvie; from now on he must take his chance with the rest of us. His way must be our way.

There was a bit of talk and argument about our line of march as we saddled up, eating our morning bannock as we did so.

'Why not by Blair, as we came, and over Druimuchdair, that's the plainest way even if 'tis a bit longer,' grumbled Tam Johnston, saddling his horse next to me. 'We've three days before the start of the gathering; and 'twill go on a good few days, even if we should be a wee thing late.'

'And a fine thing that would be, for Dundee to be a wee thing late for his own gathering,' said Pate Paterson with his mouth full of bannock. 'Beside, to go that way, now that MacKay and his lot are loose in the land, would be to risk running up against the Government troops. Delay, at the best; and wi' less than two hundred of us, I'm thinking we've no call to go asking for losses.'

'Wi' MacKay loose in the land, why will we be less like to meet him one way than another?'

'Because Highlander though he is, MacKay only thinks along roads. Mind our last near-meeting at Deeside?'

So we left the clear track just beyond Pitlochry, and with our buff coats pulled on over our uniforms for warmth, took to the mountains, and so disappeared out of the ken of the Whigs in Edinburgh and the troops they had sent out after us. It was only a two-day march, but I am thinking that none of us who made it with Dundee would ever be forgetting it.

In the lowlands that we left behind us it was spring – did I not say that the apple blossom was breaking at Glenogilvie? – but the country that we marched through seemed as though it had never heard of spring. We trudged and stumbled our way up through the Tummel and across the flank of Ben Alder – for the most part we had to go afoot, leading our horses; we were worse off than the Atholl men, who had no horses to see to – and beyond Rannoch the land itself seemed to hate us; a dark land with a strange feeling of emptiness, as though it had never known the tread of a man's foot nor the sound of a man's voice before (maybe it had not) and resented us accordingly. It flung at us every weapon that it could summon up; steep slopes of slipping scree, gullies that were over their banks in snow water running deep and fast enough to carry horse and man away; the sudden yielding of frozen earth into the bog beneath, so that horses floundered and sank and had to be shot and left there. And when all else failed, the mist came down from the high corries, closing in the world to a few feet of scree or bog-cotton, coming even between each man and the next man ahead of him in the column. And all the while the cold ate into our very bones.

At night we bivouacked in the open, a few miles short of Loch Treig, in the lee of a skein of rocky outcrops that broke like bare bones through the sour mountain grass; and woke – those of us that had slept at all – with the ice of our own frozen breath like hoarfrost on our unshaved chins, and our limbs as stiff as though we had died in the night. I was better off than most, for I had Caspar; Caspar trotting at my heels when I went afoot, riding across my saddle-bow when it was possible to ride. His paws were red-raw with the hard and frozen earth, when we made that night's camp; but he had slept inside my buff coat, so that we gave each other what little warmth we had, and so made more of it, I and the wee dog. The wee lion-hearted dog.

Dundee was a hard leader, as he always had been; but as always he demanded no more from us than he did from himself. He lay down on the same frozen ground as we did, and ate the same iron ration of stale bannock from his saddle-bag, and carried no more of comfort than we in the rolled up cloak strapped behind his saddle. And so we kept going without overmuch of complaining. Even the Highland men only grumbled among themselves in their own tongue, and looked at him with a respectful eye.

That morning, the Atholl man who acted as our guide put round the word that we would be in Lochaber by nightfall. 'If we live so long,' somebody said through chapped and blackened lips. But our hearts lifted somewhat within us.

By the time we started the long climb over the southern spur of Ben Nevis, we had forgotten we had left

Pitlochry only the day before, and felt as though we had grown old among the mountains. And eh! the smallness of us: small like a trickle of ants climbing up the empty vastness of the mountainside! But it was the last stretch. Once over the skyline that towered so high and far off above us, we should have won through!

I was just thinking that when I realised that Jock was walking lame. I spoke to Pate Paterson, and pulled aside from the column and dismounted to find out what was amiss, Caspar standing to watch me, and glad of the pause, as the rest went by. The trouble was easily traced: a small sharp stone picked up from the last stretch of scree in his off fore-hoof. I got out my knife and cleared it easy enough, the old lad slobbering at my shoulder the while. But by the time I had finished, the troop was way up ahead, and the last of the Atholl Highlanders loping by. I swung Jock to the right, further uphill, and touched in my spurs to overhaul my proper place near the head of the column.

I was watching the gold and crimson of the standard that made a shout of brilliant colour against the vast winter-bleached hillside, fool that I was, and not looking where I was going . . .

But indeed I do not think there was anything to see.

Suddenly there was a crackling, and the solid ground was gone from beneath us as the frozen surface gave, and Jock plunged forward with a squeal of terror, and next instant was floundering in one of the small deadly bog-patches, as had happened to other men and horses on that march.

I flung myself out of the saddle, and found firm – or maybe it was but frozen – ground beneath me; and flinging the bridle over his head, began to pull, shouting to him, 'Easy now – come up! Up!' Caspar, who had also jumped clear, standing anxiously beside me.

203

But Jock was floundering deeper and deeper with every moment. I have heard it said that some of these pots have no bottom to them. He could almost reach firm ground with his forehooves; but his hind legs were sinking down and down. I yelled after the column – I do not know what, some useless cry for help. And then, above Jock's squealing and threshing and the pounding of my own heart, I heard the beat of light-running feet – feet in brogues, not riding boots – odd to have noticed that – and one of the Highlanders was beside me, crying in the high-pitched voice of his people, 'Hold on! We will be needing something under his forefeet.' And I was aware without looking, that he had drawn his broadsword, and was slashing at the young heather, diving in to thrust the stuff under Jock's flailing hooves.

But the terrified beast scattered the bundles as fast as they were gathered. I leaned back, putting out every ounce of strength I possessed, and praying that the headgear would not break under the strain. The Highlander was beside me, hauling at Jock's mane, but the foul footing gave, and he was himself up to his knees with only just time to scramble clear before the hungry bog claimed him also; and I could feel the ground beginning to break away under my own braced heels.

And there were hoof-beats coming up behind me, and Pate Paterson's voice said, 'Ye'll have to shoot him.'

'I'll not—' I gasped.

'You're not the first that's had to do it.'

'This is different!' I shouted stupidly. Could he not see? This was Jock!

'Shoot him, or I will.' It was not Pate, now, but Corporal Paterson giving the order.

I snatched an agonised sideways glance, and saw his

hand already going to his holster. 'No!' I yelled. '*Wait!*'
Och, but God knows what he was to wait for. Jock was
almost haunch-deep in the black ooze. His head was
up, but his eyes, wild and white-showing, were filled
with despair; clemmed and exhausted as he had been
before, he was giving up the fight; and once that happened the last hope would be gone.

'Jock, ye old de'il!' I was almost sobbing. 'Come up,
wi' ye!' At any moment would come the roar of Pate's
pistol behind me. And then the miracle happened!

I told you before that somewhere in Caspar's tangled
ancestry there must have been a strain of cattle dog,
and whiles and whiles he thought he was a cattle dog
still. Now, the moment of sorest need, the old skill and
the old knowledge of his forefathers came upon him.
Whether or no he understood the true state of things,
he understood that there was desperate need his friend
Jock should be moved forward in the direction that I
was dragging him, and that Jock was not moving forward but only floundering in the same spot; and next
instant he had darted out on to the quaking surface of
the bog, springing, light as he was, from one frozen tussock to another where a man or even a bigger dog
would have sunk. He was barking in sharp command,
darting in and out with gadfly nips to the horse's
haunches, as I have seen cattle dogs nip at the hocks of
a wilful heifer.

And somehow the shrill torment at his haunches got
through to Jock as nothing else could do and, mad to
get free of the yapping and nipping onslaught, he gave a
terrible cry that was nearer to a human shriek than a
horse's, and put out the last dregs of his strength that
none of us, nor himself, had known that he had yet had
in him. There was a long moment of desperate, con-
vulsive struggle, a slipping back and a wild heaving

forward; and with eyes starting from his head and the tendons of his neck and shoulders standing clear as though he had been flayed, with me hauling at his head-gear and the Highlander hanging on to his mane, he came up with a hideous sucking noise, leaving a kind of ragged black wound bubbling behind him in the frozen hillside.

Caspar all but went in himself as the crust broke up behind Jock's escaping backlash; but he managed to swerve aside and come leaping and floundering from tussock to tussock, back to the safety of firm ground.

Jock stood with hanging head and heaving flanks, shuddering from crest to tail, the black ooze dripping from him. Caspar shook himself so that the black drops flew in all directions. Corporal Pate Paterson returned his pistol to his holster, and when I looked round, he was grinning. 'Insubordination, Trooper Herriot,' said he. 'Insubordination – give that poor brute a rub down, and catch up wi' the rest of us. You'll not likely lose sight of us on this braeside, but dinna go wandering into any more bog-holes on the way.' And he heeled his horse from a stand into a canter, and was gone after the rest.

I had my arm over Jock's neck that was streaked with the black sweat of terror as well as bog ooze. Across it, I looked at the Highlander, and he looked at me. He was about my own age, and short for his breed; a stocky, sandy-haired chiel with the bandiest legs I ever saw in anybody not bred on horseback. Both of us still panting for breath, we grinned at each other with chapped lips. I do not think I ever remembered to thank him, nor did there ever seem to be any need. He picked up his broadsword from where it lay among the heather roots, and sheathed it at his side, and together we began to rub down both Jock and Caspar with hand-fuls of moorland grass, and then, when I had taken off my buff coat and flung it over Jock's back, we struggled on, and hardly a word spoken between us all the while.

When we drew level with the Highlanders at the rear of the column, he checked. 'My name is Alisdair Gordon,' said he, with the air of one conferring an honour.

'Mine is Hugh Herriot,' said I; and we struck hands; and he fell in with his own kind, while I remounted and gentled Jock up towards my place close behind that red and gold standard.

And that was how I first came to know Alisdair Gordon, who was to be my friend through the weeks that followed.

I mind Claverhouse looked round as I urged Jock back into place behind him; and his face was grey-white to the lips. But there was the shade of a smile far back in his eyes. 'That's a good dog you have there,' he said, with a flick of a glance at Caspar sprawled across my saddlebow.

A little further on the slope grew too steep for riding spent horses, and we must dismount and go on foot yet again. Somehow we lurched and stumbled our way up that last slope and came over the skyline that had so long cut the drifting grey cloud-roof above us; and checked to breathe the horses – and looked down, scarce believing it, to where far, far below us, the shining waters of Spean and Roy came together and flowed down through the greenness of Lochaber. And smelled, or seemed to smell even up there on the bitter roof of the world, the springtime and the soft air that came from the West Coast.

Philip of Amryclose, standing beside the remount he

had ridden since he lost his own horse the day before, put aside the fringed corner of the standard that was blowing across his face, and said in a voice of triumph and wonder and a sort of quiet laughter, 'What was Hannibal to us?'

I have always remembered that, and he must have remembered it too, for afterwards he put it in his book, making it sound heroic, which was not how it sounded at the time.

By dusk we were back in the world of men; a world where lambs bleated and smoke curled from turf roofs and hawthorn was in flower; and folks came running out to meet us as we drew near to the clachan at the foot of the glen.

20

Summer in Lochaber

Sir Ewan Cameron, Lochiel himself, came out to greet us from his own tall grey half-fortress house nearby.

They do not grow men the like of that any more. He was tall as Keppoch, but of a finer breed, and carried himself like a king stag; and though he was close on sixty, his mane of hair and his great curling moustache were black as a raven's wing. Bright eyes, he had, and an iron mouth; and a gentle and courteous way with him beyond what I ever knew in any Highlander before or since. Yet for all that, so the story goes, fighting General Monck when he was a young man, he tore an English soldier's throat out wolf-like with his teeth.

A man once seeing Lochiel would not be forgetting him again.

Between him and Claverhouse it was a friendship at first sight. You could see it. They were like comrades in arms of twenty years' standing.

Eh well, I am wandering from my story.

Lochiel gave Dundee the use of a house near-hand his own, but Claverhouse made his quarters as he always had done, among the rest of us, in and around the clachan by the burn. The house had its uses, though, as a gathering and council place for him and all the chiefs who were already in Glen Roy and coming in more thickly as the days went by.

We were kept hard at it all through those days, as Claverhouse set about rough-training his growing war-host, accustoming them to stand firm in the face of

209

charging cavalry and the like, which is not a thing that the Highland men are used to, for it is not their way of fighting, not their way at all. But it was MacKay's way and the Government Redcoats' way, and so it must become their way too.

At the end of a week there were many still to come, but our scouts in Atholl country brought word that MacKay had sent to Edinburgh calling for more troops, and his reinforcements were coming up through the Atholl Forest to Inverness. So we could wait no longer, and the rest must just e'en follow on when they arrived in Glen Roy.

On the twenty-fifth day of May, Claverhouse reviewed all those that had arrived, along with ourselves and the Atholl men, on the common above the Spean. And all the yellow broom was in flower, filling the morning with its honey-and-almond scent to mingle with the smell of men and horses, and there was Claverhouse, sitting his great sorrel on the hummock that formed the highest point in that wide upland stretch, his friend Dunfermline at his side, and Philip of Amryclose holding the standard proud and high; and myself, the General's galloper, close behind him. Caspar I had left, as I did when need be, guarding my sleeping place in the clachan below us. And before us and a wee thing lower down the braeside, the Highland war-host went by.

There were around two thousand of them now, and their passing was a sight for sore eyes! The chiefs on horseback, in fine gold-laced coats and plumed helmets, and plaids flung on over their breastplates; their men following on foot, each man with his plaid loosely belted about him, his broadsword and round brass-studded targe; and the banners flying and the great war-pipes crying to battle . . . Only a few days before, some of the young callants must have been sitting demurely in St Andrews' lecture halls, getting a gentleman's education; others came from the forge or the fisher boats or the hunting; but you could see the fierce joy that was on all of them, to be out with their clans. Alisdair Gordon had told me who the chiefs were, as they came in over the past few days, and a good deal of what he told me I had forgotten, for there was too much to hold in my head, but not all; and so I knew the who and the wherefrom of some of those swinging by. Sir Alexander MacLean, leading four hundred men of the Isles; Glengarry with three hundred MacDonalds at his back; Clanranald, who was but sixteen, with two hundred more from the Isles and Moidart; young Stewart of Appin at the head of his father's clan. Then there was Lochiel himself with his tail of six hundred Cameron men, and old Alistair MacDonald of Glencoe with a hundred. There were the MacMartins, yellow-haired giants in plaids that glowed royally crimson and purple. Aye, and there was Coll of Keppoch and his MacDonalds in their green and scarlet, each with a sprig of heather in his bonnet, and their piper playing 'MacDonald's Salute', shameless as ever, and seeing no reason why Claverhouse should not greet them gladly.

Philip of Amryclose was fair drunk on it all. If ever you get to read his *Graemiad* (your Latin will have to be a deal better than it is now) you will know that for yourselves! I will not say that I was stone cold sober myself; but few of us were, that were young and had the hearts hot within us . . .

For close on three weeks we played hare and hounds with MacKay and the Government troops all across the southern Highlands, neither managing to bring the other to battle. MacKay with his reinforcements outnumbered us more than two to one, so that we could not afford to take him on in country of his own choosing. And he too had Highlanders with him by that time; followers of Argyll for the most part, with the knowledge of hill country in their bones, even though these were not their own hills. And indeed the game might have gone hard with us, even harder than it did, had it not been for messages, aye, and a few deserters returning to old loyalties, that reached us from the Scots Dragoons.

As it was, the game ended after a four-day hunt down Strathspey, when they reached the open lowlands of Strathbogie ahead of us, and were joined by yet more reinforcements; and there was nought to be done but to retreat in our turn, with failure sitting sour in our bellies, all the weary way back to Glen Roy, to pick up reinforcements ourselves, and wait for the long-promised men and supplies from the King of Ireland.

Lochiel greeted us warmly again, saying that while there was a stirk in Lochaber we were welcome to supper. And some of the chiefs and their tails that we had not been able to wait for in May had come trickling in. But with the waiting, they had begun to trickle away once more. You cannot hold the clansmen as you can regular troops. When there is fighting to be done, they are heroes; but when the fighting is over, their only thought, as I have said before, is to carry home their booty; and kept waiting, they grow bored and drift away home anyway, even with no booty to carry. That, or fall to raiding the country round, or start a wee bloody war between themselves. That had happened, too. And what with one thing and another, Claverhouse must have been sick at heart.

That I can only guess at, for he showed nothing; but I did once hear him say to Major Crawford that he would sooner carry a musket in a decent regiment than command such a rabble of rievers and cut-throats.

I do know that he was sick in body, whatever he was in heart and soul. Hard campaigning and bad food – and not enough of it, for often the best we had was a bannock or a handful of oatmeal in the day, and Claverhouse ate what his men ate – lack of sleep, for his nights were still spent on those everlasting letters that sought to win chieftain after chieftain for the King's cause; hardship and maybe a touch of dysentery had all taken their toll of him; and above all, now, the bitter loss of a victory over the King's enemies when it had been almost in his hands; and the waiting, the long-drawn waiting, for the help from Ireland that did not come.

And then at last it came; and that was the worst of all.

For the long-promised help was three hundred new-raised Irishmen, half-naked and all but unarmed, commanded by a Colonel Cannon in not much better state than themselves; and thirty-five barrels of powder and ball – Lady Jean had managed better than that by selling her jewels.

I saw the Irishmen march in. No, that is the wrong word; I saw them come stravaiging down into the glen, and they made even MacLean's wild islanders look like disciplined troops by comparison. I saw Dundee's face as he watched them in; that quiet, alert look of his that told nothing of what was going on behind it. Aye, and I saw his face later that evening, in the shieling where he had made his lodging-place; and him sitting at the rough table with his supper plate pushed aside – it was meat that night, too. He had taken to eating, or more often not eating, his evening meal by himself those past few nights, in order to have time for his letter-writing. Eh, those letters! I am thinking there cannot have been a chieftain in the Highlands with more than twenty men to his tail who did not receive a letter from the general of King James's forces in Scotland, before all was done!

I was busy at the small fire in the corner, brewing up an oatmeal brose with a dash of the raw heady Water of Life mixed into it, for sometimes when he could or would eat nothing else, I could get a few spoonfuls of that down him, which was better than nothing at all.

I mind the silence in the bothie; just the slow plop-plop-plop of the bubbles rising in the brose, and Caspar's soft contented breathing beside me – the wee dog was free of Claverhouse's quarters in Glen Roy as he had always been free of Dudhope – and the scratch of Claverhouse's quill moving steadily over the page.

The scratching fell silent. Sometimes sleep would come upon him in the midst of his writing, and he would let his head fall on to his left arm; only for a moment, and then wake again and go on writing through the night. I looked round, wondering if I could catch him between waking and taking up his pen again to give him the brose; but he was not asleep, just sitting staring into the shadows beyond the candle flame. It was still a luminous twilight outside, as it would be all through the short northern summer night until the sun rose again. But in the bothie with its small low-set windows, even with the door open, it was cave-dark, and I saw his face only by the light of the candle.

Old, it looked, and weary to the bone, and sick with a sickness that was of more than the body; and the eyes of him seemed to be looking out of it into shadows that were more than the crowding night-time dark in the corners.

Then footsteps came along the dirt track between the cottages of the clachan, and his face changed as life and resolution came back into it, and all that was not for other men's eyes was shut away.

Lochiel came stooping his tall head in through the doorway.

'More letters, *Iain Dhub*?' said he, sitting himself down on the creepy stool at the other side of the table. The Highlanders had begun to call him *Iain Dhub Nan Cath*, Black John of the Battles, though indeed they had shared little fighting with him as yet, only a few raids and those long desperate marches.

'More letters, for there is still the need for more,' Claverhouse said. 'But indeed I do not know how I should write them at all but for your help. At least, thanks to your gossiping tongue, I know how to write to each man, touching Glengarry in his pride and MacLoughlan in his ambition – aye, and his greed – and Glen Moidart in his loyalty . . .'

'And who, this time?' Lochiel glanced at the piece of paper half-covered with close writing. I saw the move-ment out of the tail of my eye, for I had turned my attention back to the brose, drawing it to the side of the fire, for Heaven alone knew, now, when I should have the chance to get it down him.

'Murray again,' Claverhouse said, 'there must be some way of getting through to Atholl's son, if I could but find it. The clan's sympathies are with our cause, and even Atholl himself, though he abandoned us after the Edinburgh Convention, remains carefully sitting on the fence, taking the waters at Bath for his unknown ill-ness, until the time for decision-making is safely over.

So why in God's name should his son go over to Orange William, lock, stock and barrel?' He pulled himself back from the quick rush of words. 'No, I am being unjust to Murray. To sit on the fence is the worst thing of all. At least he has his convictions – if I could but find some way to break them down . . .'

'John,' Lochiel said, 'you have had a wasted evening. One of my scouts has just come in – Murray is besieging Blair.'

'Blair? His own castle?' Claverhouse said, and I could hear the frown in his tone. For the moment, with sheer weariness, it seemed that his wits were not working.

'His own castle, his own folk who follow our cause as its garrison, and that staunch King's man, Patrick Stewart of Ballachin whom you put in to command them,' Lochiel said gently, filling in the blank in his tired mind. 'That was what I came to be telling you.'

There was a long thin moment of silence. And then I heard the sound of paper being torn across and across. And Claverhouse's voice said, 'What an upside down world we live in, that a man must needs lay siege to his own four walls.' And then I heard the scrape of his stool being thrust back and overturned as he crashed to his feet. And when I looked round, he was standing there, a man ready for action, with the sickness and weariness fallen from his shoulders, and his eyes bright and hard as sword-steel. 'Then it seems we march tomorrow.'

Lochiel had risen also, and they were facing each other across the table. 'What of Colonel Cannon and his kerns? We could be sparing a day or so to get them sorted out? And some of the chieftains who have promised have still not come in.'

216

'It would take more than one day to sort that lot out,' Claverhouse said with a snort of bitter laughter, 'and we cannot spare more than one. Lochiel, you know it. If MacKay should choose to march from Stirling now, he could be there before we could relieve the place; and standing as it does for a gateway between the Highlands and the Lowlands, Blair Castle must be still in our hands when the King comes.'

'*If* the King comes,' Lochiel said in that silken voice of his that seemed to come from the back of his throat; and they looked at each other across the candle. And I saw as though it hung between them, the thought of the pathetic rabble that had come in that day as the King's promised reinforcements.

'If the King comes,' Claverhouse almost whispered.

'This for your comfort,' Lochiel said at last. 'The prospect of fighting will do more than three regiments of well-trained reinforcements to unite the clans and make them forget old feuds.'

'That I know!' Claverhouse returned. 'That I know for my comfort, Lochiel.' He reached for his sword lying on the box bed, and then looked at me. 'Hugh, my compliments to Lieutenant Barclay, and ask him to find the rest of my officers and the chiefs, and request their presence at Glen House' (that was the house that Lochiel had lent him, and that he used for councils and the like) 'within half an hour.'

He was buckling on his sword as he spoke.

And I abandoned the brose I had been keeping with such care; I knew I could not get a sup of it into him that night; and I went to carry out the order, Caspar padding at my heels.

21

The Old Woman by The Ford

Next morning – it was the morning of Midsummer's Day – we marched out; still not much more than two thousand of us, for the desertions had more than cancelled out the Irish reinforcements; but with the promise of more clans that would gather to us at Blair. Our first day's march was to Badenoch to pick up a band of the MacPhersons, and there we bided one day, while two of our officers carried a last appeal to Murray. But they returned at evening on all but foundered horses, with news that ran through the camp like heath fire. Murray had refused to see them, and MacKay was at Perth with his army and pushing on to seize Blair Castle.

So – there was an end to waiting; and next day at first light we broke camp and marched from Cluny Castle with the handful of grey-tartaned MacPhersons that we had gained; over the pass of Druimuchdair and down the way that we had ridden on that swift raid on Perth two months ago.

Even at Midsummer Druimuchdair has no friendly air to it, and its gullies of grey granite are barren of life; but the hills beyond had woken from their winter bleakness, and the first flowerbuds were beading the heather, spilling here and there a faint shadow of smoky amethyst down some sheltered slope, and all down the south side of the pass, after we were over the saddle, the brown pools of the Garry shone through the hazels on their banks, beside the track we followed.

As we came down towards the foot of the pass, the land grew less wild, and here and there an outlying farmstead would come into view, sitting small and solitary, its peatstack beside the door, in some fold of the braeside, with the great cloud shadows drifting over.

Once we came to the place where a cattle-track dipped down from the north, to cross the river by a made ford. And on the far side, tucked in among the roots of overshadowing hazel and alder trees, looking as twisted and as rooted into the bank as themselves, an old woman in an earth-coloured gown knelt washing a pile of household clothes and linen.

I mind thinking it was late in the year for that; mostly the crofter women fling everything out-of-doors and deal with the bed-bugs and wash all things washable in May. I mind also noticing that there was something of a dark brownish-red colour among the grey pallor of the unbleached linen; a shawl, maybe; you could not see, in the cave of shadows under the alder branches.

She took no more notice of our passing than if we had not been there at all. And we marched on, and I thought no more of the thing, for the time being.

When the slopes of the glen at last fell behind us, and we came out into the open rolling country of the Atholl moors, the two scouts whom Dundee had sent ahead met us with the news that Murray, taking fright, had raised the siege of his own house and left Blair standing open to us. Nought was left of the besiegers save the traces of their camp, and the empty pasture lands from which they had had the forethought to drive off all the cattle when they left.

So we marched into Blair unopposed in the summer gloaming, to be met by another scout with word that

219

MacKay and his troops were making camp for the night at Pitlochry, ten miles or so south-east of us, beyond the pass at Killiecrankie.

It looked as though, one way or another, we should have a busy day tomorrow.

We posted pickets in the usual way, with outlying vedettes to the south and east, and pitched our camp in the broad in-pasture from which the cattle had been driven. It must have been about the place where the third Earl of Atholl built his splendid timber palace filled with flowers and rich hangings for the entertaining of the fifth King James when he came there hunting with the Papal Legate and the Italian Ambassador in his train; and as the guests departed, burned all to the ground behind them, as men today break their glasses after drinking the loyal toast.

Ours was a very different camp, but a loyal one, too.

We watered and fed and tended the horses as best we could, and set up the cavalry lines, all as we had done so many times before. As soon as the campfires were making ragged flowers of brightness through the summer dark, and the smell of cooking began to rise and spread from fire to fire; a good gipsy smell, for like all armies on the march we laid claim to anything furred or feathered that came our way, to say nothing of the odd stirk that the Highlanders brought in on a lucky day. We ate round our own fires, the Highland men for the most part according to clan or sept, and Claverhouse's Horse apart by our own horse lines; but after the food was gone the whole camp broke up, and went visiting as it often did, men drifting to and fro in search of friends at other fires, and the dark between the fires grew full of moving shadows. I mind the Gordons' piper stalking through them, found and lost and found again in the flame-light, stiff and fierce as a fighting cock, his pipes under his arm, and the music spieling out behind him like the coloured ribbons from the drones across his shoulder. *Isobel Gordon's Fancy* was the tune; and at most times men would have sprung up to dance to it, weary as they were, but that night the Highland camp was not just its usual self; there was an odd uneasiness in the air. Every man about the fires knew what tomorrow had in store, and that by next fire-lighting time he might be lying stiff and cold on the braeside with no fire to warm him ever again, but that was an old familiar knowledge, and I had never known the bright shadow of tomorrow's fighting to trouble the Highlanders before. Besides, that was a thing we all shared; this was something that hung about the clan fires, not around ours.

I felt it when I went up from the horse lines in search of Alisdair, saw it in men's eyes in the firelight, heard it behind their voices speaking in their own tongue. Caspar felt it too, and whimpered at my heels. As I checked among the Atholl men, looking about me, he stood up with his forepaws against my knee, and I felt that he was shaking, and stooped down to reassure him. His paws had hardened so much over the months that he could march moorland mile for moorland mile with us now and never get footsore; but when I took his forepaws in my hand, he picked one up awkwardly, and I saw by the light of the nearest fire that he had left blood in my palm. I rolled him over on his back to look, and found a fresh gash in one pad – a camp is a fine place for finding sharp things lying about. Alisdair would have to wait. And truth to tell, I was not sorry to leave the clan gatherings with their vague sense of trouble behind me. 'Come,' I said, 'cold water for that, my wounded sojer,' and scooped him up under my arm and made for the river.

Under the bank, a little spit of ground ran out into the current, and the light of the rising moon slanting under the low-hanging alder branches made a cobwebby paleness that was enough to see by. I squatted down with Caspar between my knees, and began to bathe his paw in the cold swift-running water. He was a good wee dog, and whimpered, but did not try to pull away, though it must have hurt him sore as I opened the cut between my thumbs to make sure that there was nothing left inside.

I was just about done when a shadow fell across me, and looking up, I saw a short squat figure blotted dark against the mingled light of moon and campfires. I could not see his face, but there could be but one such pair of bow legs in all the Highland army.

'Alisdair,' I said, 'I was coming seeking ye, by and by.'

'Ach well, 'tis I that am the honoured one,' said he, 'but I was seeing you coming down that way, and so I am come seeking you instead. What will be amiss with Skolawn, then?'

He always called Caspar by the name of Finn Mac-Cool's great hound of ancient legend, it being his idea of a joke.

'Naught but a cut paw that needed bathing,' I said, ''tis done now.' And as he scrambled down the bank I got up and we settled ourselves comfortably along the alder roots, with the wee dog at our feet.

For a while we sat in companionable silence, the sounds of the camp behind us, and in front of the lapping of the Garry water under the bank and the occasional plop of a rising trout. But Alisdair, though he sat so still, his elbows on his knees and his chin in his hands, was not at ease, but had the same odd smell of trouble about him that I had caught among the Highland fires. Whatever it was, it began reaching out from him to me . . .

'What's amiss, Alisdair?' I asked at last.

'What should be amiss?'

'I'd not be knowing. But something is. 'Tis up there –' I jerked my head back towards the camp. 'And 'tis on you, my mannie.'

'Ye've the keen nose, I'm thinking,' said he, 'ye should ha' been a Hielan' man.' And then after a few moments, almost as though he spoke against his will, 'Did ye see anything – any *one*, by the cattle ford an hour's march up-river, as we came by?'

'An old woman doing her household wash,' said I, when I had had a moment to remember.

He did not look round, and I only saw the side half of his face blotted dark against the white water. 'Aye, and you a Lowlander, ye would not be knowing.'

'Knowing what?' I said.

'The Woman of the Sidh – the Washer by the Ford.'

But I would be knowing; I who had listened to the wild tales of Philip of Amryclose. I had forgotten, but it came back to me all too clearly . . . The Washer by the Ford, and she was washing the blood-stained linen, who comes before the death of chiefs and heroes – aye, before the death of Cuchulain himself . . .

'Och, away! Dinna be sae daft,' said I, as much to myself as to Alisdair. 'She was real enough; just an old hen-wife a wee thing late with her spring washing. Aye, she was real enough.'

'She seemed real enough,' he said, 'she always does.' And I wished that I had not suddenly remembered the something dark-reddish brown among the bundle of linen; the shawl or whatever it was . . .

At first light, with the camp just beginning to stir, Claverhouse called a council of war.

In after years, I heard from this man and that what passed in the Great Hall of Blair Castle that dawn. How Dundee put the question to his chiefs and captains, should they wait for the rest of the clan muster to come in, which would likely be about three days, or go forward at once, with what we had, to meet MacKay as he came out from the Killiecrankie pass. All the regular officers, and the leaders who had been trained to command regular and Lowland troops, were for waiting. 'Wait,' said they, the hardheaded and sensible men. 'We have gained the castle and can hold it until the muster is complete. To meet MacKay with the force that we have now, half-starved and dead-weary from forced marching, would be madness.' Aye, it was good sense; but when did sense ever have a meaning for the Highland men, the likes of Keppoch? Glengarry spoke out for them, 'What matters an empty belly and a forced march to the men of the clans?'

And Dunfermline followed at his back. 'If we bide here until MacKay attacks, we shall lose the advantage of attacking first, and risk being pinned down here. And the men of the clans do not fight their best behind walls.'

And that was true as well, and nearly all the chiefs spoke up with the same voice.

But the final decision of course was for Dundee, and they sat about the table and looked to him to make it.

That must have been a stark moment for Dundee! Having followed him as I had, I'm thinking the man's own choice would lie with the Highlanders, but any man trying to drive two horses not broken to run as a pair in the same harness would know the difficulties he faced.

Och well, in the end he found a way out of the tangle; aye, and paid his debt of friendship to Sir Ewan Cameron at the same time.

'So far, Lochiel has spoken no word on the matter,' he said, 'and his experience is greater than any of ours, so much so that he cannot fail in this to make a right judgement; therefore his judgement shall be mine. Choose, Lochiel.'

And Lochiel made gracefully light of his experience of 'little sallies and skirmishes'. 'But,' said he, 'since you ask for my word, it is that we fight now. I know the Highland heart. Delay, and the clansmen will grow uneasy, remembering that the odds are more than two to one against them. But take them forward to the attack now, hungry and tired as they are, but with their blood still hot within them, and they'll gain you a victory that shall ring round Scotland, and fetch out every man who ever held a sword to King James's cause.'

And so the thing was settled, and the decision to fight that day was made. But there was one more thing, and Lochiel put the words to it. It was the opinion of the council that Viscount Dundee, on whom depended not only the fate of the army but the fate of the King and of Scotland, should not engage personally in the coming battle, but direct matters from some vantage point, as was at most times the custom.

They must have known that it was hopeless; such customs were not for Claverhouse, nor ever had been.

He thanked them for their care, both for him and the cause, admitted that indeed his death might be some loss to them. But what power would he ever have over the clans again, if he kept out of this battle? 'Give me this one *Shear Darg*, this one Harvesting-day for the King. One chance to show to the clansmen that I can hazard my own hide in King James's service as freely as the least of them, and I give you my word that I will follow the more common custom hereafter, for so long as I have the honour to command you.'

And they knew that he would not yield.

Nothing of this was known to us at the time of course; but we felt the sense of waiting that met us as we roused to the green soft gloaming of the summer dawn with the smell of thunder in the air. We – the General's troop, that is, or His Majesty's Regiment of Horse, whichever you like to call us (och, I know fine a troop is not a regiment, but what was left of one, and a proud one, and we thought of ourselves by the old name) – were seeing to the horses, ready for whatever the day might bring, when we heard the cheering from the castle; and Lochiel's pipe came swaggering down through the gate, playing some wild crying *pibroch* that calls out the claymores. Word was running through the camp from fire to fire before ever the official orders came and I mind an enormous Highlander standing with legs apart waving a flask of the Water of Life that he had got from somewhere, and bellowing challenges to come and fight him personally or run while there was still time, until he stepped backwards into the watch-fire behind him and had to be hauled out by his friends and the sparks beaten from his plaid.

And in the ready-making for battle the old hen-wife washing by the ford was quite forgotten.

I did not see Alisdair again that morning. I have always been sorry for that, for I never saw him after.

22

Dark Victory

The cheering died into the rattaplan-rattaplan of the drums and the quick clear notes of the bugles, and the wild crying of the pipes, and all the ordered chaos that is an army making ready for the march with fighting at the end of it. My own last piece of ready-making was to leave Caspar firmly shut up and in charge of the small garrison remaining at Blair.

And so, with our morning issue of oaten bannock and strong cheese barely eaten, we marched out and headed for Killiecrankie – not by the made track, och no; the road ahead and the road behind was MacKay's way; we took to the hills as we had always done, as we had done at Deeside, three long months ago. We crossed the Tilt and came over the high moors. That made a six-mile march of it instead of the four it would have been by road; but we had the time for it, so long as we met MacKay in the broad valley where the pass opens out, and he looking up the made road for us. At the Lude Burn Dundee called a brief halt to rest and water the horses – it was past midday – and of all the times and times and times that we had done the same thing, I mind that one time; slipping from Jock's back and leading him down the bank, and the water riffling about his muzzle as he drank. It was a hazy blue day, and the water was blue where it ran smooth enough to reflect the sky; peat-brown under the shadows of the bank. Most of all I mind the cold soft wetness of his muzzle when he turned his head to slobber on my shoulder.

We were still at it when one of the scouts that Dundee had sent on ahead came dropping down the braeside like a shadow, with word that MacKay was halfway through the pass; and we remounted as the Highlanders scrambled to their feet, and pushed on. We were going to meet MacKay and have our reckoning with him at last!

As we came down the final slope towards the Clune Burn, another scout came in with word that the Government army was just through the pass and debouching into the valley; and General MacKay with a small escort was riding forward to see was there any sign of us yet on the road from Blair.

'We will give him something to be looking at, though not on the road from Blair,' Dundee said, and sent forward a handful of Atholl Foresters to show themselves on the forward slopes of the ridge that we were making for, to catch the enemy's interest and draw them in the right direction.

Then we gained the true ridge ourselves – a long spur of Creag Eileich, it was – and began to form our battle line.

Even I could see how the pattern was going to work. From the long crest where we were taking up our position the hillside fell away, then levelled gently to a lower ridge about half a mile away, before it fell steeply to the Garry and the Blair road; and I had marched that way often enough to know that from the road as one came out from the Killiecrankie pass, it looked as though the lower ridge was the crest of the valley wall to the right, the higher ridge on which we were now taking station being out of sight behind it. (In the same way of course it hid the valley floor from us, but that was no great matter.) It would look like that to

228

MacKay; shame on him with his Highland name and he not knowing his own country! And therefore it must seem to him that the thing he had to do was to get his troops up to that ridge before we could gain it, and outnumbering us as he did by more than two to one, his troubles were as good as over.

And all the while, us sitting along the higher ridge and waiting for him.

We did not have long to wait before MacKay's standards topped the lower ridge, and then the heads of the cavalry and then the foot. He must have ordered Right Wheel, at sight of our Atholl men, and brought them straight up through the steep birch woods in the same order in which they had come out from the defile. And a sair shock it must have been to him to find that further ridge, and us sitting on it waiting for him.

We watched them check, and work out some kind of battle-line. The ridge was too long for the number of Government troops, and he must take care of his flanks, from the place where it sank away into marshy ground on his left to the place where it ran up into the steep wooded slopes of Creag Eileich on his right; and by the time he had done that, his regiments were only three ranks deep, strung thin and ragged as a piece of fraying rope.

That meant we must lengthen our own line, too, or risk having our flanks rolled up when it came to fighting. But for us the situation was different. We knew, all of us, as well as Dundee himself, that MacKay could not attack uphill, and therefore, when the moment came, it would be for us to make the charge. And so he lengthened our line, not by drawing it out thin, but by moving the clans apart, so that there were wide gaps between. In a charge, the gaps would cease to matter.

The run of our battle line is in my mind yet, as though we had formed it yesterday; the clan names singing in my head like an old song. On our far right stood the MacLeans under Sir John MacLean of Duart; then Colonel Cannon with his wild Irish, then the MacDonalds, with Clanranald and Glengarry and then us, Claverhouse's Horse, with the royal standard in our midst; us that had ridden into Ayrshire and Galloway behind him, and been the General's troop of His Majesty's Regiment of Horse; us that had followed him down to London to save King James, and ridden with him north again when the King failed us, because we were still Claverhouse's men to follow where he led. And on our left stood Lochiel and his Camerons; and beyond them again the MacDonalds of Sleet, and Keppoch with his cattle-rievers, and away on the far left, where the ridge ended in the up-thrust of Creag Eileich, a mixed battalion of MacLeans and Stewarts and MacNeills.

And there we waited; for it was then that the waiting really began.

Partly it was the usual custom whereby when two armies are drawn up ready for battle, they stand and stare each other in the face a while to get each other's measure as you might say, like two dogs walking stiff-legged round each other before they fly at each other's throats. Partly it was because MacKay, in his bad position, could not be the first one to move, while we in our better position were fronting west and the sun getting low; and Dundee had, I am thinking, no mind to fight with the dazzle of the sunset full in our faces. At that time of year in the northern hills there would be an hour of fighting time left after the sun was down, and we should not be needing more . . .

I mind that waiting; the first faint coolth of the evening stealing ahead of the long shadows after the heavy heat of the day; and the midge clouds dancing in the sunlight, making the horses stamp and fidget. The first heather just waking into flower; and the bees booming among the first of the little papery bells. And in front of us MacKay's troops strung along the lower ridge, black as a row of corbies, with the light behind them; and the sun westering slowly, slowly towards the distant sugar-loaf crest of Schiehallion.

Then the usual long-range firing began. Just a fitful spattering of musketry from MacKay's troops, and an occasional shot from his artillery – he had three small field pieces. It did little damage at that range, which was as well, for we could make little reply, short of ball and powder as we were. But it galled us, none the less, especially the field pieces, which to judge from the yells from the Camerons, the Highlanders thought unfair.

They began to grow as fidgety as the horses, straining like hounds in leash, and shouting to Dundee as he rode with a handful of officers up and down the line, 'Give us the word, *Iain Dhub*! Give us the word!'

But Dundee, with a buff coat under his breastplate like the rest of us, in place of his general's gold and scarlet (his one concession to the council's fear for his safety that day), did not give the word, did not slip the leash, while the sun was still above Schiehallion, dazzling into our eyes. I doubt any other man could have held them – held *us*, for the restiveness of the Highlanders was setting the blood jumping in our own veins also. And the enemy musketry was getting heavier. MacKay had plenty of powder and ball, aye, and twelve hundred baggage beasts, so I have heard, waiting below in the cornfields at the mouth of the pass.

The great bowl of the hills before us was filling with shadows; the rim of the sun in a ragged blaze of clouds that had gathered seemingly out of a clear sky was touching the high shoulder of Schiehallion, slipping behind it; and all the mountains westward standing up suddenly bloomed with sloe-dark shadows, while the last light still burned upon the hillside. For a moment, as though in a kind of breath-drawing before the next thing, MacKay's musketry slackened – the field pieces had fallen silent a while since, their carriages having collapsed beneath them – and in the silence the larks were singing overhead.

I was with Dundee by that time, sitting Jock close behind him – for was I not the General's galloper? – and for the moment almost knee to knee with Amryclose. The folds of the standard, caught by a breath of evening wind, flowed out across my face so that for a breath of time the Lion of Scotland was turned to crimson flame by the last of the sun shining through it; and when it fell back towards its shaft, the sun was half down, and turned to a golden demi-disc that you could look in the face without dazzle.

Claverhouse drew his sword, and the light of the West ran along the blade like bright water as he brought it up in the signal to charge.

'Forward in the King's name! God be with the right!'

The cheering ran along the line from the MacLeans at one end into the shadow of Creag Eileich at the other, and was lost in the bright yelping of the bugle and the sudden wild crying of the pipes that seemed to leap up from the heather as the crying of the whaups leaps skyward.

And the line moved forward.

It was slow at first, so slow that as I drew my pistol I

had a moment for a sideways glance through helmets and horses' ears along the spread of our battle-line. The clansmen were loping forward, flinging off their plaids as they came – the Highland men like best to go into battle naked, or at the most in nothing but their saffron shirts – their muskets at the ready. The enemy musket fire ploughed into them, and from the first men began to fall; but their fellows leapt over them and held on at that purposeful lope. Dundee had ordered that no man was to fire until a man of MacKay's was 'at the end of his barrel' and they carried out his order to the death. Then as the slope levelled out the pace grew quicker, gathering speed and momentum as a wave does before it breaks. The air was full of the slogans and war-cries of the clans. Away to the left, above our hoof-beats and the roar of the descending charge, I could make out the baying of Lochiel's men, 'Ye dogs of dogs, ye dogs of the breed, come here and eat flesh . . . ' And then all was drowned in the screaming of the pipes.

Ahead of us the Government battle-line, half lost in a murk of powder smoke, seemed rushing towards us, as I heeled Jock to a swifter pace. Beside me, somebody pitched from the saddle, but I had no time now to even wonder who it was. We were going full gallop now; at our head Dundee rose in his stirrups, sword up to sweep us forward. I heard his voice, the clarion voice that could carry from end to end of a battlefield, 'Follow me! Follow on! Into them, lads – charge home!'

Something like a hot iron seared my bridle arm just above the elbow, but at the time I scarcely felt it. For the first and only time in my life, maybe because it was the only time in my life that ever I was part of a Highland charge, the smell of blood came into the back of my nose, and the terrible red mist of battle-drunkenness was upon me. Most other times I have just been cold afraid.

We were into them; and half blind with the drifting powder smoke, I fired my pistol into a yelling face. All along the line rolled and ricocheted the sudden deafening crackle of fresh musketry as the Highlanders fired their one point-blank volley, then flung aside their muskets and betook them to sword and dirk. The front rank of MacKay's force was torn to red rags in that moment. Only for a few moments more, a man here and there stood struggling frenziedly to plug his bayonet into the muzzle of his discharged musket. Ahead of me, half lost in the murk, Dundee still rode with upswept sword, and we charged after him. My hand was just moving of its own accord for my second pistol when Jock screamed and reared up under me, then plunged forward like a mad thing, answering neither bit nor hand nor voice. I had one instant of knowing that we were going through the ranks of MacKay's Lowlanders like a knife through cheese, and then we were over the ridge, sky and ground changed places as Jock pitched down, going forward over his own neck, and I was flung through the air.

I must have hit my head in falling, or maybe Jock had caught me with a hoof, for the next thing I knew the fiery sunset clouds were gone, and I was lying on my back looking up into a quiet night sky made milky by a faint thunder-wrack that blotted out the stars. Around me a little night wind came hushing up through the heather, bringing with it from the valley below the terrible sound of an army fighting for its life, fighting even for the right to run; and all about me were the ugly sounds of a spent battlefield, where most of the sprawled shapes are dead, but not all.

I rolled over on to my face, and felt the rough springy harshness of the heather under me, and dragged myself up on to my knees. My head ached, a leaden thumping, but that was all. Jock lay close by, and I crawled across to him. He was trying to get up. God knows how long he had been trying; with his belly ripped up and his guts spilled out of him in a stinking bloody pile among the heather.

I mind thinking dully that somebody must have got their bayonet fixed in time.

By Heaven's Grace he had fallen on his right side, so that the left holster with my unfired pistol in it was uppermost and I did not need to leave him longer in his agony. I pulled out the pistol. I rubbed and fondled his sweating neck for the last time, talking to him – I do not know what I said. I put the muzzle to his forehead and pulled the trigger; and wished that we had not got him out of that boghole three months ago.

Then – training is a fine thing – I undid his girth, my hand slipping on the blood and filth as I freed the buckle, and pulled off his saddle, then his headgear, and bundled the lot on to my shoulder, and began to stumble back up the slope.

On the very lip of the lower ridge a group of men, one of them holding a makeshift torch, stood looking down at something – someone – lying in their midst.

The fitful light ran and flickered on the gold and crimson of the royal standard as it stirred in the night wind, and on the edge of the group someone was holding the bridle of a tall sorrel horse; and I began to know what I would see when I came up with them. But somehow it did not seem real.

Dunfermline was there, Philip of Amryclose holding the standard; Coll MacDonald of Keppoch, a few more, troopers and clansmen. I did not see who, I was looking down also, at Claverhouse, lying with his head on Tam Johnston's knee.

They had unstrapped his breastplate and done what they could for him, but there was little enough that could be done. They had torn up a dead Highlander's shirt and bound it tightly round him to staunch the bleeding, but all along under his ribs the bright scarlet stain was spreading through. I remembered my last sight of him, sword arm up to cheer us on. Just under the raised ridge of his breastplate the bullet must have taken him.

Someone began to greet. Maybe it was me; I am not sure; but I seemed too numb for greeting.

Dundee opened his eyes and looked up at us that stood about him, frowning as though he found it hard to see our faces. 'How goes the fight?' he asked, quite clear, though with not enough breath for the asking.

From far down the valley, growing fainter as it drove on into the pass, we could still hear the sounds of the pursuit; and after a moment Dunfermline answered him, 'It goes well for the King – but I am grieved for your lordship.'

A quietness came over Dundee's face. 'It is the less matter for me if – the day goes well for – the King,' he said.

The last few words we could scarcely hear.

Then a little blood came out of his mouth, and his head rolled sideways on Tam Johnston's knee.

Tam wiped the blood from his lips, as gently as any lassie could have done; and as gently laid him down.

There was a long, long stillness. Even the wind seemed to die away into the heather and the thin moorland grasses. It was Keppoch of all men, 'Coll of the

Cows' as Claverhouse had called him, who broke it, wiping his eyes and nose on the red-haired back of his hand. '*Iain Dhub Nan Cath*,' he said, 'Black John of the Battles; we'll not be following his like again; and there's something of ourselves that he's taken with him, the night.'

23

Lament for Iain Dhub

Little by little the sounds of the pursuit died into the night, and the Highlanders came trickling back, to be met by the sorest news that ever met men returning from battle with the hot sweet taste of victory in their mouths. Strangers there were in the torchlight, too; chiefs of the clans that had come in to the muster since we left Blair, and followed on, too late to draw sword in the battle.

Below on the slope, where the dead lay tumbled among the birken trees, men were using their broadswords for another purpose, hacking down saplings and whippy branches to make a rough litter for carrying Claverhouse back to Blair. The leaves were still on the branches; small bright spangles of leaves in the torchlight when they set it down and lifted him on to it. They had buckled on his breastplate again by then, to cover the hole in his side and make all decent, and folded a couple of plaids about him, laying the folds back from his face to leave it bare.

Six of us, of his own troop, lifted him on our shoulders, and the rest followed, leading our horses with their own. The Highlanders followed after, each clan or sept behind their chief, and Lochiel's piper stalked ahead, playing as we went, 'Lochaber no more – Lochaber no more . . .'

And so we set out to carry himself back to Blair; and the soft gusts through the heather bringing the first fine spattering of rain.

It was grey dawn with the whaups calling and the soft swathes of rain hushing in from the West when we came into the town. Runners had carried the news ahead, and the folk had turned out, townsfolk and garrison with spluttering torches that showed murky red as flame does when the daylight is coming. There was a sorrowful murmuring of voices, and the low keening of women, and always ahead of us, the crying of the pipes 'Lochaber no more . . . Lochaber no more . . . ' until they ceased under the dripping yew trees at the door of the little kirk beyond the castle gates. St Bride's, they call it.

The door stood open, waiting for us, letting out a glim of candlelight. And we carried him in and set the litter down before the altar, close behind the gash of darkness where the flagstones had already been raised and set aside, waiting too.

It was only when we set the litter down that I felt the hurt of my left arm, or at least that I became aware of it. And I looked down and saw the rent in the sleeve of my buff coat, and the dark stain about it, and felt my hand sticky and stiff, web-fingered with blood. But the bleeding seemed to have stopped; and that seemed important because I did not want to foul the kirk floor – always wipe your muddy boots on the house-place threshold, never bleed on a kirk floor. Did I not say that training was a wonderful thing?

They set candles at his head and feet; it was dark in the kirk; and the flames stirred in the soft wet gusts of air from the open doorway so that it seemed his face moved and he was on the point of waking. But it was only the stirring of the candle flames. We stood our guard round him, the men of his own troop. And the rain spattered against the windows and hushed among the branches of the yew trees outside; and other men came in, the chiefs and their clansmen, as many as the narrow walls would hold, while the rest I could hear gathering outside.

Presently, men came in carrying a hurriedly made coffin-kist, and set it by in the shadows; and then the minister in his black gown with an open book in his hands took up his place, and the service began; the unfamiliar burial service of the Episcopalian kirk, 'Man that is born of woman hath but a short time to live . . . He cometh up and is cut down like a flower; he fleeth as it were a shadow . . .'

And the windows darkened to a new squall and the wind drove the rain whispering against the glass.

Four chiefs, Lochiel and Glengarry, Keppoch and young Clanranald lifted him into the kist. We had carried him back from Killiecrankie, but he was theirs too, and the clans must be allowed some part in him. But it was I that drew the fold of the plaid across his face. It was of the ancient MacDonald tartan, the colour of the bell heather that he would not see in full flower that year, nor any year.

The armourers hammered home the nails, and the ropes were slung into place, and we lowered him into his grave.

And when the last solemn prayers were said and the last responses spoken and the kirk was silent of men's voices, and the flagstones laid back over the dark hole that had gaped like a wound in the floor, Philip of Amryclose, who had stood unmoving all that while, gave the royal standard into the hands of Lieutenant Barclay and turned to Lochiel's piper, holding out his hand.

'By your courtesy,' he said, 'I have that within me that must be given voice, and my own pipes are far away.'

I saw the other hesitate an instant. It is a great thing for a piper to lend his pipes to another man. Then with a deep and splendid courtesy, he set them in Amryclose's hands.

And Amryclose stepped forward to the place where the crowbars had left a few scratches on the stones. There he stood a while as though deep in thought; no, as though listening to something that none of us could hear, then he settled the bag under his arm and the blow-tube in his mouth, and began to inflate it. And the narrow kirk filled with the deep strong voice of the bass and tenor drones as the great warpipe seemed to wake; and then the tune-voice of the chanter leapt up from under his moving fingers as he began to play.

He played slowly at first, a little uncertainly, feeling his way as though he were listening still and echoing what he heard. Then he grew more sure, finding his theme and then beginning to develop the variations that grew from it as the flower grows from the branch or spindrift from the breaking wave. For it was no mere gathering or marching tune he played; it was the true *Piobairaechd*, the *Ceol Mor*, the Great Music, wild and stately and fit to tear the heart out of the breast with its swoops and swirls of sound that rose and filled the kirk with its lament for *Iain Dhub Nan Cath*.

I had never heard Amryclose play like that before.

But I knew the theme. And as I listened the hair rose on the back of my neck, and I was back in Glenogilvie on Midsummer's Eve, among the elder trees by the burn; and Darklis's voice in my ears, 'I have had the oddest tune running in my head ever since I came here . . .'

241

24

The Black Tents of the Tinkler Kind

We had lost a third of our men, and one of them was Alisdair Gordon. I had only known him three months, but I missed him sore. Even in the midst of my grief for Claverhouse I missed him sore. But of MacKay's troops, only seven hundred got back to Stirling with him, and his stores and equipment and ammunition were all left in our hands.

But we had lost Dundee, and there was no one to make proper use of them. Colonel Cannon, being the most senior officer left to us, took over the command; but within days the clan chiefs were falling out among themselves, old feuds flaring up again. Lochiel and MacDonald of Sleet were on their way home again with their followers before ever we marched from Blair. It was not Cannon's fault I daresay; no Lowlander could ever handle the Highland men save Dundee, and maybe Montrose before him.

Aye, we had had our victory for King James, but to build on it was one man's task. It is always one man's task. And the one man was gone from us.

The wound in my arm was only a deep gash that had barely nicked the bone. The Blair surgeon probed it for splinters and bound it tight to stop the bleeding that the probe had started up again; and when in a few days we marched out, I was judged fit to leave with the troop; what was left of it. I had a remount between my knees, a rawboned brute with a mouth of solid brass and the manners of a Leith fishwife; and Caspar was with me still – the one good thing in a world that seemed very driech and drear.

I am not sure to this day where we were heading. MacKay was still at Stirling, frenziedly gathering fresh troops, and maybe it was against him that we marched. But I was not over clear about anything then, what with the fiery throbbing of my arm, which did not seem to be doing just what it should under the stained and grimy bandages, and the kind of buzzing haze that I had in my head.

And I am not at all clear, and never have been, as to how I came to lose the foraging party that I was out with next day. There was a sudden mist; the kind that seems to come just smoking up out of the ground, and that did not help. One moment the others were within sight and sound, and the next, they were gone . . .

The thing to do would be to get back to the main force, I thought; but with no sight of the sky or the surrounding country, my sense of direction was lost to me; and there was no coolness in the mist, no slaking for the thirst that had begun to burn me up.

I reined in my horse and sat listening, hoping for some sound that would give me my direction, maybe even a voice or a whinny or the jink of a bridle bit from the foraging party. I tried to shout in case they were within hearing, but my hot throat would only produce a kind of croak, and no answer came back; only a bird calling somewhere in the mist. But as I strained my ears to listen, I thought at last I caught the chime of water over a stony bed. There must be a burn close by; a guide down off the high moors – cold clear water to drink!

But mist plays strange tricks with sound; the burn was way further off than I had thought, and the sound drew no nearer until when I found it at last I all but rode into it. And there it was, peat-brown and cool and bright, calling to the thirst in me, I slid to the ground, and holding to my horse's bridle, scrambled down the bank, and went full length with my face in it, Caspar crouching beside me. My hat went bobbing away downstream, but I cared nothing for that. I cupped my hands and drank and drank, and dashed the blessed coldness of the water over my head and neck.

And in that instant a jack-snipe got up from the long burnside grass and came zigzagging along the bank almost under the horse's nose.

The brute shied violently, squealing between fear and temper, and whipped free his bridle, which was lying carelessly looped over my wrist – it was the wrist of my sound arm at that, so I have no excuse – and bolted off into the mist.

I scrambled to my feet and started after him, hoping that when his panic died he would come to a halt. But the dull pounding of his hooves died into the distance, and he was gone as though the mist had swallowed him or the Hollow Hills opened to let him through, and my pistols and food wallet with him.

I was alone, save for Caspar, and lost and with a fog inside my head to match the fog that swathed the moors around me. And by the time I had given up hope of finding my horse again, I had lost the sound of the burn.

We passed that night in the lee of a peat hag, Caspar huddled in the crook of my sound arm, and next morning wandered on again. Maybe we went in circles at times, I would not be knowing. The mist had cleared from the hills, but not from my head, so that all places and all skylines looked strange, and my clemmed belly did nothing to help. Caspar could have hunted for himself, he had learned the way of it in the past months, but he would not leave me, and stuck as close to my heels as my own shadow. Sometimes, more often as the day went by, I pitched over a hummock or a heather snarl, and lay where I fell for a while before dragging myself up and pushing on again. There seemed nothing to keep going for, anyway; but my body kept going, as a body does that does not want to die, even when its owner does not care much either way. And on the edge of the gloaming, I realised that I had left the open moors and was among trees.

And not long after that, at least I think it was not long, I saw through the crowding trunks of birch and hazel the glimmer of firelight. A vague idea gathered itself in my mind that I had found the camp. I lurched on towards the ruddy flicker, and began to catch the smell of food cooking. Dogs were barking, but there were often dogs about the camp. I stumbled out from among the trees into the firelit clearing, and saw a couple of dogs straining at the ends of the bits of rope that tied them to the wheels of covered carts, a few tethered ponies, the black domes of tents. I was in a Tinkler encampment.

I took another step or two, and my legs gave under me, as figures leapt up from beside the fire and came running.

I was heaved over on to my back, and they were bending above me. Caspar sprang valiantly to my defence, and I heard his warning snarl break into a string of agonised yelps as somebody kicked him aside. I tried to shout at them to leave my dog alone, but my tongue seemed made of wood. Ruthless hands were on me, turning out my pockets – it was little enough they

245

would find there except an empty purse and a pewter tinder-box – dragging my sword belt over my head. 'There's a good bit of steel there!' someone said; someone else was tearing my shirt open. Everything seemed swimming away from me, but I made a last desperate effort to protect Darklis's silver pin with the amethyst flower-sparks that I wore fastened inside it.

And there was a kind of check in time. 'Yon'll fetch a bonnie penny,' a boy's voice said.

And an older voice that seemed to have some authority over the others said, 'Dinna be more of a gap-wit than ye were when your mother spawned ye! We'd bet get word tae Captain Faa, I'm thinking.'

And a woman's voice cut in, 'And meanwhile let ye get him up to the vardo; I'll see to him. An' have a care tae that arm; canna ye see he's wounded?'

The next thing I knew was lantern light, and a feeling of enclosed space all round me, and a close warm smell of an animal's lair; and a man with agate eyes set in a face of gilded leather bending over me with a knife in his hand. I struggled to fend him off, but the searing pain in my arm held me back, and the man said in a soft sing-song voice, "Twould have been easier had he stayed out of his body a while longer,' and then 'A-a-ah now, that will let the evil humours out of the wound.'

And I went out into the blackness again.

For a long time I was lost in the blackness; a blackness that was suffocating and hot; and swirling with dreams. One above all others: again and again the old dream came back on me, and there, out of the dark, the drummer laddie would be staring up at me with that terrible third eye in the middle of his forehead. Once I seemed to wake from that dream, to see other eyes looking down at me; two, not three, yellow as the sun-shot eyes of a fish-eagle. I was sure that I had seen them before, but almost at once I lost them again, sinking back into the tangled swirl of dreams and darkness.

Once, maybe twice. I was aware of the world moving under me, jolting and creaking. I suppose that the Tinkler folk were moving camp. And then, little by little, the darkness lightened, and the tangle of dreams began to let me go. I was aware of feeling cool, which struck me as being interesting and unusual, I had been hot so long. There were dim memories in the back of my mind, of the taste of strange herb drinks; of constantly pushing down the animal-smelling rug that was spread over me, and somebody pulling it up again as often as I pushed it down. I began to be aware of light shining through a hole in the tilt above me, and sounds of life going on in the world outside my small dark shelter, voices and the barking of dogs and the stamp of ponies; the scent of bruised woodruff and watermint that I was lying on, sometimes a figure bending over me, pouring broth into me, doing things to my arm. Above all, Caspar lying pressed against my flank, and the silver pin still safe inside the breast of my filthy shirt when I fumbled up a hand to feel for it. The heat and throbbing had gone from my arm; but I remembered quite clearly that I had been wounded in it. I remembered the battle, and the bees booming in the young heather while we waited for the onset. I remembered that Dundee was dead, and Alisdair, and old Jock; but it all seemed a long way off and a long time ago. And I had an odd feeling that so long as I did not move, it would not wake and become real and hurt me more than I could bear. So I did not move. Even when I was strong enough to crawl out of the straw with its mingling of watermint, and sit with the tattered rug wrapped about me and my

247

legs dangling over the back of the tilt cart, I took care not to move deep inside myself, not to wake up, not to ask for news.

I do not know how long it lasted, the kind of half state that I was in. But a morning came when I woke to find the life running through me again, and hurting – hurting. When I was a wee lad I used to wonder whether it hurt the sallows to wake up in the springtime, that they flushed so darkly red when the sap rose in them . . .

The camp was already astir, the morning stew cooking, and the women making ready their baskets of clothes-pegs and laces to take into the nearest village, wherever that might be, the men busy with the tools of the tinklers' craft or whistling their dogs to heel and setting off after the evening meal.

I slid down from the cart without waiting for anyone to come as they had done before to help me, and stood clinging to the side of the tilt to save myself from landing in a heap. And when I had more or less found my balance, whistled Caspar down after me, and set out in the general direction of the fire. My legs were like withies and the ground swam a little under me, and the grief was rising in me; but the foremost thing in my mind was that I must find out how to get back to the troop.

The folk gathered about the fire were talking together in the strange tongue that they used among themselves – I suppose it was a mixture of Lowland Scots with the Romany, for I could understand after a fashion much of what they said. But they stopped when they saw me, and a tall woman whose face and hands I knew, for they seemed to have been part of my sickness, swept two bairns and a lurcher bitch out of the way to make room for me. 'Come,' she said, 'eat'.

I sat down in the cleared space, because sitting was easier than standing just then. But it was not food that I had come for. 'My coat,' I said, 'I'm wanting my coat an' my breeks an' my boots; I must be away back to the General's troop.'

They looked at me, neither friendly nor unfriendly.

But I thought the woman looked sorry. 'Not yet,' she said. 'Let ye wait a few days until ye can walk three paces wi'out falling over your own feet.'

And a man looked up from the kettle he was mending and said, 'And e'en then, ye'd best not to stravaigling around the country in a coat the like o' that one, ma mannie.'

And a second woman, much older than the first, took her pipe from her mouth and leaned forward to lay a narrow brown claw on my knee, and said in a voice of velvet, 'Laddie, there's nae general, and there's nae general's troop to be away back to.'

The grief that I knew was bad enough; the threat of more to come was more than I could bear, and I flung her hand off my knee as though it was something loathsome, and cried out on her, 'What d'ye mean, ye old hag? We won! The General died for it, but we had the victory!'

They told me the truth of the matter kindly enough. Indeed I think there was something of sorrow on them also, for though they cared as little for King James as they did for Orange William, they had a certain caring for Dundee – had the Tinklers not acted as our scouts before now? – and felt it a sorry thing that his death should have been all for nothing.

They told me how at first there had been panic in Edinburgh, the Government knowing of the Loyalist victory, but not that Dundee was dead; and how appeals for help were sent post-haste to London, for the rebels were masters of all beyond the Forth, and if Stirling fell would be masters of all Scotland. And how, when Dundee's death was known, they had taken heart again, making little of MacKay's defeat, since the man who had defeated him was gone.

They told me how MacKay, taking heart also, had brought his freshly gathered troops up to Dunkeld, and Colonel Cannon with the disheartened remains of our own troops (the sorry crumbling, that I had seen the beginning of, had gone on since) had found them barring his way across the Tay. How there had been a battle, and the new Orange regiment had stood its ground manfully for a while, until, just as they had taken all the steel they could, and were on the very point of yielding, Cannon had called his own men off.

'Why?' I cried. 'Why?'

The man who had taken up the story shrugged. 'Och now, who can be telling with a Highland army? Mebbe the heart went out of them, and they lacking their leader. Mebbe they remembered the Woman of the Sidh that so they tell was washing her bloody linen at the Garry ford as ye came down to Blair, which is no' a pleasant thing to be thinking of once the blood is cooled in ye . . . They're gone now, melted back into their own hills. That's the way 'tis when one man builds an army, and he's no' there any more.'

'Aye, and so MacKay is in command in the North, now.' The younger woman pushed a wooden bowl of stew towards me. ''Tis all in the past and over, for good or ill. Come, eat, and be glad that you are still alive to taste the rabbit.'

But I could not eat; not just then.

I got to my feet and lurched back to the tilt cart and

crawled up into it like a sick animal seeking the darkness and solitude of its lair, and lay down in the straw with my head in my arms. Something in the shadows under the tilt was greeting; drawing its breath in long harsh gasps. Caspar was huddled against me, shivering, but it was not Caspar. I did not know that it was me, until the cart lurched and subsided under a new weight, as somebody else climbed in beside me, and the sound stopped as I froze rigid. A dry bone hand was laid leaf-light on the back of my neck, and the velvet voice of the old woman said, 'Husheen, husheen now, my dearie.'

A quietness seemed to flow from the hand on my neck, and slowly the black wave of misery ebbed a little. Because I could not bear to speak of the thing itself, I turned to my own personal grief and perplexity, and asked without lifting my head from my arm, 'What'll I do, Grannie? What'll I do now?'

She said, 'I was hearing that already there are men slipping away to the west coast. To the Outer Isles, they will be going, and then across to Ireland to join King James. If ye had a mind, ye could go that way, when ye're a wee thing stronger.'

And I knew, without the need for thinking, that that was the way I would be going. I rolled over under her hand, and lay propped on my sound arm, looking at her as she sat in the opening of the tilt. She was a very ugly old woman, shapeless with sagging flesh and wrinkled as a walnut; only her eyes under their shaggy grey brows were bright and soft; a lassie's eyes still, and I mind seeing, between one breath and the next, that she was one of those women – there are not many of them – who are ugly the first time you see them, and less ugly the second, and by the third, are beginning to be beautiful.

251

She had begun to sing; the merest thread of outworn song, but bonnie –

> 'Good Sire I pray thee
> For Saint Charité,
>   Come dance with me. In Ireland . . .'

It was a song that I had heard Darklis sing, time and again.

She broke off singing in a little, and pulled forward a bundle that she had brought in with her. 'I have brought ye some clothes. Ye must promise me on the sun and the moon that ye'll not go stravaigling off the moment that ye have them, an' you as dwaibly as an hour-old calf. But a man feels more a man when he has his breeks on and a coat tae his back.'

'On the sun an' the moon,' I promised; and then, 'Grannie, would we be anywhere near Glenogilvie? I must take my leave of Lady Dundee and – and her kinswoman – Darklis, before I go.'

She looked round at me, 'Darklis? That would be the Rawni – Mistress Ruthven?'

I nodded.

'None so far. But in five days, my son Balthazar and his woman are for a wedding, Glamis way. There's always siller for a good fiddler at a wedding, and for his woman, telling fortunes for the bonnie ladies. Gin ye go with them, they'll pass but three–four miles from the place, and ye can drop off, an' join them again later. By God's Grace ye'll find my lady and the Rawni still there.'

'Still there? Why would they no' be still there?' I asked quickly.

'There's talk that Dudhope and Glenogilvie are to be

stripped from the Grahams for their part in what the Government will be calling the Rebellion.' The old woman looked up from her pipe that she had taken from some pocket among her rags. 'Have a care in going there, my dearie. There's sorrow enough on that house, and harbouring rebels is a crime; see that ye dinna lead any more trouble to it.'

'I'll take care,' I said.

25

Farewell to Glenogilvie

Five days later, clad in a tattered plaid and breeks, and
an old greasy bonnet in which Balthazar's woman had
stuck a bright knot of rowan berries for luck, I got
down from the Tinkler cart where two tracks crossed
each other, not far from Glenogilvie and, after arrang-
ing a trysting place for first light next morning, set off
with Caspar padding joyfully at my heels.

My full strength was not yet come back to me, and
though it was but the three or four miles to go, my legs
were beginning to weary under me when I came into
the head of Glenogilvie in the gloaming. I came down
through the high orchard, dropping towards the house;
and as I drew near I saw lights moving in the stable-
yard, and a general cheerless bustle about the place,
and yet there seemed to be fewer folk around than
usual.

There was a dim taperlight in the windows of the
bower, and with a vague memory of the old woman's
warning, I went in by way of the garden, through the
overgrown rose trees. The nearest window stood a little
open to the heavy August night, and from inside came
the murmur of women's voices. I knew them well; but
Darklis and my lady might not be alone; I reached up
and beat lightly with my fingers on the panes, hardly
louder than the wing-flutter of a big night-moth. Inside
the room the voices ceased; but nothing moved. After a
few moments I drummed again, and Caspar whimpered. Quick footsteps came towards the window, and

there above me in the opening stood Darklis. I could scarcely see her in the dusk, but I mind how the candles behind her made a bright cloud round her soft brown hair. 'Who is it?' she demanded, and then, 'Is it—'

'Darklis,' I said, ''tis me. Me and Caspar. Can we come in?'

She gave a small sound like a sob, and leaned out to take Caspar in her arms as I handed him up to her. 'So he found you? Och, ye wicked wee dog, we thought ye were lost for sure!' she said, her face buried in the feathery top of his head. She stood back, and I got a grip on the windowsill and hauled myself up, making somewhat heavy work of it, for my left arm was not just that good, and climbed in. And Darklis with her free hand pulled the shutters across behind me.

My lady Jean had just risen from the great carved chair beside the empty hearth, and stood looking across the room to me, with eyes that seemed sunk into her head. She was gowned in stiff black silk, and her hair was as elaborately dressed as ever I had seen it. That will have been for pride's sake. The cradle beside her chair was still swaying gently where her foot had only just left the rocker, and a contented snuffling came out from under the carved canopy. Otherwise, save for a table and a creepy stool and a couple of half-packed kists spilling over on to the floor, there was nothing left in the room at all.

'Hugh!' she said, warmly and gently. And then, 'How does your arm?'

'All but well,' I told her, surprised that she should be knowing.

And I suppose she saw my surprise, for she said, 'Captain Faa sent word to Darklis. We half expected you to come.' She glanced round the room, seeming to see its state of bareness and chaos for the first time. 'But you are only just in time. Tomorrow we shall be gone from here.'

'Where do you go to, Jean?' I asked. It was the first time ever I had called her by her name alone, but it seemed natural, then, to all of us.

'My mother has offered us sanctuary. We shall go to her for a while at Auchans.'

I minded that iron woman who had turned away from her daughter's wedding. 'But this is your home,' I said stupidly.

'I have no home now. I am the wife of a rebel – the widow of a rebel – who died with a price of eighteen hundred good Scottish marks on his head! Dudhope and Glenogilvie are both forfeit. The Marquis of Douglas is to have them.'

So the old woman had been right. But – Douglas again, with his two days' seniority; always Douglas!

'Dudhope I do not grieve for,' she said after a moment. 'But this – this was John's home.'

Caspar whimpered, and Darklis set him down.

Jean seated herself again and folded her hands carefully in her black silken lap and looked at them for a moment; then up again at me. 'Were you with him? They say his last words – his last thought was for the King's cause.'

I thought, 'She is hoping that there was some word for her – something I might have heard that nobody else did.' And for the moment I wanted sore to tell her a kind lie. It would not have been hard to invent something. But I knew that only the truth, however hard, was good enough for my lady Jean.

'He asked how the day went,' I told her. 'And Lord Dunfermline said, "It goes well for the King, but I grieve for your lordship." And himself said, "It is the less matter for me if the day goes well for the King," and then he died, with his head on Tam Johnston's knee that had caught him when he fell.'

She must have seen the fear of hurting her that was on me, for she said, 'Dear Hugh, I had my own last word from him. He left it with the Commander of the Blair garrison, in case . . . ' And she put up her hand and touched the breast of her gown, as though to be sure that the letter was still safe in the place where she carried it. And I saw Dundee's signet ring on her finger. It was not the kind of thing one would miss, in time of battle, and his hands had been covered by the plaid when we carried him back to Blair . . . Too loose for her finger, it was, and she wore a ring of her own beneath it, to keep it safe. 'For young Jamie when he is a man,' she said, as though I had spoken. And then, careful of any hurt that might be on *me*, 'I am not doubting that he would fain have left it in your charge, but you were as like to be killed as he was.'

And then she said quickly, 'But I am keeping you standing and hungry. Sit ye down. And, Darklis, do you go see what there is to be found in the kitchen.'

'I cannot be staying long,' I said, 'I've a tryst to keep with the Tinkler folk that gave me a lift here. But I could not go without taking my leave.'

Darklis made a small sharp movement that I saw out of the tail of my eye.

'And where would you be away to, then?' asked my lady Jean.

'To join King James. I was hearing that men are getting away by the Western Isles to Ireland and the King's cause.'

'You can stay long enough to eat, at all costs,' said my lady, 'so sit ye down, Hugh.'

So I sat down on the creepy stool and fell to fondling Caspar behind his silky ears, he standing up with his forepaws on my knee and singing like a kettle. And I mind the end-of-summer scent of the Four Seasons roses when a breath of warm air through the crack in the shutters set the candle flames to fluttering. And the faint rhythmic sound as she set her foot again to the cradle rocker.

She was gazing into the empty hearth as though there were a fire in it, and she seeing faces in the flames.

In a few moments Darklis came back with bread and cold meat and a bowl of mulberries and a flagon of wine and set them on the table, and a bowl of scraps for Caspar, too, that she set down beside the hearth.

And when I had eaten – it was a silent meal; there was so much to say between us, and yet so little that could be said, though I told them something of the days in Lochaber and the march down to Blair – my lady rose and went to one of the open kists and delved within, and brought out a small velvet pouch drawn up at the throat with scarlet cords, and came back with something in her hand.

'You will be needing money to get you to Ireland. I want you to take this.'

I saw the glint of gold in her palm as she held it out to me.

I shook my head. 'I'll manage.'

'How?' she said, levelly, not taking her hand away. 'I could spare you no more than this if you were my brother; but such as it is, I ask you, as though you were my brother, to take it. John would wish you to take it, to speed you on your way back to the King's service.'

Aye well, I took the gold, and stowed it in my pocket, and made shift to thank her. And as she returned the velvet bag, I saw among the things in the kist, where her rummaging had turned it up, a little picture half spilling out from the piece of crimson silk in which it had been wrapped. The little rough portrait sketch that I had made of Claverhouse that summer evening six years ago.

That was almost the undoing of me.

She took up the square of board and carefully and gently refolded the crimson silk about it. 'Now go,' she said, 'and God go with you, Hugh Herriot. Darklis, take him out by the side door; it is not good for that arm of his to be climbing through windows.'

I mind the sense that I had of grief hanging in the room, tangible as the scent of the Four Seasons roses. I looked back once, and my last sight of Jean, she was standing by the empty hearth in her black gown, her head up, and Claverhouse's ring loose on her finger catching the taperlight.

I left by the side door, Caspar padding at my heels; Darklis came with me, and together we went up to the head of the orchard.

It was a soft night with a young moon faintly thunder-hazed, but giving light enough to show the old trees heavy with ripening apples that had been blossom when last Darklis and I came that way.

We checked among the last of the apple trees, by the gate, and turned to each other.

'Need you go?' Darklis said.

'I'll not be William's man,' I told her. 'Besides, am I no' on the run for a rebel?'

'The Tinklers would shelter you till all's blown over.'

I shook my head. 'I'm going away to follow King James.'

'So you said ... Ye dinna care a straw for King James.'

'No,' I said, 'but Claverhouse did.'

'And so ye'll follow King James because 'tis the nearest ye can come now to following Claverhouse?' Her voice had a kind of flash to it in the dark. But then she put a hand on mine that was already resting on the top bar of the gate. 'You always have to follow someone. 'Tis time ye learned to be your own man, Hugh.'

'Mebbe,' I told her, 'but I'll not learn it hiding with the Tinkler kind.'

And she sighed in the dark, and very gently drew her hand away.

'I'll come back for you one day, if I live,' I heard my own voice saying, and startled myself with the raw longing sound of it.

'If I live . . . ' she echoed. 'No, dinna promise. Dinna come back. I could not be leaving Jean so long as she needs me.'

And she the one that had been bidding me learn to be my own man!

'And if she stops needing you? She might, one day.'

'Then mebbe God will be gentle to us and lead us together again. There's naught to be gained by hovering and hankering.'

'Take Caspar for me,' I said after a moment, through the knot that was in my throat.

'Yet again? I said not to come back.'

'Not just to care for, this time. For a gift. He's all I have to give. Only take better care of him than ye did last time.'

'I will that,' she said. 'And my silver pin – ye have it still?'

'Inside my shirt, where I've worn it since ye gave it to me.'

She put her arms round my neck, and kissed me the

once, sweet and fierce and quick on the mouth, then thrust me away. 'The sun and the moon on your path, my bonnie dark laddie,' she said, and swooped up Caspar into her arms and turned away.

I stood, hearing Caspar's protesting whimper, and watched her go, down through the apple trees towards the light that shone dimly amber in the chinks of the bower window that tomorrow would be dark.

And it came to me that I had bidden goodbye to Darklis too many times in the past years. Well, this was like to be the last time of all.

I went out through the gate and turned towards the head of the glen, and my next dawn's tryst with Balthazar and his woman; and not even the sound of Caspar's paws behind me for company.

26

Study of Hands with Almond Blossom

So I left my own hills behind me and got away to Ireland, and joined the army that King James had gathered there, and fought through the sorry campaigns of that autumn and the next year's spring. I was at the Boyne; and after that last battle was fought and lost, and the last hope of James's cause dead with it, and the King faded away back to France, I was one of those that followed him.

The Wild Geese, they were calling us. There have been many since to bear the name, but we were the first of them.

St Germain just outside Paris became the home of James's court in exile. A pleasant enough place, but somehow shadowy; and the court that James held there was somehow shadowy, too. From time to time men would be coming from England or from Scotland, among them the few that remained of the General's troop. It was good to see Pate Paterson again, and I felt a little less alone after his coming.

In name, we were in the service of our own king, but in fact the French king fed and paid us – so far as we were fed or paid at all – and so we managed as best we could. But in the end – och well, we could not be expecting Louis to keep us for ever, and we ourselves were sore pressed, and James's kist was empty; and maybe it was Scottish pride, maybe just that we were tired of going threadbare and hungry, we went to James and asked leave to enter the French army as private soldiers.

At first he would not be hearing of any such thing, but in the end we brought him to see reason and let us go.

He reviewed us for the last time, in the palace gardens; a hundred and twenty of us, already wearing our stiff new privates' uniforms and glad of their warmth after our old threadbare gear, for it was January and bitter cold. But though the decision had been taken by us all, some of us wept at the last, and felt ourselves shamed; and the King wept, too, thanking us for our loyalty.

We redeemed the shame later. Aye . . .

We were sent down to Roussillon on the Spanish border, where the Pyrenees come down to the Mediterranean Sea – France was at war with Spain as well as England and the Low Countries – and there we were joined by two other Scottish companies, and together we served through three campaigns among the high, fanged, clear-cut mountains that looked always as though they had bitten their own shapes out of the sky. We were at the taking of Rosas in Catalonia – that was a name any regiment might be proud to carry among its battle honours. They say that when Louis got the news of it, he went out to St Germain himself to take word of our part in it to our own king.

But honour seldom comes free; our losses were sore and Pate Paterson among them.

I was shot in the left elbow in the last stages of the fight. Och well, the old wound that I had in that arm always ached in the east wind. The trouble is that it still does; which is odd, though I believe not unusual, with an arm that is not there any more.

At first it did not seem likely that I would live through the surgeon's butchery and then the long jolting journey in the ox-carts that brought our wounded

263

back to Roussillon and the half-ruined monastery at Perpignan that was our base hospital. And at first, truth to tell, I did not want to. Dying would be a way of escape from pain and the sounds and sights and smells of that awful place; and it did not seem to me, in the odd times when the pain drew back a little and my head was clear enough to think at all, that I had much to live for, anyway. But it seemed that whatever I might feel about it, once again my body did not want to die. And little by little the pain and the fever fell away behind me, and the tarred stump below my left shoulder ceased its foul discharging and healed clean.

I began to thrust out towards the living world again. But it was a world that had, so far as I could see, no place for me.

A day came that was towards the winter's end, and it was towards sunset of that day. The evening meal, such as it was, cabbage soup and some nameless meat that a huntsman would not have fed to his hounds, was cooking over a couple of fires in the old cloister garth; and a few of us were huddled close round the flames, with old coats and tattered blankets about our shoulders against the icy wind from the Pyrenees that was stripping the first blossom from the old twisted almond tree in the corner. It would have been warmer inside, but there are worse things than cold; and as soon as any of us were strong enough to drag ourselves out of our make-shift beds, we crawled outside, where at least there was air to breathe, away from filth, and the stink of other men's pain. Scottish and English and French wounded huddled round the fires, and the usual hangers-on; a few camp-followers (we should have done ill without their nursing, for all that kirk-folk have to say about such lassies!), beggars drawn in off the streets by the fires and the smell of cooking food; a stray garbage-eating goat with yellow slit-pupiled eyes and a piece of rag hanging from its mouth – if it did not wander out again by dark, there would be goat stew next day; we foraged for ourselves, those of us that were able, and we were always hungry.

The place was not much of a refuge, and there was no one there who meant a straw in the wind to me, now that Pate Paterson was gone; and yet, glancing round at the figures huddled in their blankets and old army coats, a black despair was on me, because they were my own kind, and soon I would be losing them also. Any day now, I would be given my discharge and cast adrift to fend for myself. I was a sound man again, only not just sound enough; and my soldiering days were over. I was good with horses, but who was going to want a one-armed groom? I could turn beggar, the maimed soldier's last and most common resort. But even my begging would have to be done in a foreign land; I could not get back to Scotland; not for years yet, any-way. Maybe, I thought in the black mood that was on me, the simplest thing would be to go down to the foreshore and make myself a hole in the water and be done with it all.

One of the English soldiers began to sing, crooningly as though half to himself:

'Who passes by this road so late?
Compagnons de la Marjolaine,
Who passes by this road so late?
Always gay!

Of all the King's Knights 'tis the flower,
Compagnons de la Marjolaine,

> Of all the King's Knights 'tis the flower,
> Always gay! . . .'

I roused up and looked round me to see who could be fool enough to sing in such a howling wilderness of a world. And it was so that I saw the beggar woman who must have just come in from the street; and she sitting with her back against the almond tree.

Now the very blackness of my despair came, I am thinking (for I am not the despairing kind), at least partly from my weakness, and the long time that it had taken my wound to mend. I was in the odd state that comes to a man that has been long sick and near to death, when the living world first lays hold of him again. It is as though he has one less skin than usual between himself and that world, and he is more piercingly aware of everything, sight and sound and smell and touch – aye, and joy and despair; and the shadow of a falling leaf and the distant notes of a fiddle and the glance of a passing stranger can all invade him as they cannot do when he is a whole man with his full number of skins.

It was in that way that I saw the beggar woman.

Miserable old crone that she was, sitting with her head tipped back against the trunk of the almond tree, the last reflected brightness of the sunset shining into her withered gargoyle's face. But it was not her face that held me; it was her hands, lying together in her ragged lap. Old, gaunt, coarse hands, dirt-coloured and cracked like earth in a drought. But they had once been beautiful. I could see the beauty in them, as maybe I would not have done at another time or in another mood, for it was a long time since I had sought below the surface of things with a painter's eye, which is a little like a lover's. I saw the beauty of the bones; how when she was long dead and her hands were a skeleton's, they would still be beautiful. There was beauty, too, in the way she moved them, turning and twisting between her fingers a sprig of almond blossom torn off by the wind. I saw the shadow of her hands and the almond spray sharp-etched on to the rusty blackness of her lap; I saw the thick knotted blackish veins on the backs of her hands, and was aware of how they must have branched, blue and scarcely visible, delicate as the veining on a damsel-fly's wing, when they were young.

Suddenly I was minded of Darklis's hands moving light and sure on the strings of her lute, for Jean's amusement while she sat for her wedding portrait.

In those few moments, something began to wake in me that had been a long while sleeping; a kind of sap-rise that was kin to the buds breaking on the almond tree; a stir of old longings almost forgotten. I began to think how I should paint the old woman's hands; how to catch the strong life and the weariness in them, as well as the hidden beauty, and make it all part with the almond flowers that were fragile as white shadow, yet strong with life also . . .

She was staring at the food, her gap-toothed mouth hanging a little open. Somebody threw her a hunk of bread, and she dropped the almond spray to catch it, and thrust it into her breast under her filthy shawl; then scrambled to her feet and hobbled out through the doorway that gave on to the old monastery forecourt and the streets beyond. Maybe the crust was for someone else, that she did not stay to eat it by the fire.

It seems strange, now, that she never felt my gaze upon her. Her eyes never met mine for an instant; but if she had not wandered into the cloister that evening, I am thinking it quite possible that I might have made my hole in the water. As it was, when they gave me my discharge three days later, I set out to make a new life for myself, with a reasonably clear idea of how I hoped to do it.

I had a few coins in my right-hand pocket; not many, for was there ever a soldier whose pay was not in arrears? And the end of my empty sleeve was stuffed into the left-hand one – there are few things more provoking than an empty sleeve flapping loose. And so I went down into the town. I was no stranger to Perpignan, for our headquarters had been there since we came down from St Germain the best part of two years before. I went straight to a certain tall and tottering wine-shop whose creaking sign showing the seven stars of its name arranged in a triangle had been badly in need of repainting ever since I had first known it, and was now so washed out by the storms of the past winter that the stars seemed to be sinking through the board to the other side even while you watched. I went in and spent the smallest of my coins on a measure of raw red wine; and spinning out the drinking of it as long as possible, managed before the last drop was downed to persuade the landlord to let me repaint it for my food while I was on the job, and the cost of the paint, with enough over for another sign.

Seeing the painted house-timbers of the town and the boats in the harbour, I knew that there must be paint to be got, easy enough, in Perpignan.

Having agreed, though unwillingly, that the old faded sign was unworthy of the good wine he sold, the landlord sent his potboy with me to show me where to get what I needed, and to make sure that I did not cheat him and run off with the money.

So, I painted my first shop sign.

I settled down to work, with the old sign rubbed down and propped against the wall, with the walnut oil and my couple of brushes and my shells of colour. (I had bought my pigments ready-ground and only requiring to be worked up with oil, which is a thing no painter should do; but I needed time and practice to work out how to grind my colours one-handed, and meanwhile I needed to eat.) And oh, but I was feart! It was so long since I had last put brush to board, and though the old love had woken in me, there was no saying whether I had yet the old skill. Lacking that, I should just have to paint up the sign as it had been before, and be content with that. Only I should not be content, for the loss in me would be not just the loss of my new bonnie plans, but something deeper and more sore.

But with the first brush-strokes I knew that all was well. The old skill was rusty with lack of use, but it was still there . . . I laid on a background of a dark blue-green, the colour of a clear sky at twilight seen from a lighted room, and against it painted a wreath of twisted stalks and leaves in solid black, and set my seven stars among them – white, with yellow hearts to them, like white roses in a garland. It was clumsy work, and I was beginning to know by the end of it how often a painter uses his left hand without even knowing that he is doing so. But the thing was bonnie enough in its way.

The landlord was inclined to grumble that nobody would recognise the new sign; but his fat wife wept at sight of it and said that it was a garland of stars for the Mother of God. I had not thought of it that way, but if it pleased her, where was the harm?

And it got me another sign to paint, for Monsieur

Dupont, a crony of the landlord's and a shoemaker by trade. I struck the same bargain with him, and painted him a fine pair of buckled shoes with high red heels, such as I had seen often in London Town, three–four years ago.

And then, with enough pigments in small membrane-covered pots for at least two more signs, I took to the road, for I had no mind to spend more time within a bugle-call of the regiment.

I painted my way across France, teaching myself the craft as I went, and discovering how best to carry it out one-handed. More than a year it took me, painting shop signs for the most part, though from time to time somebody would ask me to paint their dog, and once it was a village bull, and once a girl on the bottom of a wine cask. And there were times when I had money to jingle in my pocket, and times when I came uncomfortably near to starving. More than a year, come to think of it, for it was March when I changed the rags of my French soldier's coat for the rags of a decent brown on that I had found hanging on a blackthorn bush, its owner busy at the spring sowing in the field beyond, and crossed the border into what they used to call the Spanish Netherlands, by a suitably lonely woodland track, no one seeking to bar my way.

Life was more difficult after that, making my way through a countryside that had been fought over for the past five years, and was being fought over still, in a fitful way, though I kept well clear of the guns. Nothing of that was part of my life any more. But it seemed strange after my years with the French, with Spain and the Low Countries and the England of Orange William for the enemy, to be in a world to which France and King James's England were the enemy after all.

I minded my tattered French coat that I had left hanging on a blackthorn bush, and away past that, far, far back, till I seemed to catch the waft of hawthorn flowers, and the light bitter mocking of Alan's voice: 'The De'il's greeting to ye, Hughie lad, here's turning your coat with a vengeance!'

But I was not turning my coat; I was one of the Wild Geese, whose loyalties are not bounded by frontiers. I had followed Claverhouse, and I had followed James for Claverhouse's sake, and now King James's service was closed to me, and I went to find another life for myself in the only way that I knew.

Life was more difficult also, for the very simple reason that I did not know the language and must get along as best I could by shouting and dumb-show. But once across the second border into the Dutch Republic, I found help that I had not expected, though I suppose I might have done so if I had thought, for in the sea-port towns there were Scottish and English merchants and seamen. It was good to hear my own tongue again. And if any of them guessed that I was one of the Wild Geese, they asked no questions, but set me on my way.

And so at last I came to Utrecht, and to Silver Spur Street, and found the third house above the kirk, with the swans carved on its gable, and asked the feather-bolster-shaped serving maid who opened to my knocking at the door, was Mynheer Cornelius van Meere at home.

She stared at me as though I were the Man in the Moon, and when I repeated the question, made shooing gestures at me that were understandable in any language, and would have shut the door in my face. But at that moment, luckily for me, another woman came across the hall behind her, and paused to ask a question. The two spoke together quickly in their own tongue, the maid holding the door still half-closed. Then it opened a little wider, and the maid, with a disapproving sniff, moved back a pace, though remaining ready to give support if need be, and the other woman, who was clearly the mistress of the house, took her place in the doorway.

She asked me something – I suppose it was my business; and I repeated my own question again.

She stood and looked at me, like a bright-eyed robin, her head a little on one side, and I saw that she understood no more English than her maid did. Fool that I was, because Mynheer spoke English, I had thought that his wife would, too. 'Cornelius van Meere,' she said, and nodded, and waited again; and I thought that maybe, just maybe, she might know my name. Mynheer had said all those years ago, that if ever I changed my mind I was to come to the house with the carved swans, and if he was from home, his wife would take me in until he returned. So, if he had meant it, and he *had* meant it, he would surely have told her all about me, told her my name.

But it was all a long time ago.

I slung my bundle higher on to my shoulder, and made her a small bow with my hand on my chest, and said, 'Hugh Herriot,' and waited in my turn.

I saw blankness in her face, and then questioning, and then a small struggling memory. And the memory opened like a flower.

'Hugh Herriot,' she said; and then flinging the door open wide, 'Com!' And as I came in over the scrubbed white step, she put out a hand to my free arm and found only an empty sleeve to my ragged coat; and I saw her plump kind face flinch with shock, and crumple. But I

272

was too tired to mind. Then she was shooing the maid off in her turn, calling behind her into the depths of the house, a quick string of guttural words in which I could make out only three, 'Cornelius!' and my own name, and she was thrusting me across a wide dim hallway.

And then, not quite sure how I got there, I was in a room with black-and-white tiles on the floor; a very cool calm room through which the light seemed to wash like water into every corner; standing with my bundle at my feet. And Mynheer, looking more than ever like a toad in a vast curled wig, was pumping my hand up and down between both of his.

'Hugh!' he said. 'Hugh – after all these so many years!'

And suddenly my mouth felt dry. It was so many years, as he said; too many years to leave an offer lying and then try to take it up again, expecting it still to be there. I said nothing, and in a little he stood back and looked at me. 'And zo you change your mind,' he said, as though it was only last week that we had spoken of the thing.

I swallowed against the dryness of my mouth. 'If you will still take me, Mynheer.'

And after a troubled moment, he said, 'Can you still paint, my Hugh?' He was not surprised by my arm, somewhere in that stream of words his wife must have told him. But I could see that it might raise problems.

'I'm right-handed,' I said.

'Ach, that I know. Lacking an arm you will contrive; but there are other things to cut off the gift – the flow – the fire.'

I shook my head. 'I have painted my way across France – shop signs and the like, and learned to grind my own colours one-handed as I came, but whether I can still paint as ye mean it, I do not know.'

'We shall find out,' said Mynheer, seemingly from rather a long way off, through the fog of weariness that was gathering about me. 'But first you must eat, and then you must sleep; and then tomorrow we will talk of many things such as how you came to be painting your way across France and whether you can still paint other things than shop signs.'

And so I ate and slept, and next morning answered a great many questions over a hot thick bowl of chocolate – I had never tasted chocolate before. And then Mynheer took me up to a long light room at the top of the house, where two apprentices were already at work, one grinding colours while the other was preparing a canvas, and at the far end a big canvas stood on its easel, covered with a cloth. Mynheer spoke to them, and they went on with their work. Then he showed me where the pigments and oils, the pestles and mortars and grinding slabs were kept, the spare pieces of board for sketching, and all the ordered chaos of brushes in jars and the like, and said, 'Now paint.'

'What would you be having me paint?' I asked.

'Whatever you please. But you will grind and work up your own colours first.'

He went away; and the two apprentices left me alone, as I make no doubt they had been ordered.

I looked round the room to see what I should paint. There was a bowl of fruit on the table, the dense glowing rind of oranges contrasting with the thin old-woman-withered skin of long-biding apples; there were striped and feathered tulips in a crystal jar that caught the light from a nearby window and focused it in a silvery blot at the heart of its own shadow, on to the white cloth on which it stood. There were three peacock's feathers in a narrow-necked jar of translucent green porcelain.

I considered them all as I began to grind my pigments, holding the mortar between my knees as I had learned to do.

But when the colours were ready, I began to paint from my inner eye the gaunt hands of an old beggar-woman lying in her black lap, with a sprig of almond blossom between the fingers.

I worked all day, until the light began to fade. And then I came back to myself, and stood back to see what I had done.

And it was bad. It was so bad that I could have put my head on my knees and wept. The brush in my hand was still loaded with paint, and I made to slash it across the painting, but suddenly Mynheer's hand came down on my wrist. I had not heard him come, and had no idea how long he had been standing there behind me.

'Do not spoil it,' he said.

But it seemed to me that there was nothing there to spoil. ''Tis not what I saw,' I said, ''tis not what I saw.'

'It never is,' he said, half sadly, half amused. 'Even when you do not choose a subject that would tax Rembrandt – and let us admit that neither you nor I are Rembrandt – it never is. If you are to become a painter, Hugh, you must accept that always there is a falling short between the vision and what we poor mortals make of it. You must accept it, but you must never cease to strive against it. When you think that you have captured the vision whole and perfect, when you become satisfied with your work, that is when you will cease to be a painter.'

'I'll never be a painter,' said I.

'You will, and maybe a better one than I – when we have got rid of all the bad habits that you have picked up with too much sign painting.' His voice ran up, and cracked in exasperation, 'Got in Heaven! Have you had hands of your own for – what, twenty-two, twenty-three years? And still you do not know how a thumb bends into its socket? Ach vell, that can vait till tomorrow. Clean up those brushes and the palette, and come down to supper. The other two vill haff begun without you.'

27

Autumn in Utrecht

Two and a half years later I got my first commission –
the wife of a small merchant who could not or would
not afford Mynheer's price.

Mynheer told him that he had a journeyman in his
studio who could paint nigh on as well as himself, and
since he was *only* a journeyman, at half the fee. I
should have been grateful, but I was not, for I had seen
the woman. She had a fat foolish face like a bun with
small dead currants in it for eyes; and I said so.

'If you paint landscape or bunches of pretty flowers,'
Mynheer told me, 'you can choose for your self your
own subject, trusting to God that you will be able to sell
it and so continue to eat afterwards. If you are a portrait painter you can occasionally, *ferry* occasionally, do
the same. But for the most part you will paint people
who come to you with the price of the portrait in their
hand: and occasionally, *ferry* occasionally, that will be
one with a face such as Viscount Dundee, but more
often it will be one with a fat foolish face like a bun with
small dead currants in it for eyes. Then you will set
yourself –' his voice was rising to a roar – 'to find what,
if anything, lies behind the fat and the foolishness! I
have said that you will wait upon Mevrow de Fries at
two o'clock on Tuesday.'

So at two o'clock on Tuesday, I waited on Mevrow
de Fries and began to work on my first commission.

Aye, it would have been a momentous day in my life,
if that had been all. But it was to be a day when, light or

dark, kind or cruel, life gathers itself together in a kind of peak, and comes crashing down in a new pattern.

Mevrow wished to be painted with her little dog in her lap. It was a fat and foolish little spaniel, but she loved it, and in return it gave her the love that I think she lacked from Mynheer de Fries. And when I had cleaned my palette and brushes and made all ready for the next day's sitting, and was on my way home in the early dusk, I found myself thinking of Caspar, and away back through Caspar, of many other things and places and people . . .

News trickled through to us in Utrecht from time to time, and so I knew that the Earl of Balcarres had escaped to France. And I knew that the bairn, Jamie, had died in that black Covenanting house of Auchans, only a few months after his father at Killiecrankie. Dundee's only son, and Jean's. Poor Jean. I knew that less than two years ago she had married again – Colonel Livingstone, when he was released into banishment with his health broken after all those captive years under the death sentence, and they were somewhere in the Low Countries now. How could she, I wondered, she that had been wife to Claverhouse? I had wondered that so often. Eh well, it could not hurt Dundee, seven years in his grave at Blair.

I fell to wondering where in all the Low Countries they might be. I had half heard that they were in Brussels before the French bombardment; but now . . . There was a tightening in my belly, for wherever my lady Jean was, there surely Darklis would be also; and the foolish fancy woke in me that they might be here in Utrecht as well as any other place, and I might meet her round any corner of the cobbled street. I did not think of her so often these days, but suddenly the feel of her

278

was so close to me that it was as though in another moment I would be able to conjure her up out of the shadows.

A fresh spattering of autumn rain in my face brought me out of my day-dream; and I realised that I must have been dawdling, for here I was but just passing the Castle of Antwerp Inn, no more than halfway home, and the candle-light from the open-shuttered windows beginning already to be reflected in the still waters of the canal.

And there I had to stop for a few moments, late or not, for they were loading peats for the winter, swinging the great creels of it up past the lighted windows on ropes and pulleys from the projecting gable beam for storage on the turf-floor under the roof, and a couple of creels were blocking the narrow way. I mind noticing that the rain – and there had been a deal of rain in the past week – had damped the turfs through, so that there was not so much dust flying around as there generally is at such times, but it had made the stuff heavy to handle. I suppose that was why they were still at it, shouting directions and the odd curse to each other, so late in the evening.

They shifted the last two creels, and I dodged past and went on my way.

A few hundred yards further on, a bridge crossed the canal and in the fading light and the shadows of the poplar trees that lined the bank at that point, I was quite close before I noticed that a woman in a dark cloak was leaning over the balustrade, watching the water and life of the barges tied up alongside; a moment more before I realised that she had a wee dog with her. Her hood was pulled forward and I could not see her face; but I think I knew, in that moment, without seeing . . .

In the same instant the dog let out a sudden piercing whine; and then a shower of shrill, half-joyful, half-desperate barking, and tearing its leash from her hand, came flying along the bank towards me, ears, tail and leash all flying behind. And the woman looked up, startled, so that her hood fell back, and I could see her face.

Then Caspar was clamouring and scrambling at my knees, and even as I stooped to greet him, he swerved and darted back to the woman on the bridge, then came tearing back to me again. And so kept on, weaving a kind of shuttle of joy to and fro between us while the distance shortened as I walked forward, not hurrying – somehow it did not seem a time for hurrying.

The woman never moved at all, until I came beside her on the bridge. Then she said, 'Hugh,' and nothing more.

'Darklis!' I said, 'Darklis! – Darklis! . . . ' and having begun to say her name, did not seem able to stop. But Caspar was scrabbling at my knee and wailing for my attention, and I squatted down to greet him. I could not be making him a pocket of my hands to bury his nose in as I had used to do, so I cupped the one hand I had under his muzzle, and saw as he thrust into it that his muzzle was feathered with white. I gathered him on to my knee while he licked my face from ear to ear, singing like a kettle in his old way.

And then Darklis was on her knees beside us, with a little half-quenched sound as though for some pain deep within herself. I suppose she had seen from the way I took Caspar's muzzle that I had but the one hand to take it in; and she put her hand on my left shoulder, and felt downward. I'd not have let anyone else in the world do that, unless it were himself. Even with Darklis I am thinking I stiffened a little.

'Was that in King James's war?' she asked softly.

'In a way,' I said.

'Oh Hugh,' she said. 'Did they hurt ye sore?'

'Aye,' I said, 'but 'tis rising four years gone by.'

For a while we bided, crouched against the balustrade of the bridge with Caspar between us, seeing nothing of the folk that went by save once or twice when someone all but fell over us. Darklis asked me how did I come to be in Utrecht, and I told her. 'D'ye mind Mynheer van Meere that painted my lady's wedding portrait? I'm back to the craft he would have had me follow. I'm his journeyman now, but I'll be my own man in not much over a year.'

'Oh, Hugh!' she said. 'Ye'll mind I always said ye'd make a better painter than ye would a sojer laddie.'

''Tis to be hoped so,' I said, playing with Caspar's ears. 'But I made none so bad a sojer laddie, a' the same.'

I knew that, at least in part, we were only talking of surface things, in the way that we had so often done before, held back from talking of things that went deeper by the old barrier that was still there. And suddenly the fear came on me that at any moment she would be gone again; and I left off playing with Caspar's ears, in a panic, and reached to find her hand under her cloak. 'Oh, Darklis, I was thinking of you as I came along the way – I felt ye so near that it was as though I could call ye up out of the shadows – I havena done that, have I?'

She laughed softly, and left her hand lying in mine. 'I'm no shadow, my dearie.'

'No,' I said, 'and you're with my lady Jean – we heard that she and Colonel Livingstone were somewhere in the Low Countries; but I was not knowing where.'

'Moving about . . . We only arrived here the day. We're lodged at the Castle of Antwerp, back yonder.' She gave herself a little shake inside her cloak and began to draw her feet under her. 'Hugh, I must be getting back to see to the bairn.'

'The bairn?' I said stupidly. 'The bairn died, long syne.'

'Not Jamie. Colonel Livingstone's bairn.'

That brought the marriage home to me as it had not quite come home before. 'Oh, Darklis,' I said after a wee while, 'how could she? She that had had Claverhouse for her man!'

Darklis was looking down through the balustrade, and I mind the last reflected light from the water on her face, mingling with the glow of a street lantern that someone had just hung out close by. The voice of the town seemed to have gone very far away. 'Mind ye, he'd always been there, before ever she knew Claverhouse,' she said. 'And when they let him out of gaol he was awfu' sick, and she tended him – she and I together, and after – he was there, and he was kind, and he'd always loved her. And she was so lonely, Hugh.'

'Is she happy?'

'Happy is a chancy word. She's content.'

A poplar leaf, still green at the heart but edged with gold, came eddying down in the quiet air and landed on my shoulder and clung there. Darklis picked it off and put it into my hand. 'Keep it,' she said. 'When a leaf comes to you like that, 'tis a gift from the People of Peace.'

She got up and shook out her skirts. 'I must go. Come you and see her, Hugh. Not tonight, she is tired; but come.'

'If it willna make her sad,' I said, getting up also.

'Not the kind of sad that will harm her. Did I no' tell ye, she has her contentment,' and then she said, very low, 'Which of us keeps Caspar?'

'He's yours,' I said; and the heart was sore within me, not only for Caspar's cold nose in the hollow of my hand, but because still it seemed that there was no way in her mind that we might both be keeping Caspar. 'I gave him to you, as you gave me your bonnie siller pin.'

But in that moment there came a kind of dull roar, a rumbling and booming sound. Once in the Pyrenees, I heard a landslip after heavy rain. It was like that, maybe, but smaller and with the cracking and tearing of timbers in it, and not lasting so long. There was shouting and screaming horribly mingled with it, too; and looking back the way I had come, I saw a cloud of dust in the light of the street lanterns engulfing the Castle of Antwerp.

And Darklis and I were running, it seemed all Utrecht was running, in the direction from which the shouts and cries and the cracking and subsiding of timbers still came. 'It's the Castle of Antwerp,' somebody was shouting. 'I told them last year the turf-floor needed shoring up – and with all this rain to make the peats heavy . . .'

Darklis was crying out as she ran, 'Jean! Jean! I am coming!'

There were torches, and beyond the torches only darkness – we must have been longer on the bridge than we knew – and the whole front of the inn bulging outwards and dragged askew; and we were through the gaping doorway into choking clouds of dust. Timbers were still falling, and for a splinter of time I was back beside the burn in Glenogilvie on Midsummer's Eve, and Darklis clinging to me and crying of death-darkness and torches, and the world falling; and a fierce faery wind blowing out of nowhere; and the tune of a pipe lament somehow caught up in it all, as things are mingled and caught up together in the tangles of a nightmare. Then I was back in the ruins of the Castle of Antwerp, and the torchlight flaring on Colonel Livingstone's unconscious face with a great broken place on his temple, as we dragged him out from under the wreckage of an inner doorway; and a serving-man was shouting over and over again to anyone within earshot. 'He'd come out to speak with me in the doorway, or he'd have been under that lot, too!'

And all beyond was fallen beams and broken plaster and a mountain of sullen black peat.

People were fetching spades and crowbars, and meanwhile we all began to dig with our bare hands, like terriers at a rat hole – like Caspar.

But we knew that it was no use. No use at all.

A few days later, my lady Jean and the bairn with her were buried in the shadow of the Buurkirk at the heart of Utrecht. It was a very gentle day, though there had been rain earlier, with a sky of watered blue and dove and silver arching above the town, and the leaves drifting down from the poplars and the linden trees around the kirkyard.

There were not many folk to see her laid in her grave. Colonel Livingstone stood at the graveside, a bandage round his head; and with him Sir Andrew Kennedy, the Conservitor of Scottish Trade in the Netherlands, who was an old friend and had come over from Rotterdam to take charge of all things; a few more; and Darklis and myself standing back a little from the rest because we had Caspar with us. But Darklis went forward at the last, and knelt to scatter a handful of rain-wet autumn crocuses and late Four Seasons roses on the kist before the grave was filled in.

When all was over we set out to walk home together. I looked back once from the kirkyard gate, and saw the dark figure of Colonel Livingstone standing as though he had taken root in the rank graveside grass; and for all that Sir Andrew was still with him, I never saw a man look so utterly alone before, nor have I ever seen one since. I turned away to where Darklis had checked and stood waiting for me, and we started to walk back to Silver Spur Street and the house with the carved swans on the gable, which was the nearest thing to home that either of us had since I had taken her back there to Mevrow van Meere on the night that the Castle of Antwerp fell in.

At the first, we walked a little apart, but in a while she moved in towards me. 'If I had not been taking Caspar for his evening walk, I would have been with her,' she said in a small hushed voice.

I put my arm around her and felt that she was shivering; and that was not from cold, for have I not said it was a gentle day? There was another thing that I felt, too. In all the days since Jean's death, she had been frozen, like the creature that the People of Peace leave behind in the place of a stolen human being; but now the ice was melting, and with it something else, the strangeness, the holding back, that had always been like a defence-wall around her. Whether it was because Jean was dead and had left her free and lonely as Claverhouse had left me; whether it had to with that terrible flash of the Sight, that had come to its last cruel flowering, and dropped away into the past, leaving her like other lassies . . .

'Not that it matters either way,' she was saying in the

same small desolate voice. 'She doesna need me now. Nobody needs me now.'

I stopped, and turned her towards me. Her face was curd-white in the shadow of her hood, and her eyes huge in it, and darker than I had ever seen them.

'I need you,' I said. 'I've always needed you, my bonnie love.'

We did not even kiss each other, not then; but I held her close, and she refuged her face in the hollow of my neck. And we did not care that all the good burghers of Utrecht could be seeing us as they went by; and all the while, Caspar was weaving himself in and out around our feet; and the poplar leaves drifting golden all about us in the quiet autumn air.

Aye, that was your grandmother when she was young. You will have known it all the while, of course; no need to guess. But I did not write all this down to keep you wondering and spring surprises on you in the end. I wrote it that you might know, and pass the knowing on to your grandchildren after you, what manner of man was General John Graham of Claverhouse, Viscount Dundee; him they called Bloody Claver'se; him they called Black John of the Battles; and what it was like to be one of those that followed him.

A little also, maybe, what it was like to be young Hugh Herriot. But that is by the way.

I have always had the knack of catching a likeness from memory.

Other great reads *from* **Red Fox**

Further Red Fox titles that you might enjoy reading are listed on the following pages. They are available in bookshops or they can be ordered directly from us.

If you would like to order books, please send this form and the money due to:

ARROW BOOKS, BOOKSERVICE BY POST, PO BOX 29, DOUGLAS, ISLE OF MAN, BRITISH ISLES. Please enclose a cheque or postal order made out to Arrow Books Ltd for the amount due, plus 75p per book for postage and packing to a maximum of £7.50, both for orders within the UK. For customers outside the UK, please allow £1.00 per book.

NAME_____

ADDRESS_____

_____

Please print clearly.

Whilst every effort is made to keep prices low, it is sometimes necessary to increase cover prices at short notice. If you are ordering books by post, to save delay it is advisable to phone to confirm the correct price. The number to ring is THE SALES DEPARTMENT 071 (if outside London) 973 9700.

Other great reads ✦ *from* **Red Fox**

Fantasy fiction—the Song of the Lioness series

ALANNA—THE FIRST ADVENTURE
Tamora Pierce

Alanna has just one wish—to become a knight. Her twin brother, Thom, prefers magic and wants to be a great sorcerer. So they swop places and Alanna, dressed as a boy, sets off for the king's court. Becoming a knight is difficult—but Alanna is brave and determined to succeed.

ISBN 0 09 943560 8 £2.50

IN THE HAND OF THE GODDESS
Tamora Pierce

Alan of Trebond is the smallest but toughest of the squires at court. Only Prince Jonathan knows she is really a girl called Alanna.

As she prepares for her final training to become a knight, Alanna is troubled. Is she the only one to sense the evil in Duke Roger? Does no one realise what a threat his steely ambition poses?

ISBN 0 09 955560 3 £2.50

THE GIRL WHO RIDES LIKE A MAN
Tamora Pierce

Alanna has proved herself equal to the men around her but now faces fresh challenges when she becomes shaman to a fierce tribe of desert dwellers.

ISBN 0 09 981340 8 £3.50

LIONESS RAMPANT
Tamora Pierce

With this fourth book, Tamora Pierce brings her Song of the Lioness quartet to a stunning climax and conclusion.

ISBN 0 09 981350 5 £3.50

Top teenage fiction from Red Fox

PLAY NIMROD FOR HIM Jean Ure

Christopher and Nick are each other's only friend.
Isolated from the rest of the crowd, they live in their
own world of writing and music. Enter lively, popular
Sal who tempts Christopher away from Nick . . .
ISBN 0 09 985300 0   £2.99

HAMLET, BANANAS AND ALL THAT JAZZ
Alan Durant

Bert, Jim and their mates vow to live dangerously –
just as Nietzsche said. So starts a post-GCSEs summer
of girls, parties, jazz, drink, fags . . . and tragedy.
ISBN 0 09 997540 8   £3.50

ENOUGH IS TOO MUCH ALREADY
Jan Mark

Maurice, Nina and Nazzer are all re-sitting their
O levels but prefer to spend their time musing over
hilarious previous encounters with strangers, hamsters,
wild parties and Japanese radishes . . .
ISBN 0 09 985310 8   £2.99

BAD PENNY Allan Frewin Jones

Christmas doesn't look good for Penny this year. She's
veggy, feels overweight, *and* The Lizard, her horrible
father has just turned up. Worse still, Roy appears –
Penny's ex whom she took a year to get over.
ISBN 0 09 985280 2   £2.99

CUTTING LOOSE Carole Lloyd

Charlie's horoscope says to get back into the swing of
things, but it's not easy: her Dad and Gran aren't
speaking, she's just found out the truth about her
mum, and is having severe confused spells about her
lovelife. It's time to cut loose from all binding ties, and
decide what she wants and who she really is.
ISBN 0 09 91381 X   £3.50

Teenage thrillers from Red Fox

GOING TO EGYPT   Helen Dunmore

When Dad announces they're going on holiday to Weston, Colette is disappointed – she'd much rather be going to Egypt. But when she meets the boys who ride their horses in the sea at dawn, she realizes that it isn't where you go that counts, it's who you meet while you're there . . .
ISBN 0 09 910901 8   £3.50

BLOOD   Alan Durant

Life turns frighteningly upside down when Robert hears his parents have been shot dead in the family home. The police, the psychiatrists, the questions . . . Robert decides to carry out his own investigations, and pushes his sanity to the brink.
ISBN 0 09 992330 0   £3.50

DEL-DEL   Victor Kelleher

Des, Hannah and their children are a close-knit family – or so it seems. But suddenly, a year after the death of their daughter Laura, Sam the youngest son starts to act very strangely – having been possessed by a terrifyingly evil presence called Del-Del.
ISBN 0 09 918271 8   £3.50

THE GRANITE BEAST   Ann Coburn

After her father's death, Ruth is uprooted from town-life to a close-knit Cornish village and feels lost and alone. But the strange and terrifying dreams she has every night are surely from something more than just unhappiness? Only Ben, another outsider, seems to understand the omen of major disaster . . .
ISBN 0 09 985970 X   £2.99

Other great reads ⌐*from* **Red Fox**

Sigh and swoon with our romantic reads

IF IT WEREN'T FOR SEBASTIAN   Jean Ure

Sensible Maggie's family are shocked when she moves into a bedsit to learn shorthand and typing. Maggie herself is shocked when she meets enigmatic, eccentric Sebastian – the unlikeliest of housemates. But a cat called Sunday brings them together – then almost tears them apart . . .
ISBN 0 09 985870 3   £3.50

I NEVER LOVED YOUR MIND   Paul Zindel

Dewey Daniels and Yvette Goethals seem the unlikeliest of couples – he thinks she's an adolescent ghoul, and she despises him for being a carnivore. Yet despite himself, Dewey finds himself falling in love with her – which leads to utter disaster!
ISBN 0 09 987270 6   £3.50

SEVEN WEEKS LAST SUMMER
Catherine Robinson

Abby's only plans that summer were to catch up on her revision for the mock exams and enjoy the sun. Instead, the summer becomes a time of change for Abby, her family and her friends, too.
ISBN 0 09 918551 2   £3.50

I CAPTURE THE CASTLE   Dodie Smith

In this wonderfully romantic book, Cassandra Mortmain tells the story of the changes in the life of her extraordinary and impoverished family after the arrival of their rich and handsome young American landlord.
ISBN 0 09 984500 8   £3.99

Other great reads from **Red Fox**

Leap into humour and adventure with Joan Aiken

Joan Aiken writes wild adventure stories laced with comedy and melodrama that have made her one of the best-known writers today. Her James III series, which begins with *The Wolves of Willoughby Chase*, has been recognized as a modern classic. Packed with action from beginning to end, her books are a wild romp through a history that never happened.

THE WOLVES OF WILLOUGHBY CHASE
ISBN 0 09 997250 6   £2.99

BLACK HEARTS IN BATTERSEA
ISBN 0 09 988860 2   £3.50

NIGHT BIRDS ON NANTUCKET
ISBN 0 09 988890 4   £3.50

THE STOLEN LAKE
ISBN 0 09 988840 8   £3.50

THE CUCKOO TREE
ISBN 0 09 988870 X   £3.50

DIDO AND PA
ISBN 0 09 988850 5   £3.50

IS
ISBN 0 09 910921 2   £2.99

THE WHISPERING MOUNTAIN
ISBN 0 09 988830 0   £3.50

MIDNIGHT IS A PLACE
ISBN 0 09 979200 1   £3.50

THE SHADOW GUESTS
ISBN 0 09 988820 3   £2.99

Other great reads from **Red Fox**

Paul Zindel is the king of young adult fiction

Sad, but comic and seriously off-the-wall, Paul Zindel's books for young adults are unputdownable.

A STAR FOR THE LATECOMER
with Bonnie Zindel

Brooke's mother would give anything for Brooke to be a star – but her mother's dying.

ISBN 0 09 987200 5   £2.99

A BEGONIA FOR MISS APPLEBAUM

'Miss Applebaum was the most special teacher we ever had . . .'

ISBN 0 09 987210 2   £2.99

THE GIRL WHO WANTED A BOY

Sybella knows more about carburettors than boys – but she wants one, badly.

ISBN 0 09 987180 7   £2.99

THE UNDERTAKER'S GONE BANANAS

No one will believe him but Bobby knows he saw the undertaker strangling his wife.

ISBN 0 09 987190 4   £2.99

PARDON ME, YOU'RE STEPPING ON MY EYEBALL

A tender tale of two mixed-up misfits falling in love.

ISBN 0 09 987220 X   £3.50

MY DARLING, MY HAMBURGER

'If a boy gets too pushy,' says Maggie's teacher, 'suggest going for a hamburger.'

ISBN 0 09 987230 7   £3.50

Other great reads from **Red Fox**

Superb historical stories from Rosemary Sutcliff

Rosemary Sutcliff tells the historical story better than anyone else. Her tales are of times filled with high adventure, desperate enterprises, bloody encounters and tender romance. Discover the vividly real world of Rosemary Sutcliff today!

THE CAPRICORN BRACELET
ISBN 0 09 977620 0   £2.50

KNIGHT'S FEE
ISBN 0 09 977630 8   £2.99

THE SHINING COMPANY
ISBN 0 09 985580 1   £3.50

THE WITCH'S BRAT
ISBN 0 09 975080 5   £2.50

SUN HORSE, MOON HORSE
ISBN 0 09 979550 7   £2.50

TRISTAN AND ISEULT
ISBN 0 09 979550 7   £2.99

BEOWULF: DRAGON SLAYER
ISBN 0 09 997270 0   £2.50

THE HOUND OF ULSTER
ISBN 0 09 997260 3   £2.99

THE LIGHT BEYOND THE FOREST
ISBN 0 09 997450 9   £2.99

THE SWORD AND THE CIRCLE
ISBN 0 09 997460 6   £2.99

The Pick of the Poets from Red Fox

THEM AND US
Jennifer Curry, illustrated by Susie Jenkin-Pearce

Pairs of poems – one by an adult and one by a child – on the same subject can mean very different ideas, as this warm, humorous, and sometimes surprising anthology shows.

ISBN 0 09 995110 X   £3.50

IT CAME THROUGH THE WALL
Tim Healey, illustrated by Tony Ross

What is the huge hairy horrible thing that comes through the wall one night? All is revealed in this deliciously spooky rhyme . . .

ISBN 0 09 922621 9   £2.99

FOR LAUGHING OUT LOUD
Edited by Jack Prelutsky, illustrated by Marjorie Priceman

"If you have got a funnybone, and I've no doubt you do,
Then this completely silly book is sure to tickle you!"
A collection of the funniest, silliest poems around – guaranteed to have you in giggles!

ISBN 0 09 923731 8   £6.99

SINGING DOWN THE BREADFRUIT
Pauline Stewart, illustrated by Duncan Smith

Tropical rain showers, hurricanes and bluebottles, coconuts and mangoes: all the smells, sounds and colours of the Caribbean are vividly captured in Pauline Stewart's first collection of poetry.

ISBN 0 09 928821 4   £3.50

WONDERCRUMP POETRY
Various prize-winning children

All the best entries from the NECA/Dahl Foundation/School Book Fairs Poetry Competition are in this wonderful new collection of poems, covering such wide-ranging topics as school, the family and growing up . . .

ISBN 0 09 930328 0   £3.50

Griping Red Fox Fiction for Older Readers

BETWEEN THE MOON AND THE ROCK
Judy Allen

Shy Lisa feels that she has finally found a voice when she joins the Christian fundamental group that have recently moved in next door – but her best friend Flora feels that there is something frighteningly evil behind their mesmerising services.

ISBN 0 09 918651 9   £2.99

TINA COME HOME
Paul Geraghty

New to England, Murray is fascinated by Tina, the most unusual, interesting girl he's ever met. Not daring to approach her, he starts secretly trailing her home from school . . . which is when he stumbles upon her secret.

ISBN 0 09 971710 7   £3.50

PAUL LOVES AMY LOVES CHRISTO
Josephine Poole

Paul and his sister Amy have always been the greatest friends, and he takes it for granted that he is the most important person in her life. When she falls in love, his whole world is suddenly shattered, and he has to face the violence of his emotions.

ISBN 0 09 974040 0   £3.50

YOU'LL NEVER GUESS THE END
Barbara Wersba

Joel's black sheep brother has hit the bestseller lists with a novel Joel knows is rubbish. Life's not fair, and it's beginning to get him down – until a bizarre chain of events lead Joel into the spotlight . . .

ISBN 0 09 911381 3   £3.50

Join the RED FOX Reader's Club

The Red Fox Reader's Club is for readers of all ages. All you have to do is ask your local bookseller or librarian for a Red Fox Reader's Club card. As an official Red Fox Reader you only have to borrow or buy eight Red Fox books in order to qualify for your own Red Fox Reader's Clubpack – full of exciting surprises! If you have any difficulty obtaining a Red Fox Reader's Club card please write to: Random House Children's Books Marketing Department, 20 Vauxhall Bridge Road, London SW1V 2SA.